HER
FIRST
MISTAKE

BOOKS BY CAREY BALDWIN

HER
FIRST
MISTAKE

CAREY BALDWIN

bookouture

Published by Bookouture in 2021

An imprint of Storyfire Ltd.
Carmelite House
50 Victoria Embankment
London EC4Y 0DZ

www.bookouture.com

ISBN: 978-1-80019-655-1
eBook ISBN: 978-1-80019-654-4

For Dottie, Sue Ellen and Suzanne
With love

PROLOGUE

Twenty years ago

Somewhere in the woods—
San Diego County, California

Mia covered her mouth with her hand; she mustn't cry out. Her mother had promised this would be the last time she'd lock her in the shed, and Mia believed her—or at least she was trying to.

Tonight or maybe tomorrow I'll tell Arnie all about you.

Mia's heart fluttered at the remembered promise. She couldn't wait to meet Arnie, and not only because it was dark and cold in here. Shivering, she adjusted the blanket, spreading it to better cover her shoulders, and then tucked it beneath her arms to make a coat. Her teeth chattered, and the tips of her fingers tingled. She hated the cold, but the dark was so familiar she hardly minded it. She had a flashlight for when she really needed it, but she knew better than to waste the batteries. They cost money, and money was hard to get. If she used the batteries too fast, it made life hard for Mommy.

Mommy talked about Arnie all the time. She said he was tall and had dark wavy hair and a scar on his cheek he got fighting bad guys when he was in the Navy. By now, Mia knew her mother's Arnie speech by heart:

I couldn't tell Arnie about you straight off because I figured he didn't like kids. You remember my friend Sid left on account of he didn't want the burden. Said he wouldn't trust himself to look after a dog, much less a little girl. I told Sid you didn't need looking after, and he left me anyway. But turns out Arnie isn't like Sid at all. He smiles when I talk about having kids someday. Mia, I finally got a man who likes children!

Next, her mother would clap her hands and hug her. *So tonight's the night. I'll wait 'til he's had his whiskey and is in a real good mood so he won't be mad I fibbed to him. Then I'll tell him all about you and what a good little girl you are, and you won't have to hide when he comes over anymore. Why, next thing you know, he'll be taking us both out for ice cream. What kind do you want, baby?*

Then Mia would answer, *chocolate*, even though she couldn't remember how chocolate ice cream tasted. Mommy talked about chocolate scoops on top of a sugar cone the same way she talked about Arnie. Like nothing else in this world could beat them. Ice cream and Arnie. Arnie and ice cream. These were the things her mother's dreams were made of.

Mia secretly wished her mother would go on and on about her to Arnie like she did about him to her. But that couldn't happen because he didn't know Mia existed. The hope chest in the front room was used to hide her things—coloring books, a bear with the stuffing leaking out, and clothes usually kept folded in the bottom drawer of the dresser in the bedroom she and Mommy shared when Arnie wasn't around.

Tears stung her eyes, and she sucked in a breath. She was not supposed to be jealous of Arnie.

Mommy loved them both the same—that's what she always said to Mia right before she locked her in the shed and told her to be good.

Make Mommy proud.

Mia fought back her tears.

Mommy would come for her soon.

But where was she? Though Mia didn't know how many days had passed, she was sure Mommy had never left her this long before.

Mia moved her thumb over the button of the flashlight. She hesitated before pushing it. After Mommy had closed the door, and the board that bolted it had groaned into place, Mia had kept the flashlight on until she could see better in the dark, then quickly switched it off. Now, its light looked yellow, and she understood that meant the battery was almost gone, even though, after those first few minutes in the shed, she'd only used it when she had to eat or drink or needed the baby potty in the corner. She swung the dull light around letting it bounce off the row of opened cans lined up against the wall.

One, two, three… eight cans.

She counted them after every sleep. There wasn't much else to do, and she liked counting. She was six and a half years old and could already make it to one hundred. And because she could make it to one hundred, she knew if she had to, she could get all the way to infinity.

Mia, a smart girl like you can do anything you put your mind to. That's what Granddad used to say.

She didn't go to school, but whenever Mommy wasn't saucing it up, she worked with Mia on letters and numbers. *Saucing it up* was what Granddad called it when Mommy drank beer until she couldn't walk straight.

Last year, after he caught a cough that wouldn't go away, Granddad died, and Mia and Mommy got kicked out of his apartment. That's when they found the cabin in the woods where they lived now. Mommy said the cabin was a blessing, and that someone must've left it especially for them because they had no place else to go.

Mia thought a real house would have been more of a blessing, but still, she liked the woods, which were filled with fast, furry rabbits and chattering squirrels and chirping birds—even a deer now and then. The woods reminded her of walks with Granddad. He had one book with photographs of plants and another with animals. Mia would try to spot as many creatures as she could and match them to their pictures.

She missed Granddad.

Trying not to think about his scratchy whiskers and his big laugh and the way he called her his brave little soldier, she rubbed her legs, which felt funny from sitting too long. She stood up and wobbled over to the cans and aimed the light, but she didn't have to look inside them to know her food was gone. Like the batteries, she'd tried to make the beans last. Whenever she'd woken from a long sleep, she'd made herself eat from only one can—no matter how loudly her stomach growled. This past wake-up, she'd eaten from the very last can, and she'd cut her finger when she'd dipped it inside to get the juice.

That hurt, but she hadn't cried because brave little soldiers don't cry over cuts and scrapes. Now, there was crusted blood on her hand, and her finger felt raw and sore, but she didn't care.

Where was Mommy?

If only Mia could go back to sleep and not wake up again until Mommy opened the door. But Mia couldn't fall asleep because her tummy was empty, and she was very, very thirsty.

Like the cans, her water feeder was empty.

She pressed her palms against her hot eyes and hoped as hard as she could that Mommy was coming for her right this minute.

Then her flashlight flickered out.

The beans were gone—all eight cans.

The water, too, and Mommy had filled the big feeder jar clear up to the top.

Mia had taken so many long sleeps.

Her chest suddenly felt tight, like she'd outgrown her shirt. It was hard to breathe. Her legs shook.

Even if Mommy had been too scared to tell Arnie the truth, she would never leave Mia this long. Something was very wrong.

Mommy's hurt!

It was time to stop wishing.

It was time to *do* something.

Mia crept around the shed, trying not to bump into things, until she came to the group of cardboard boxes she'd been searching for. She didn't like to touch them because they had bugs and spiders inside. Shaking out her hands, she gulped before thrusting her arms deep into one box and then another, checking for anything that might help her, but all she found were rags and old clothes.

What if Mommy had been saucing it up and hit her head again, like the time Mia had to call 911? What if she was sick with a cough like Granddad?

Mia heard whooshing in her ears, tried to take a deep breath, and noticed her chest fighting against her again.

I have to help Mommy.

But there was no way to do that while she was trapped in this shed.

Do not make a peep!

Mommy made her promise. And Mia had kept that promise. Though many times she'd wanted to cry out, she never did. But what was the point of being a good little girl if she couldn't help her mother?

She raised her fist to her mouth and bit down hard.

Then she tossed away the dead flashlight, straining her ears as it rattled across the dirt floor. Careful not to cut her finger again on the jagged metal top, she grabbed an empty can and squatted. Propping one shoulder against the cool, splintery wall of the shed, she ground the can's sharp edge into the dirt, then scooped up as much as she could, dumped it out and did it again… and again… and again.

She could no longer stop the tears from rushing out of her eyes and dripping onto her shirt, but so what? Being a brave little soldier hadn't helped any more than being a good girl.

Gritting her teeth, she kept working.

She'd promised her mother not to scream… but she hadn't promised not to dig.

CHAPTER 1

Present day

San Diego, California

Mia Thornton wasn't a ghost, but people so rarely noticed her she was often tempted to rattle a picture on the wall or creak open a door just to make her presence known.

However, tonight was not one of those occasions.

Seated alone at her table, on a Friday night, she stuck out like a bruise on the tender white throat of a lily. The Piano Man, one of the Gaslamp Quarter's trendiest establishments, had a reputation for fine cuisine and an ambience that practically guaranteed a happy ending. Here was where a man brought a woman for a third date, an anniversary, or after he'd taken her for granted once too often. The dining room, as advertised, boasted a piano man as well as low lighting and ubiquitous handholding. On the patio, multiple fire pits and an hors d'oeuvre and cocktails bar lured both romantic pairs and singles. But the singles, too, came in multiples—gangs of friends ready to mix and mingle.

Are you celebrating a special occasion? Had been the host's question before guiding her to a table reserved for two in the dining room.

She'd told him *no*, but that had been a lie. When Ruth Hudson had invited her to dinner—and at such a nice place—her heart had galloped into her throat. Tonight was to have marked the beginning of a new friendship, and in Mia's world that definitely qualified as a special occasion.

In preparation for this evening, she'd brushed her medium-length brown hair until it gleamed and applied red lipstick—a color she never wore. She'd only purchased the shade because a clerk at the MAC store suggested she could use a little more pizzazz. But she'd never called *Siren Red* into service until this evening. After trying on and discarding half her wardrobe, she'd eventually settled on a pretty blue dress and bone-colored pumps.

She checked her watch.

It had now been forty minutes and two chardonnays since the waiter had pulled out her chair. Her mouth felt cottony, and she reached for her water glass but found it empty.

Ruth isn't coming.

Blinking away the stinging sensation in her eyes, Mia tucked two twenties under the saltshaker and scraped back her chair as noiselessly as possible, intent on slipping from the dining room before any more pitying glances came her way. And she would have, perhaps, succeeded, if her cell phone hadn't sounded, causing many nearby patrons to turn and glare.

Funny how fast pity can change to indignation.

Although her phone was softly chiming "Crystals", from the looks she was getting you'd think it was blasting the drum solo from "Wipeout". She stopped dead in her tracks and fumbled in her purse. An excruciating length of seconds passed before she found and silenced her cell and read the message from Ruth.

Something came up. Rain check?

A wave of relief swept over her. Ruth had not forgotten. She simply couldn't make it tonight.

No big deal.

Mia tapped out her response: *No worries. How about next Friday?*
One second passed and then another.

She stared, but no scrolling dots appeared on the screen.

A reply was not in the offing.

Keeping her gaze on the floor, she made her way to the door. Not until she'd crossed the threshold of the dining room did she glance up—only to find Jane Glasgow entering the restaurant. Too late, Mia ducked her chin.

Jane had seen Mia see her.

Her cheeks heated, followed by the tips of her ears.

Could Mia pretend she hadn't seen her? Would Jane?

"Mia!" Jane smiled and waved. "Hello!"

Oh, well.

At least it was Jane. She wouldn't go blabbing on Monday morning about bumping into *poor Mia* all alone on a Friday night. Mia's shoulders loosened. Come to think of it, Jane seemed to be on her own, too.

Not likely.

Popular Jane would surely be meeting someone.

"Hello, yourself." Suddenly aware she'd been blocking the door, Mia stepped out of the way of traffic and made an effort to smile. She liked Jane who worked with her at the preschool and had a gentle manner perfect for putting the little ones at ease. Early on, Mia had dared hope the two might become friends, but more than a year had passed, and they hadn't yet shared a coffee—in or out of the break room.

Of course that was Mia's fault, not Jane's.

Mia had never been adept at making friends.

"Are you here with a date?" Jane peered past her.

"Yes. I mean, no." Why couldn't she answer a simple question without stumbling? "I was supposed to meet Mrs. Hudson—Ruth—but something came up."

"Tennyson's mother?" Jane lifted one eyebrow, clearly surprised.

And why wouldn't she be? Their posh preschool catered to a crowd teetering on the edge of the upper class. Unless it concerned their children, the moms and dads rarely talked to the staff, much less dined with them on a Friday night. "Like I said, Ruth couldn't make it. I'm just leaving."

A look of comprehension crossed Jane's face. She stuck her index finger in the air. "That's right! She recently split with her husband. She must be lonely."

More like desperate if she'd resorted to going out with Mia. Ruth might have lost her friends in the divorce, or perhaps she didn't want to discuss her failed marriage with them over the main course. In the corner of her mind, Mia understood this. But to her, desperation seemed as good a basis for a friendship as any. "I guess. Anyway, I'll see you Monday," she said, her knees locking as she sensed someone behind her.

"Jane! Get your ass over…" a lively voice trailed off.

Jane stepped forward, and Mia rotated the upper half of her body while her legs remained facing the door.

With one hand on her hip, the other waving a purple drink in a martini glass, Celeste Cooper approached, gorgeous auburn hair shimmering over bare shoulders, a billion-watt smile illuminating her path. And she *would* have an $800 Michael Kors snakeskin tote, just like the one Mia had been admiring for months, dangling carelessly from her arm. The bag gaped. Its glittering contents, lipsticks, breath spray, a big, fluffy pom-pom keychain, and what appeared to be condoms, hinted at a world Mia could only imagine.

A world Mia coveted.

In truth, Celeste Cooper didn't just have Mia's dream purse; she had her dream *life*.

Mia commanded her jaw to unclench.

"Look who I found!" Jane exclaimed.

Celeste frowned, but made a quick recovery. "Hey, Mia."

"Hey. I was just—"

"Why don't you join us?" Celeste asked, extending an arm toward the patio.

Mia peeked outside, and there, seated around one of the fire-pit tabletops, she spied the remaining unmarried staff members of Harbor Youth Academy—all the single teachers, save Mia, gathered for a night on the town.

"We're just getting together for our monthly..." Jane's tone turned apologetic "... for drinks."

"You do this every month?"

"Only for the past year," Celeste said.

There was a brief silence during which tension leaked into the air like moisture from a rain cloud before it bursts wide open.

Jane shifted her weight. "It's, er, very informal. We didn't think you'd be interested or we would've mentioned it."

That couldn't be true.

Perhaps Jane wasn't as nice as Mia had supposed. Or maybe Jane went along with the others for fear she'd be ostracized, too. But this was no oversight. It was a deliberate exclusion that had been backed up by a code of silence. To think of the effort it had taken to conceal a year's worth of outings from her. Not to speak in front of her, even once, of the fun they'd had, the bands they'd heard, the men they'd flirted with. All those conversations that had stopped when she'd walked into the teachers' lounge suddenly made sense.

She managed a tight smile, hoping the scalding embarrassment she felt hadn't reddened her face. "No worries. Like I said, I have to get home because..." She paused, scrambling for an excuse, but there was no need to invent one—the women who worked alongside her five days a week at the preschool, and who were the closest things to friends she possessed, had already turned their backs.

As she watched them go, tears pricking her eyes, she spotted something on the floor.

She crouched and quickly scooped up Celeste's fluffy, pom-pom keychain.

Then, instead of calling out to Celeste as she should, she closed her fist around the keys and stuffed them into the cotton tote she'd been carrying around since college.

CHAPTER 2

Saturday

When Mia raised her head, heavy with sleep, off the vanity, the reflection staring back at her in the mirror made her breath catch. Her dark image, lit only by slats of moonlight stabbing through the shutters of her bedroom window, seemed more ghoul than woman. She dropped her chin and let her gaze travel down her Coldplay T-shirt to her hands, fisted on her knees, her legs crammed into last summer's too-tight jeans, and finally to her feet clad in white tennis shoes. She could feel the damp seeping through the canvas shoes onto her sockless skin—the shoes were wet, from dew, maybe? She pinched her shirt to sniff the dank, woodsy smell, and her fingers transferred dirt to the fabric.

What time was it?

Her phone lay on the vanity, and she tapped it.

The screen lit up:

4:43 a.m.

A deep breath later she pulled her hands through her hair, her fingers catching on a twig, which she flicked away. Then she got up and walked to the kitchen, filled a water glass and chugged it, killing the fire in her throat. From the kitchen window she could see the front yard, short spikes of grass dusted with porous yellow light, and a reassuringly empty driveway.

Her Jetta was still in the garage.

Her hunched shoulders eased into a more natural position.

So this wasn't a repeat of the last "incident"—though she'd have to check the gas gauge on her car to be sure.

About three years ago, Mia had gotten up in the middle of the night, dressed, and driven downtown. Aunt Misty heard the car grinding out of the driveway, and when Mia didn't answer her cell, Aunt Misty used *find my phone* to locate Mia and then sent the police to check on her welfare. The cops founding her astride a carousel horse at Seaport Village, seemingly awake, but unresponsive to their questions until they brought her around by splashing water in her face.

There had been two previous, less troubling, incidents. One in which Mia cooked bacon and eggs in her sleep and another where she'd cleaned the bathroom; but the Seaport Village excursion was the last straw for Aunt Misty who'd insisted Mia seek help before she killed herself or someone else while sleep-driving. Considering the fact that Mia was afraid to drive, at least while awake, and, at the time, didn't have a license, she'd readily conceded.

That's when she'd started up with her former psychiatrist, Dr. Alessandra Baquero.

After a battery of tests, including an MRI of the head and an EEG, Dr. Baquero announced that Mia did not appear to have any *organic* problems with her brain. No tumor, no seizure disorder, etc. The sleep disturbances were probably related to a combination of post-traumatic stress and the sleeping pills Mia's primary care doctor had prescribed. Dr. Baquero changed her medication, initiated weekly therapy sessions, and that had put an end to the sleepwalking—until now.

It was only last week that Dr. Baquero pronounced Mia mentally safe and sound and released her from therapy. She was going to be disappointed when she found out about this. Sleep problems were nothing to be ashamed of—Mia knew that. Still, when you can't remember where you've been or what you've done, it's easy to imagine it might have been something awful.

Mia checked her phone.

4:49 a.m.

She'd wait until 7 o'clock before calling Dr. Baquero's service.

*

"Thanks for seeing me on short notice." Mia met Dr. Baquero's steady eyes.

"Of course, that's why I keep Saturday hours open. I want to be there for my patients if an urgent matter comes up."

Mia felt her cheeks flush. As relieved as she'd been when the answering service told her Dr. Baquero could fit her in, Mia worried, now, that she'd taken a slot from someone who might need it more. Her own problems seemed far less urgent once she'd discovered, just half an hour ago, the three-year-old bottle of sleeping tablets spilled open in her nightstand drawer.

Though she didn't recall doing so, it seemed obvious that after tossing and turning for hours over taking Celeste's keys last night, she'd resorted to swallowing one of her old pills. She wasn't sure which was worse—what she'd done to Celeste or keeping an old prescription that had been considered a prime suspect in her sleep disturbances. Nor did she care to admit she might have driven her car in an altered state. This morning the needle on her gas gauge hovered just *under* the half-full mark, and though she couldn't be certain, she thought it had read slightly *over* half-full when she'd returned from the Piano Man last night.

"What's going on?"

"I know last week was supposed to be our final session."

"Let's circle back to that, okay?" Dr. Baquero said. "You told the service you needed to see me right away, so how about you fill me in?"

Mia's gaze traveled the lilac-colored walls of Dr. Baquero's office, littered with diplomas and awards, then paused to linger on her desk, crafted from polished walnut and adorned with a computer and oversized mug proclaiming *Keep Calm and Kick Ass*.

A framed picture faced away from Mia.

Many times, she'd paced the office just to get herself in position to look at that photograph. It was of Dr. Baquero's daughter—a teen with cropped, silken black hair framing a round face, flawless skin and intense dark eyes that promised to keep your secrets—a young, shorter-haired version of her mother.

She fell back into the depths of the sofa she'd sat upon almost every Wednesday afternoon for the past three years. Her fingers stroked the supple leather. She inhaled its familiar scent, considering. What would Dr. Baquero think of her when she found out Mia had taken a prescription she'd expressly instructed her to throw away? Mia had hung on to the pills as a fail-safe, but since when did the risk of a potentially sleepless night outweigh the danger of wandering around like a zombie, maybe even driving? There was no point in bringing up the sleepwalking now that she knew all she needed to do was throw away those pills.

No.

She would use her time to talk about the keys instead. That was a mess she did need to sort out.

Dr. Baquero studied her—eyes crackling-smart and, as always, charged with empathy.

"I did something I'm ashamed of."

"Mm hm."

No alarm in her voice at all. If only Mia could be so cool. "Something pretty rotten."

"I see."

Last week, she'd been so proud, albeit a bit anxious, when Dr. Baquero released her from therapy, and now, just days later, here she was asking for help. She wanted to go back to being a success story, but since she couldn't, she might as well get on with it. "I played a trick, sort of, on someone I wish I could be friends with. I guess you could say I self-sabotaged again. And the worst part is that what I did was unkind."

Dr. Baquero didn't flinch. Didn't even blink. "We've talked about this. You're not going to be perfect. No one is. If you slip up and do something self-destructive that's not the end of the world. You can review the situation and take the steps needed to prevent a recurrence. But I must say, as often as you put your foot in it in social settings, it's not like you to be unkind." She tapped her pen against her teeth. "Suppose you tell me exactly what happened."

So she did. And twenty minutes into the story it occurred to her that Dr. Baquero had a point. What she'd done wasn't nice, but it wasn't terrible either. After all, Mia had quickly realized her actions had been wrong, and that they'd taken her further away from her goal of making friends with the other women at the preschool.

"So what were your thoughts when you slipped your friend's keys into your own purse?" Dr. Baquero asked.

"I wasn't thinking at all. It was pure impulse."

"That's a cop out. Impulse implies you weren't in charge of your behavior, and we know that's not true. So what about before? What were you thinking and feeling a few minutes earlier?"

Mia knew where this was going. Dr. Baquero wanted her to identify her triggers so she could head things off *before* they went south. Use her deep breathing to offset anxiety, replace irrational thoughts with realistic ones. But that was the tricky part—thinking and behaving rationally. "I guess I felt bad."

This drew a half-smile from Dr. Baquero. "Care to elaborate? You can do better."

"Bad. Weird. Anxious. Not good enough. Worthless—I should have stopped that chain of thinking when I came to *worthless*. I'm not worthless just because someone left me out." Looking up, she was relieved to find Dr. Baquero nodding approval. "And

I wished I had Celeste's life. That I could be like her. You could say I'm jealous, but I guess another way to look at things is that I admire her."

"See what you did there?"

"I reframed jealousy into admiration—a negative into a positive."

"Fantastic! Now let's keep moving that direction. In what ways do you admire Celeste?"

"She's glamorous and fun. People love to be around her. She says what's on her mind. Never takes any guff. Not from the preschool director, not from the other teachers, not from anyone. Celeste Cooper is fearless and fabulous." So fearless and fabulous that Mia had been studying her from afar, trying to emulate her style.

"I understand why you'd want to be like her. But maybe her life isn't the perfect one you imagine."

Celeste's perfect world was hardly a figment of Mia's imagination. It was right there in the society pages for everyone to see. A quasi-celebrity father, a mother celebrated for her charitable work with at-risk youth. And even if Mia hadn't read a word of such things in the papers, she'd still recognize the difference between her world and Celeste's by the telltale, life-is-good smile Celeste always flashed.

"You never know until you walk a mile in someone's shoes what struggles she may face. For example, I'm sure she doesn't have any idea what you've been through." Dr. Baquero came out from behind her desk, and then she sat next to Mia on the couch. Something she'd never done before. "Think back to when I first met you. You spoke so quietly I had to threaten to get you a microphone so I could hear you. You were having nightmares several times a week—and then there was the sleepwalking."

"I'd still be having those nightmares if you hadn't changed my meds."

Dr. Baquero nodded. "Yes, but you've been off all medication for years. And still, you speak up, and you're no longer afraid to look me in the eye. No more sleepwalking."

Mia cast her gaze to her lap. She couldn't bring herself to interrupt this litany of praise with the truth. Last night had been an aberration. And the minute she got home, she'd flush the rest of the pills.

"You've got a license, you drive your own car, and soon enough you'll be in your own apartment."

"I know, but—"

"No buts, remember? Give yourself the credit you deserve. A year ago, you'd have been too ill at ease to accept a dinner invitation from a casual acquaintance. But last night you found the courage to show up. Then, when you ran into the other teachers, out-on-the-town without you, instead of pretending not to see them, you stood your ground and engaged them in conversation. I agree that what you did later—keeping those keys—was wrong. But it was also human. The way I see it, this is a good opportunity for you to pick yourself up and figure things out. So tell me, how do you plan to handle this setback?"

Mia raised her chin. Snatching up Celeste's keys wasn't that big of a deal. Everyone does foolish things now and then. The sleepwalking was a one-off. None of it meant she was a failure or that she'd been released from therapy too soon. She could handle this. "I have to make things right. I have to make amends to Celeste."

"Bravo."

"I can tell her I found her keys, but I didn't realize at first that they belonged to her. I'll return them, and then I'll come up with some way to make it up to her—maybe I could take over her class field trip next week—that would give her the afternoon off." She fiddled with the hem of her blouse. "Is that enough? Do I have to admit I took them on purpose?"

"I'll leave that to you. But as well as you've been doing, I'd be remiss if I didn't caution you against saying more than you need. You're not even sure of your own motives for keeping the keys, so why go into a lot of detail with Celeste—unless you really believe it's the only way to make things right?"

Dr. Baquero was leaving the choice to her. "You still think I'm cured?"

"I think you're ready to handle life's daily problems on your own. You need to trust yourself. But like I said, don't expect to be perfect, because I guarantee none of us are. In truth, I suspect this keychain incident resulted partly from my releasing you from therapy last week—that you were testing me."

Of course, that was probably why she took that pill, too. She was testing Dr. Baquero—and herself. "You think I'm too dependent on you."

"I think you can stand on your own two feet. By the way, how did your aunt take the news when you told her you were moving out?"

Mia shifted on the couch. "I haven't. She cried when I turned off location sharing on my phone last week, and then I couldn't bring myself to upset her again after she made such a fuss about not knowing where I am every second of the day. After what I've told you, do you still think I'm ready to fly without you?"

"You already have your wings, Mia. All you have to do is keep spreading them. Like that book club you started. Keep that kind of thing up and you'll be far too busy for weekly therapy."

Mia frowned. She'd put a notice up in the break room at work inviting anyone who was interested to join a "classics" book club. The inaugural selection was to be *Jane Eyre*, and the first meeting was set for Friday after next—only so far, no one had signed up. "I hope so," she said, deciding on optimism—there was still time for people to join.

Dr. Baquero rose and stuck out her hand. "You know, releasing you from treatment doesn't end our relationship. You can call and schedule a booster session any time you like. If you need me, I'm still here. I'm truly sorry if I didn't make that clear before."

Mia stood, shifting her weight from one foot to another. She stared long and hard at her therapist's hand before grasping it so tightly the poor woman nearly dislocated her elbow getting free.

But then, to her great surprise, Dr. Baquero went in for a hug.

On the way home, Mia held her head high, even hummed under her breath, all the while considering ways to return Celeste's keys and make up for the inconvenience she'd caused. If Dr. Baquero believed in Mia, then she should believe in herself. She shouldn't keep running to others to solve her problems.

When her phone buzzed in her hand, she looked at it right away, hoping it was Ruth Hudson texting to reschedule dinner, but then she noted the caller ID, and her toe caught on a paving stone.

Unknown number.

Her stomach instantly churned. Devastating thoughts played in her head: someone had seen her take Celeste's keys. She was being fired from her job. She was never to approach Celeste or Jane again. She'd never make a real friend.

STOP.

No one knows you took those keys. You'll give them back. Everything is going to be okay.

She took a calming breath, and then read the message:

Mia, I got your name from Jane Glasgow. This is Angelica Cooper—Celeste's sister. Have you heard from her? Celeste is missing!

CHAPTER 3

Monday

Mia hesitated outside the wrought-iron gate leading into Pocket Park—an outdoor square adjacent to San Diego's historic Gaslamp Museum. Since getting that text from Angelica Cooper, Mia had been in a complete tailspin, barely able to eat or sleep. Yesterday, the news had featured a story about Celeste and put out a call to anyone who might have seen her. Mia tried to convince herself there was nothing to fear, that on Monday she'd show up to work and find a beaming Celeste returned from some grand adventure. But this morning, when Mia arrived for work at the preschool, she found a note taped to the door:

> *Harbor Youth Academy will be closed today. Preschool hours will resume tomorrow morning at nine o'clock. Anyone wishing to volunteer in the search for Celeste Cooper should meet at Pocket Park. Authorities will be available throughout the day to assign duties.*

When Mia's mother had gone missing, the police had assumed she'd run off with a boyfriend, leaving her six-year-old daughter locked in a shed. Foul play had been considered but quickly and conveniently dismissed. The community hadn't rallied around. No volunteer searches had been organized, and, to this day, Mia still died a little inside each time she saw someone who, from a distance, resembled her mother.

She didn't know if her mother had abandoned her or become the tragic victim of a psychopath, and not knowing was paralyzing, because every step she took toward the truth had the potential to plunge her into total darkness. Sometimes, she prayed that her mother *had* left her alone to die, because that would mean she was still out there, somewhere—alive. But most of the time, she simply tried to forget. Over the years, she'd learned the less she thought about her mother, the less it hurt.

But now, with Celeste missing, Mia could barely keep the ghosts of her past at bay, and she couldn't stand to think her own actions might have played a part in Celeste's disappearance.

What if Celeste had accepted a ride with a stranger because she didn't have her keys?

Unlikely.

Celeste was a smart woman who knew how to take care of herself. And she had plenty of friends around that night to give her a lift. Mia had nothing to do with Celeste going missing. That was just her guilty conscience messing with her head.

She was truly sorry for what she'd done, but *sorry* didn't help anyone. Volunteering, on the other hand, might. The community was really pulling together for Celeste, and Mia planned to do her part—whatever it took. She understood, too well, what the Coopers were going through.

She shook out her shoulders.

Crowds of strangers weren't exactly her thing, but she owed it to Celeste to be here—even though it meant facing her fear of social gatherings. It'd taken her two hours and three cups of coffee to work up the nerve. If the other teachers turned out, maybe she could join them, but if there'd been a group text or other information sharing, Mia hadn't been included. No one had filled her in about what happened, and she was hungry for details. Thank goodness for the note on the preschool door. Otherwise, she wouldn't have even known about today's search.

On a deep inhale she opened the gate, hands jittering from all the caffeine, and entered Pocket Park. She fixed her gaze on a red-brick border surrounding a circle of gray cobblestones. Feet clad in shoes of all sorts—heels, hiking boots, tennis shoes, and even flip-flops, greeted her. After a few beats, she found the courage to look around and size up the crowd. At this point about thirty or so people milled beneath the park's giant magnolia trees. Blow-up photos displayed on easels were strategically placed between the benches around the park's perimeter. Mia spun, and images of Celeste, with her shiny auburn hair and lovely hazel eyes, kaleidoscoped around her. Unnerved and dizzy she came to a stop, steadying herself by focusing on the nearest stationary object: a bronze statue of a dog.

"You know the story of Bum, the mutt?" A white-haired woman, her steps buzzing with energy, approached.

"I'm reading it now." Mia pointed to the engraved placard bolted onto the statue. "Bum sounds like quite a character."

"San Diego's town darling and its biggest mooch. I'm Cora, by the way."

"Mia."

"Did you get one of these?" Cora handed over a packet of papers in a laminated folder.

"Not yet." As she accepted the packet, the knots in her stomach loosened, just a little. This woman seemed to welcome Mia, without question, into the volunteer group, and that gave her a good feeling. "Thank you, Cora." She smiled, happy she'd remembered to use the woman's name. Focus on the other person, not yourself, Dr. Baquero always said.

"Thank *you* for coming." Cora's gaze swept the park. "A lot of the volunteers have already gone out but there's still plenty of time left."

Mia wasn't sure what duties volunteers would be given, but she was prepared to do whatever was asked of her. "Gone out?"

"Door knocking. The sign-up table is over there." Cora pointed as she hurried past Mia to greet another newcomer.

Mia opened the folder Cora had provided. On the first page she found a handwritten thank you note from Celeste Cooper's mother, Alma. Imagine writing so many thank you notes at a time like this. Alma Cooper was living up to the image Mia had gleaned from the papers. "People have big hearts," she said aloud.

"Some people do." Paul Hudson, Ruth Hudson's soon-to-be-ex, shaded his eyes from the late morning sun and sidled up to Mia.

Other Harbor Youth parents would, no doubt, be volunteering, too. It was especially good of him, the vice president of a local bank, considering he must've had to take the day off. "Good to see you, Mr. Hudson."

He arched an eyebrow. "Under these circumstances?"

Her face grew hot. "I didn't mean... This is truly awful. I shouldn't have said... I'm so sorry. I was being polite."

"And I wasn't." He towered above her, blond, broad-shouldered and handsome, wearing just the right expression: worried but not overwrought; confident but not arrogant. "I don't know why I said what I did, either. This is all so unsettling. Please forgive me."

She blew out a breath, relieved the tension had dissipated as quickly and unexpectedly as it'd come. Obviously, she wasn't the only one on edge. "There's nothing to forgive. It's hard to know the right thing to say or do in such a terrible situation."

"Thanks for being a sweetheart." His gaze swerved away from hers. "We'll talk more, Mia, but if you'll excuse me, I need to find my wife. Have you seen her?"

Strange. Ruth had told Mia she wouldn't take Paul back if he swam naked through a sea of electrified eels to get to her, but the way he'd said *my wife*—his whole demeanor, in fact—made it seem as though nothing were amiss between them. "I haven't bumped into her, yet. But I just got here."

"Well, good to see you." Then he half-laughed, apparently realizing he'd reenacted her initial gaffe, and disappeared back into the crowd.

*

As she headed for the sign-up table, Mia kept an eagle eye out for anyone or anything that didn't fit in—a routine she'd developed partly because she held out a secret hope her mother would magically appear one day, and partly because Aunt Misty had taught her danger might be lurking around every corner. Dr. Baquero discouraged what she called post-traumatic hyper-vigilance, but Mia hadn't quite managed to lose the habit. Suddenly, her gaze boomeranged back to a group of trees providing cover for a man, who, from his concealed spot, peered surreptitiously between a magnolia's branches.

Just the kind of behavior that set her teeth on edge.

Watching, while trying to appear not to, she saw him lift his arm, something shiny in his hand. It could be a knife... or a gun.

Her pulse ratcheted up along with his arm.

The glinting object touched his lips, and she exhaled.

Just a flask.

But what was he doing hiding out in the trees? In case she was ever asked to give a description, she made note of the furtive man's appearance: muscular, golden hair in need of a cut, about six-feet tall.

"Hey, there. You here to volunteer?"

She jumped at the sound of a man's voice, and then turned—it was the guy behind the volunteer table trying to get her attention.

"Yes, hello." She walked over. "Is this where I sign up for duty?"

"If you're at least eighteen," he said, openly assessing her.

"I'm twenty-six."

"Do you have identification?"

She slipped her purse from her shoulder and rummaged for her wallet. "Do you mind if I ask why?"

"Routine."

Were the cops looking for suspects among the volunteers? She'd heard criminals often inserted themselves into investigations, helped search for the very victims they'd abducted. She certainly hoped the police wouldn't waste time looking in her direction. She held her ID up for his inspection.

Apparently noting her discomfort, he smiled. "At ease, Mia Thornton. We can't be responsible for minors is all."

Well, that made sense. They couldn't have a kid coming across morbid evidence or, heaven forbid, a dead body. Hoping he wouldn't notice the tremor in her hand, she slipped her license back into her wallet and her wallet into her purse. She couldn't keep blaming the caffeine. She needed to get her nerves under control.

"I'm Detective Griffin Samuels."

Detective. He looked the part: shiny suit, no tie, close-cropped hair, a stare that dissected you like a scalpel. If anyone could catch a killer, it was this guy.

But Celeste wasn't dead. She couldn't be.

Turning her attention to the sign-up sheet, Mia picked up the pen.

Put it down.

Picked it up.

"Whatever you can do, the Coopers will be grateful," the detective said. "Even if it's something as simple as putting the hotline number in your email signature."

"What a good idea. Where do I get that number?"

Detective Samuels pointed to the packet tucked beneath her arm.

"Of course, thanks." She scrawled her name on the paper and filled in her phone and emergency contact information. "But what do you need me to do right now?"

"Today is about increasing awareness and gathering intelligence. We're doing a door-knock and bar-crawl in the Gaslamp Quarter since Celeste visited a restaurant here on Friday. But if you're not comfortable talking to folks, there are plenty of other ways to help. You could bring food for the other volunteers or pin information on your social media outlets. You'll find suggested wording for tweets and messages in your packet. And we've placed flyers with Celeste's photo in your materials. You can make copies and tack them up on windows, trees, any place conspicuous as you move through your normal day. Like I said, if you don't feel comfortable talking to people there are plenty of other things that need doing."

This detective seemed to have sized up her skills in the space of a minute and found them wanting. But she wasn't going to let him dissuade her from helping where help was most needed. "I can knock on doors and crawl the bars. No problem."

"Do you have a partner? Everyone needs to buddy-up for safety."

"Can't you assign me one?"

"If another single becomes available, we can, but right now everyone else is paired up."

"I'll be fine on my own."

"Sorry, but you can't go out by yourself."

Mia's shoulders stiffened. "I can do this, no problem."

"There's a good reason for the buddy system, and we have to stick to the safety rules." He crossed his arms over his chest. "No partner, no door-knocking, no exceptions."

His look told her he wouldn't bend, and she hoped hers told him the same.

"I couldn't help overhearing." A pretty woman, around Mia's age, maybe a bit younger, walked over, and Detective Samuels made room for her beside him. Her shoulder-length auburn hair shimmered in the midday sun.

Those hazel eyes.

She looked like…

"I'm Celeste's sister, Angelica, and I need a buddy, too." She extended her hand across the table to Mia.

"That's awfully kind of you," Mia said, suddenly finding it hard to keep her feet under her. The sight of the sister somehow made reality sink in.

Celeste was *gone*.

Just like Mia's mother.

Mia gripped Angelica's hand too tightly, then released it too quickly.

"You're the kind one for volunteering," Angelica said. "I'm sorry, but I didn't get your name."

"Mia Thornton. I teach at Harbor Youth Academy."

"Oh, right. You were at the Piano Man with Celeste on Friday."

"Like I said in my text, I just bumped into her. I'm so sorry I couldn't fill in any details. We work together, but we don't really hang out or anything."

"Well, she's spoken of you. I remember her mentioning that you were especially good with one little boy. Tennyson?"

Mia couldn't conceal her surprise. "Celeste talked about me?"

"She did. You just missed Jane and the others, but I'm happy to go out with you."

"You're sure?" Mia could hardly believe Angelica Cooper would want to be her buddy.

"Absolutely. I planned to go out with Isaiah—our brother, but I can't seem to find him. I think he might be deliberately avoiding…" She stopped talking mid-sentence, and her brow furrowed.

Mia followed Angelica's gaze to the man who'd been hiding among the trees, now zigzagging his way over, a failed sobriety test waiting to happen.

"And speak of the devil," Angelica said in a tight, quiet voice as Isaiah bumped into Mia.

"Who are you?" Isaiah asked in lieu of *excuse me*.

"Mia Thornton. I'm a friend of—I mean I work with Celeste." She stuck out her hand, and it hung in the air for what seemed a lifetime before he finally touched his palm to hers in a sloppy shake.

Angelica said, "You remember Celeste mentioning the teacher who had a magic touch with that difficult pupil. Mia is the Tennyson whisperer."

Isaiah swayed on his feet. "Tenny who?"

"You're drunk." Angelica turned away from her brother.

"Possibly," he said, words slightly slurred, "but at least I'm not in denial, running around passing out flyers like we're going to find Celeste chilling on the beach, a piña colada in hand and no idea the whole town's looking for her."

Isaiah wobbled forward, another step closer, and then stumbled, the flask tilting in his hand. Something wet and warm ran down Mia's chest, pooling between her breasts, dampening her shirt with a sweet-smelling liquid.

She groaned, easily identifying the offending substance as tequila—Mia would know that smell anywhere.

Although Aunt Misty declared herself a teetotaler to all who inquired, every year, on the anniversary of Mia's mother's disappearance, Aunt Misty would get good and soused with Jose Cuervo, and Mia would have to maneuver her safely into bed.

She stared down at her shirt.

Detective Samuels rounded the table and offered her a handful of wadded up napkins. "Sorry about that." He turned to Angelica. "Maybe you should take your brother home."

Isaiah's face reddened. "Don't apologize for me, Detective. Guess you think I'm the bad guy for stating the obvious. No one has seen her since Friday, and you told us yourself the first forty-eight hours are the most critical if a missing person is going to be found alive. This doesn't look good."

"Unless she took off on her own." Angelica's voice shook.

"Stop kidding yourself." Isaiah scoffed. "She's never set a foot out the door without sending Mom her itinerary in triplicate. There's no way she'd go off the grid. And the last time her social media went dark was never."

Mia shuddered. Not just because what Isaiah said rang true—she didn't think Celeste would take off without a word either—but because, deep in her heart, she didn't believe her own mother would've left her locked in that shed if she hadn't planned to come back for her.

And yet no one had searched for Emily Thornton.

Watching tears slide down Angelica's cheeks, Mia felt the weight of her own loss pressing against her chest. She drew herself up as tall and straight as she could. "Celeste is out there somewhere. We're going to do everything we can to find her."

"If you want to drink yourself into oblivion, Isaiah, that's on you. But I'm going to keep knocking on doors and passing out flyers," Angelica said soggily, then she covered her face. "This is all so surreal. If only Celeste hadn't lost her keys."

Lost her keys.

The words echoed, ringing in Mia's ears, making her dizzy. "What do you mean?"

"Celeste walked home because she lost her keys," Isaiah said, unsteadily.

Mia shook her head, trying to clear it. "Didn't Jane drive her? Or one of the others? I-I don't understand."

Angelica, more composed now, said, "They offered her a ride, but Celeste said she'd prefer to walk. Her house isn't far. The police found her purse in an alley behind the restaurant, and since there was no blood or sign of a struggle at her place, we think she never made it home on Friday night."

"It appears someone grabbed her off the street," Detective Samuels said.

"Because she walked home? Because she lost her keys?" Mia heard her own words floating around in the air. Her vision went gray, and her knees softened. The world rushed around her, and soon she was spinning—inside a giant kaleidoscope papered with photographs of a beautiful young woman with shiny auburn hair and lovely hazel eyes.

CHAPTER 4

Mia reclined, with her head and shoulders propped on satin pillows, on a bed in a small, femininely appointed room.

Celeste Cooper's bedroom.

Inside Celeste Cooper's *darling yellow Victorian cottage just steps from San Diego's famous Gaslamp Quarter.* That's how Celeste described her house on a vacation rental website—and she'd bragged around school about getting top dollar for it on the occasional weekends when she left town. Mia had studied the website photos, relishing the sneak peek into Celeste's home. She'd even purchased a similar, pinch-pleated duvet cover for her own bed. She'd hoped, someday, she might see the place in person, but she'd never imagined her invitation would come about like this.

From a pair of pale-blue bedside chairs that matched the room's chintz curtains, Angelica Cooper, along with her mother, Alma, kept watch over Mia. Though her auburn hair was cut short, and her hazel eyes were edged with the faintest of lines, Alma Cooper greatly resembled her daughter—if Mia didn't know better she could easily mistake them for sisters. Alma must have been a very young woman when she became a mother. Now, Angelica and Alma wore the same concerned expression, as if they owed something to Mia, and the irony of that tightened around her heart like a noose, as she mentally replayed the events of the past hour over in her head.

At the park, after Angelica had mentioned the keys, Mia's vision had gone blurry and her knees wobbly. The next thing she'd known,

Detective Samuels was lifting her off the ground. Angelica, she recalled, had fed her water and talked to her in a low, soothing voice, apologizing profusely for Isaiah. He'd reportedly been about to take a drunken swing at Detective Samuels when Mia had fainted, and his fist had glanced off her chin instead. Isaiah had grabbed her by the blouse, presumably to break her fall. In the process of *not* catching her, he'd managed to rip Mia's buttons and empty the remainder of his flask onto her slacks. Angelica had rushed to comfort Mia, and though it seemed an awful thing to admit, Mia had greatly enjoyed the attention.

Next, Detective Samuels had suggested Mia go to the emergency room, and Mia had pulled herself together enough to convince him that was unnecessary. But when Angelica had mentioned Celeste's house was nearby, Mia's tongue had grown thick and she hadn't been able to muster a refusal. Angelica had tilted her head, just the way Celeste often did, looked at her with large, hazel eyes, and for one heart-stopping moment it had seemed Celeste herself was imploring Mia to come home with her.

So she'd let Angelica drive her here, where they'd surprised Alma, who was supposed to be at her own home resting, but instead turned out to be sitting on the sofa pressing a framed photo of Celeste to her chest. After a brief introduction, which was less about Mia and more about Isaiah's sins, Alma and Angelica had steered Mia to Celeste's room where she'd promptly dropped her purse on the floor next to the bed...

Her purse!

Mia suddenly felt nauseous.

Celeste's big, fluffy, pom-pom keychain, a highly recognizable and damning piece of evidence, was still inside. Mia could only imagine what the Coopers would think of her if they found out what she'd done.

Nabbing those keys had turned into much more than a selfish mistake. It had set in motion the chain of events that had led to

Celeste's disappearance. But returning the keys would be of no use now.

So how would she ever make things right?

A new wave of nausea rolled over her, and she sat up clutching her stomach.

Alma rose and approached Mia with a fringed cashmere throw, tucking it around her stocking feet. "Are you okay?"

Mia tried to make her voice sound normal. "Perfect. I was just clearing my throat."

"May I get you more tea?"

"No, thanks." Mia unwrapped the throw Alma had just arranged and swung her legs off the side of the bed. She'd caused enough trouble already. "Thanks for everything, but I feel fine. I really should go. I don't want to be a bother any longer."

"But you're not a bother at all. A little rest. A little more tea. It's the least we can do after what my son did," Alma said.

If anyone should feel guilty, it was Mia. "His fist barely grazed me. I'm good as new. Honest," she said, gingerly touching a sore spot on her chin.

"If you're absolutely sure you're okay," Angelica said, "I would like to get some door-knocking in before it's too late. I don't expect you to come with me after the day you've had, but I can drive you to your car."

"She can't leave in those clothes." Alma turned to Mia. "I'm so sorry about Isaiah. I hope you understand spilling that flask was an accident, and when he grabbed your blouse he was only trying to help."

"Did he get drunk by accident, too?" Angelica scoffed.

Her mother's face fell. "Your brother is crazy with worry."

"I'm crazy with worry. You are, too. But neither one of us got drunk."

"Let's not do this in front of Mia." Alma leaned over to pat Mia's hand. "You know, dear, you remind me of Celeste. So sweet."

Mia's throat constricted, not only from the comparison but also because Alma was so quick to defend Isaiah.

A mother who stood up for you, who loved you—that was what every child longed for.

Did her children realize how lucky they were?

Angelica touched her forearm to her head. "Sorry, Mom. You're right. We should all take a page from your book and be more understanding."

"Thank you. Now then, let's get Mia fixed up. She can wear something of Celeste's."

Angelica's lips tightened into a strained expression. "Mom, really. I don't think we need to—"

"We can't send her home in torn clothes reeking of alcohol. And you'll come straight back after dropping Mia? Let the police handle the door-knocking. I don't want to have to worry about where you are."

"I've got *find my phone* turned on so you can track me." Angelica flung open the closet and, seemingly carelessly, grabbed an outfit that turned out to be a stretchy skirt and sheer top. She held it out to Mia. "I think these will fit."

Mia shook her head. She didn't have what it took to pull off a look like that. Yes, she might have the figure, but she lacked the nerve. "I-I can't."

Angelica sighed. "Okay. Maybe you'd feel more comfortable in something a little less, um, you know…"

Hangers rattled and clothes whooshed.

By now, all three women stood staring into Celeste's closet where a bookshelf leaning up against the wall caught Mia's eye. Sitting on the top shelf, opened and turned over, as if to quickly mark one's place, was a copy of *Jane Eyre*. Mia's hand flew to her chest where she felt a sharp, stabbing pain.

Celeste had been planning on joining Mia's book club.

Angelica pushed aside more garments. "This isn't so racy. Will it do?"

Mia gaped at a classic black dress with pockets. "It looks expensive. Are you sure it's okay for me to borrow this?"

Angelica looked at the frock, as if reconsidering, and then back at Mia.

"We insist," Alma said, just as the silence was becoming awkward.

Angelica handed Mia the dress. "Not to rush you, but I want to get started on my section of the Gaslamp Quarter before it gets dark."

There was a hint of consternation in Angelica's voice that Mia resolved not to take personally. She scrambled out of her clothes and into the little black dress while Angelica stood by with folded arms. Then Angelica scooped up Mia's things along with her purse.

"I'll take those." Mia snatched at the clothing, nearly upending her bag in the process. If those keys fell out, she would never be able to look the Coopers in the eye again.

Thankfully, the keys stayed put, and Mia clutched the purse to her body.

"Are you ready? I can drop you at your car before I head out on my own," Angelia said. The way she emphasized the *on my own* part made Mia wonder if she'd done something to offend.

Alma shot a pleading look at her daughter. "I'll ask you again to cancel your plan of going door to door. It's not right to put me through the worry. You may drive Mia to her car, but then I'd like you to come straight back."

"Fine. I don't want you stewing—but you have to promise me you're going to follow doctor's orders and get some rest."

Alma's face brightened with relief, and she pulled Angelica in for an embrace. As mother and daughter said their farewells, Mia wiped a palm over her hip, and then, noticing a bump in the dress pocket, reached in and took out a tiny cardboard square.

Lacy's Gentlemen's Club.

She quickly closed her hand to conceal the object. What was a matchbook from a strip club doing in the pocket of Celeste's dress?

CHAPTER 5

Mia kept her chin up, her eyes fixed on a framed photograph hanging above the sofa in the living room of the house she shared with her Aunt Misty. Shortly before her grandfather had fallen ill, he'd taken Mia to a flea market and let her pick out her own special treasure.

She'd chosen a photo of stars blitzing the night sky.

A wise choice, he'd said. *It takes a dark night to reveal heaven's beauty.*

To this day, every time she looked at that photo, she thought of Granddad—and remembered how to hope.

If only Aunt Misty could do the same.

She hardly seemed like the same woman who used to bring Mia gingerbread men and play tea party, back in the day before Granddad died—before Mia's mother whisked her away to the cabin in the woods. Back then, Aunt Misty's eyes had danced with mischief; now they darted guardedly about, their former bright blue dulled to a near gray. Her gaunt face aged her beyond her years, and her short, bobbed hair, though stylish, did little to mitigate a chronically beleaguered expression.

Aunt Misty wet her lips, preparing to speak.

Mia's entire body stiffened in anticipation.

"Why would Angelica Cooper take you to her poor sister's house and lend you her clothes? It's downright macabre. That family gives me the creeps." Aunt Misty shuddered.

Mia had known her overprotective aunt would be less than pleased about her visit to Celeste Cooper's home, but she hadn't expected her to turn it into something sinister. But that was Aunt Misty for you: she dreamed up ulterior motives for the cable repair guy, the postman, and the pharmacist. There was nothing strange about the Coopers' kindness. "They're not creepy. They're nice."

"Too nice, if you ask me."

Mia cringed as the four walls of their living room closed in. She tried to tune out her aunt's words. She already knew them by heart: *You can't trust them—them* meaning anyone in the world other than Aunt Misty or possibly, on a good day, Dr. Baquero.

"Mia, are you listening? I said I think someone followed me home today. I'm certain of it. I can *feel* someone watching us."

"You mean like yesterday? And the day before? What about last week when you called the police because the Pembertons didn't answer their phone, and a strange car was parked in their drive?"

"That was their fault for not picking up my calls and for not telling me they'd bought a new Mustang. But I'm getting off track. I'm relieved you're okay, but I still don't understand why Angelica Cooper took you to Celeste's house. It just doesn't feel right."

"She wanted to make sure I was okay." Mia touched her chin, where a bruise was beginning to form. Better not mention that Isaiah had punched her. That would simply be too much for her aunt. "Celeste's place is very near the park, and Angelica felt bad about her brother ripping my blouse."

"He tore your blouse?" Aunt Misty twisted her hands.

"Don't give me that look. He was trying to break my fall—it was an accident. I'm a friend of Celeste's and—"

"You're *not* her friend."

"Celeste talked to Angelica about me. And Mrs. Cooper, Alma, said I remind her of Celeste. I think maybe they wanted to look after me because they hope that, somewhere out there, someone is watching over Celeste. What if Celeste fainted? What if she hit her head and can't remember who she is? Maybe she has amnesia and a kind stranger is nursing her back to health right this minute."

"You've got a wild imagination."

"I'm your niece, aren't I? Now, please, please, *please*, stop worrying. I'm tired, and I'm going to my room." It was past time to get Celeste's keys out of her purse. After parting ways with Angelica, Mia had made copies of flyers and handed them out before heading home. But every time she'd reached in her bag, she'd thought of those keys, lying in wait, ready to strike like a poisonous snake. She'd considered tossing them in the ocean, but that felt all wrong—like she'd done something criminal and like a further betrayal. If Celeste came home—*when* Celeste came home—Mia might still be able to sneak them back to her. Better to hide them someplace safe.

"Then go lie down, and next time, call me."

"I will. And here's fair warning; I'm going out again tomorrow after work."

"But—"

"There's no point arguing. I intend to do all I can to help find Celeste. If anything happened to me, you'd want the whole world out there searching and you know it."

"At least turn on the location sharing on your phone again. I need to know you're safe. I can't shake the feeling that someone's been following us."

She sighed. If anyone was stalking Mia, it was Aunt Misty. "We've been through this. You don't get to track my every move. I'm not six anymore."

Aunt Misty crossed the room and pulled the curtains aside just enough to peek out the window at the street. "It's for your own safety. What if—"

"What if what? My mother's out there spying on us? She's come back to steal me away from you? I should be so lucky."

Her aunt stumbled back, clutching her chest, filling Mia with regret.

"I only meant that then we'd know she's *alive*."

"I want to believe your mother's alive, too. She's my sister. My flesh and blood. And yes, when you were little, I did worry she'd come back and try to take you away from me. But Mia, she locked you in a shed." Aunt Misty's voice cracked. "I'll never forgive myself for that. I shouldn't have let a falling out with *her* keep me away from *you*. If only I'd visited you at the cabin, I would have seen what was happening. I should have known. I should have kept you safe."

"But you didn't know, and once you found out, you did everything for me. Now I'm an adult. So you've got to back off and let me live my life, and it wouldn't hurt for you to get one of your own while you're at it. Besides, I don't even remember the shed." Not much of it anyway. Only around the dark, dark edges—a flash of memory here and there. In truth, she had very little recall of the years in the cabin—but the past was always there, lying in wait. She did have a few good memories, and she clung to them for dear life. "What I remember is Mother reading to me and singing. She had such a pretty voice."

"I hope she still sings. But we don't know if she ran off or… or…" her aunt's throat worked "… if someone hurt her, they might still come after you. I don't mean to scare you, but I'd rather you be frightened and safe than carefree and in danger."

"That makes absolutely no sense. I wish you could hear your words with my ears. When I was a little girl—"

"They found you unconscious in the woods, half-starved and totally dehydrated, hands bloodied and blistered from digging yourself out of a shed with a tin can. So if I'm protective, you can't blame me."

"I get that. I do. When I was a child, when you first took me in, this whole *someone dangerous is out there* thing made sense. But that was twenty years ago. There's nothing to be afraid of anymore." Her heart quivered in her chest, making her even more determined to convince—for her own sake as well as her aunt's. "No one is coming for me. No one is watching."

*

Once in her bedroom, Mia closed the door, wishing again for a lock, something her aunt would never allow. She hurried across the room and knelt in front of her mother's hope chest, placed both hands on the lid and then jerked them away. Years had passed since she'd touched this relic because, along with old clothes and coloring books, it contained memories she'd didn't want to face.

But it was those very memories that made her mother's hope chest the perfect hiding place for Celeste's keys.

No need to padlock a box that could kill your soul with its contents.

And it wasn't only Mia who acted like the thing was cursed.

Aunt Misty would rather hand a serial killer an engraved invitation to tea than go poking around in that chest from the cabin in the woods. It must've been hard for her to stomach having it in her home, but a social worker told her Mia might want it someday.

That chest was all she had left of her mother.

Mia reached out, once more, laying her hands on the lid. Her nails dug into the cedar, releasing an odor that took her back to a time and place when life was made bearable only by her love for her mother, and her innocent faith that things were going to get better.

Steeling herself, Mia pushed up.

The lid resisted, but eventually creaked open.

She felt the braces lock into place and closed her eyes.

She counted to ten, then twenty.

Don't be a baby.

Who knew how long she had before Aunt Misty would barge through the door, eager to resume their argument?

Mia opened her eyes and swatted away the dust motes. There, before her, lay Breezy—a half-eviscerated teddy bear with one eye and no nose. Her childhood friend should've brought a smile, or a tear, but she only shivered from a prickle of cold. She lifted a folded shift, a pair of child's pajamas, some patched clothes that didn't ring a bell. Was she the same girl who'd worn these? Her skin felt numb, her palms clammy, but this was nothing compared to the cold sweats she experienced every time she imagined opening the lid to her past.

Her shoulders relaxed.

Maybe the old saying was true.

Nothing to fear but fear itself… or getting caught with a missing woman's keys.

She yanked her purse off her shoulder and crammed her hand inside, searching for the pom-pom keyring. Once found, she laid it on the bottom of the chest and began tossing clothes on top, until eventually, inevitably, the past came crashing over her.

Suddenly, she couldn't breathe.

Gazing down, she took in the mess she'd made. Breezy's legs stuck straight up from a pile of wadded shirts. A woman's cotton smock with blue roses careened over the side. The smell of Mommy's perfume filled the room—but that had to be Mia's imagination. Her mother's scent couldn't possibly survive twenty years stuffed in a box, could it? She rocked back on her heels, pulse thumping in her throat. As her head cleared, she spied an object at the bottom of the chest: a shiny paper square wedged in a corner crevice, only a sliver of it visible.

She squinted at its white border. It looked like…

Was that an old Polaroid?

Careful not to tear the fragile paper, she worked the photo loose: a young girl, she must've been around five or six, wearing socks and a too-big dress, probably from the Salvation Army or handed down from a neighbor.

Mia's hand began to shake. All the photos Aunt Misty had of her were either from before or after Mia and her mother lived in the cabin. Studying the little girl's eager smile, Mia blinked hard. She'd never seen a picture of herself at this age before. She didn't even know what she looked like back then. There were far too many things she didn't know—like what had really happened to her mother.

Reaching up, she wiped away a tear.

Maybe it was time to stop hiding from her past.

Maybe it was time to start looking for it instead.

CHAPTER 6

Tuesday

Unlike Aunt Misty, Mia didn't find it disturbing to wear a missing woman's clothes. In fact, in Celeste's dress, she felt like she could do anything she wanted, *be* anything she wanted. After work this afternoon, before heading back out to search for Celeste, Mia had hesitated only a moment before changing into it. Alma had insisted she borrow it, so there was nothing wrong with wearing the dress one last time and pretending, just for a single day, that she, not Celeste, was the fearless and fabulous one.

Now, just steps ahead, the flashing neon lights of Lacy's Gentlemen's Club beckoned. Mia halted in front of XXX Videos to inspect the item she'd found in Celeste's pocket. The matchbook's corners were frayed, and the ink between the silhouetted legs smeared as though someone had rubbed a thumb in a very strategic spot.

She imagined the silhouette gyrating, the matchbook coming to life in her hand. Face burning, she quickly dumped the thing in her purse and looked up to find a man with decaying teeth leering at her. "Way to class up the neighborhood, babe."

He was a stranger, big and tall, with acne scars and a creepy stare—a man any woman might reasonably fear.

He took a step toward her, setting her heart racing in her chest.

Her first instinct was to turn and run, but instead she held her ground, grasping the fabric of Celeste's dress between her fingers, savoring its rich feel, trying to channel the woman who'd worn it before her.

"Wanna have some fun?" The man was still staring, his hand on his crotch now.

"Not interested," she said firmly. "And I've got pepper spray in my purse."

The way he jumped back, and then all but ran into the video store was more than a little satisfying. Part of her had worried this might not have been the brightest idea—going to a seedy area, asking around about a missing woman in a strip joint—but facing down this man boosted her confidence that, after weighing all her options, she'd landed on the right course of action. She'd considered going straight to Detective Samuels with the information about the matchbook—but there was no real reason to think there was a connection between it and Celeste's disappearance. The police didn't have time to knock on every door and follow every lead. That was why they'd asked for volunteers to help canvas the neighborhood. She could've told Angelica and Alma what she'd found, but if Mia had been hanging around a strip joint, she definitely wouldn't want Aunt Misty to find out. Or she could've simply tossed the matchbook and let Celeste keep her secret—but someone at this club might have seen something.

And if there was any chance of that at all, she owed it to Celeste to follow up.

Besides, there was nothing to be scared of.

It wasn't yet dark, and Lacy's was a legitimate place of business. Like any other bar, they had to have a license and were subject to inspections and strict operating rules. Establishments like these were tightly regulated—when you really stopped to think about it, strip clubs were probably among the safest haunts in the city.

Unless the movies had it right: dirty cops on the take, looking the other way, permitting all sorts of debauchery. And she *had* found Lacy's matches in the clothing of a missing person.

She tightened one hand into a fist.

Celeste was gone, and that was on her—at least in part.

If only she'd called out to her: *Wait, you dropped your keys!* Celeste might be home with her family tonight or reading *Jane Eyre* for book club.

But there was no turning back the clock. So from here on out Mia was going to have to do everything she could to help find Celeste. Joining the search was hardly a sacrifice—it would bring her closer to the Coopers.

She pulled her shoulders high.

No reason to linger on the sidewalk. It was pretty sketchy out here, and inside Lacy's, at least there'd be witnesses to any mayhem that might befall her.

Onward.

She marched ahead until she reached Lacy's Gentlemen's Club, determined to track down any witness who might've seen Celeste.

The front door was glass with a blackout curtain. A *Help Wanted* sign hung atop a silver cardboard cutout of a nude female.

Forcing her breathing to slow, Mia heaved open the door and crossed into a world unlike any she'd ever been a part of. The smell of air freshener hit her first, then, beneath, she detected high-octane sweat. Her gaze flew to the stage where spotlights encircled naked breasts, tattooed legs, and writhing bottoms. Glitter fell like colored snow onto a black runway.

Heart thumping in time to the music, she inched forward, halting in front of a densely muscled man, dressed in black, who stood with legs spaced wide behind a velvet rope hooked between two posts.

She stepped back, trying not to stare at the man's ears, adorned with giant gauges that stretched the lobes. His skin was thick and reddened. His stubble-covered jowls, like his ears, hung slightly lower than what she considered standard. From the depths of his sockets, yellow eyes flickered like spelunker lights.

"Welcome to Lacy's. Twenty-dollar cover. Two-drink minimum." The doorman made his gravelly voice heard above the din of drunken conversation and Lady Gaga.

She hadn't considered a cover charge. "You take credit cards?"

"Yeah."

While she fished in her purse, he unhooked the rope and shifted his weight, setting off a small earthquake that rattled her feet and reverberated up her legs. By now, she had her wallet, but his impatience made her fingers clumsy. "Sorry, just a second."

His gaze traveled appraisingly from her shoes up her torso and finally lighted on her face. "If you're here for the job, you don't have to pay."

"You mean…" her gaze locked onto a woman slithering around a pole.

"The waitress job."

"Oh." She flushed, suddenly embarrassed at where her mind had gone. "No…"

He wiggled the fingers of his outstretched hand, and she took a deep breath.

Why not save the twenty dollars?

It wasn't as if they would offer her the position. But maybe the pretense would help her accomplish what she'd come here to do. Maybe it was time to start thinking outside the box.

Fearless and fabulous, remember?

"Oh, no. I meant to say, yes. *Yes.* I'm here to apply for the waitress job—and I'm also looking for someone." She dropped her wallet in her bag and pulled out a flyer. "Have you seen this woman?"

He stepped forward, then hung his head over her shoulder, eau de Marlboro leaking from his pores. She coughed, but he continued to stand too close, staring but not taking the offered flyer from her hands.

Maybe he didn't want to give her a chance at his fingerprints.

At last, the doorman spoke. "Yeah."

"Yes, you've seen her?" His response set off a chain reaction of pounding pulse, shortness of breath and trembling knees. "Where?"

"On the news."

The guy hadn't admitted to seeing Celeste, but that didn't mean she hadn't been here. "Okay. Like I said, I want to apply for the server position, so I don't have to pay?"

"Yeah, you don't have to pay. I'll call the manager."

As he talked on the phone, she strolled, head held high, over to the stage and positioned herself in front of one of the dancers. And then, impossible as it seemed, she worked up the nerve to look the woman directly in the eye and smile.

In return, she got a wink.

A jolt of electricity buzzed through her. Afraid to look longer on the stage, she whipped around and found herself face to face with a tall man who, in contrast to the refrigerator guarding the door, was all lean, sinewy power. Despite his lined visage, he was handsome in a dangerous, tough-guy kind of way.

"Let's have your name, please."

Understanding she oughtn't give her real name, she frowned. Then, she thought of one of Aunt Misty's favorite Reba McEntire songs. "Fancy."

"Okay, Fanny. Follow me."

She winced, but didn't correct him. He was already on the move, leading her to a small table in a corner. Surprising her with his manners, he scraped out a chair for her.

"Thank you." She sat and clasped her hands in her lap.

He took the opposite seat. "So, Fanny, where do you see yourself in five years? What are your long-term goals?"

Her mouth went dry. She'd been unprepared for that. In fact, she was unprepared for all of this: the smells, the sounds, the raw sexuality on display. But most of all, she was taken aback by the way she responded to this assault on her senses.

She *liked* it.

"Sorry. Five years? Um. Could you repeat the question?"

"Take it easy, doll. I was being funny." He reached over and laid a hand on her wrist, setting her skin on fire. "You got a look our guests will like, Fanny, and we need a waitress. You got experience? I'm asking for real."

She wet her lips, wishing for a glass of water—or something stronger. "I have a bachelor of arts in English literature from San Diego State." She'd graduated *summa cum laude* but, regardless of how it was pronounced, she didn't relish using the word *cum* in this setting, so she held back that detail.

He tapped his fingers. "No problem. We got some other college girls here working the poles. But I mean do you have any waitress experience? What you been doing for a living? English degrees don't pay the rent."

They didn't. Teaching at a preschool barely did either, but that wasn't the answer he was looking for. And even though she was only pretending to apply for the job, she wanted to nail this interview, just to prove she could.

Reflected in one of the mirrored walls, she noted the emblem on the back of a guest's T-shirt. "I'm currently on hiatus, but I've waitressed at Hotties." She knew nothing at all about waiting tables and could only hope he wouldn't ask any technical questions like whether saltshakers should be filled at the beginning or end of one's shift.

"Hiatus, huh?" He grinned. "English majors. But I like you, doll." He was jotting notes. "Hotties downtown or Oceanside?"

Would he try to check her references? She pulled the fabric of her dress away from where it stuck to her back. "Oceanside. Two years. I left because the customers were handsy. A little is okay, but the managers let it go too far. What's your policy?"

"Strictly no touching. No worries on that count. Galen—" he glanced at the doorman "—will take care of any problems you have. I run a tight ship."

"And the pay?"

"Minimum plus tips. I expect you'll do real good for yourself—I mean real *well*. See, I know grammar, too. I just don't always get the point."

This was going better than expected. "You don't need a reason to use good grammar."

He handed her a pen and shoved his pad over. "Write down your number, and I'll get back to you, Fanny. I got someone coming in tomorrow so I can't offer you the job yet. I pride myself on being fair."

She scribbled her real number and got to her feet, making a mental note to change her voicemail to an anonymous message. "I'll give it some thought, but I have a few other offers already, so don't take too long." Then, refusing to be bested by a man who didn't see the point of good grammar, she added, "By the way, my name isn't Fanny, it's *Fancy*."

He stuck out his hand. "Suits you."

On that note of approval, it seemed a good time to do what she'd come to do. "You've heard of the woman who went missing Friday, Celeste Cooper?"

"Who hasn't?"

"Yes. Well, you see, I'm a friend of the family's, so I'm asking around wherever I go. Have you seen her?" She searched her bag. "I've got this flyer I could leave with you."

Like Galen, the manager didn't touch the paper. "I haven't seen her in here. Just on the news."

"May I put up this poster near the door, in case someone else might have spotted her? There's a hotline number and a reward and everything."

"Sorry, but, no."

"We're trying to get the word out." She held his gaze, hoping to transmit the urgency she felt.

Unfazed, he shook his head. "I'm afraid it's a hard no. Someone might get the idea one of our customers had something to do with her disappearance. Don't ask me again." His voice started out neutral, but ended on a note of steel. Raising his hand high, he opened and closed his fist twice.

A secret signal?

"Will you call me if you do see her?"

"Fancy, if I bump into a missing person, it's the cops I'll be calling." Galen materialized at Mia's side.

Figuring she was about to get bounced, she dodged his reach, turned and made a break for it, praying he'd allow her to leave under her own power. She wove her way through the gauntlet of customers, and made it about halfway to the back door before someone tapped her on the shoulder, freezing her in place.

"Good luck with the job, sweetie," a female voice purred.

Mia whirled.

That dancer, the one who'd winked at her earlier, turned out to be the owner of the sultry voice. She'd thrown a gauzy wrap, which did little to conceal her nudity, over her shoulders. With nowhere safe to fix her gaze, Mia decided to study the floor.

"I said good luck with the job!" Then, in a low, low whisper, the dancer added, "I saw her."

Mia jerked up her head. "Celeste Cooper? Where?"

The dancer adjusted her G-string, making a show of angling her body away from Mia, as if no longer addressing her, but continued whispering. "At the club. But you didn't hear it from me, okay?"

Mia's gaze darted around until she spotted Galen and the manager engaged in deep conversation. "Hear what? No idea what you mean."

"Perfect. Now get out of here."

Not yet. No freakin' way. "I'll give you my number so we can talk later."

"No. That's all I know. Just go."

Mia peeked around again, and this time found Galen giving her the eye. Her brain told her to head for the door, but her feet remained stubbornly rooted. "Maybe we can meet up later. After your shift?"

"You gotta go *now*."

"First, tell me your name, then I'll leave."

"Shoshanna."

As the dancer dove into the crowd, Mia's pulse started racing. Shoshanna *knew* something.

Struggling to regain her composure, Mia checked on Galen again. He was occupied, breaking up a row between two gentlemen. With the bouncer busy, it seemed like the right time to make her getaway. But the adrenaline rush that, up until now, had been keeping her afloat, abruptly wore off. Her muscles wilted, making it difficult to push her way through a crowd of stirred up men and past a long hallway lined with private chambers.

What went on behind those curtains?

She felt a magnetic pull in her solar plexus. Perspiration beaded between her breasts. Pausing, she closed her eyes, imagining ordinary people doing exotic things in those dark spaces. Then a hand closed over her mouth, and simultaneously, a powerful arm clamped her waist.

Her eyes flew open.

Unable to scream, she kicked and clawed at her captor's arms.

Uttering a soft curse, he hoisted her off the floor and hauled her into a pitch-black chamber.

CHAPTER 7

Mia sucked air through her nose, drawing in a burst of oxygen that revved her system like a shot of epinephrine. Her muscles jerked; her body steeled, preparing her for the fight of her life. Twisting, she wrenched one arm free, grabbed the hand that covered her mouth and bit down.

"What the hell!" To her utter amazement the man released her.

She heard a click and a lamp switched on, flooding the darkened space with eerie blue light. Panting, heart pounding, she screwed her fists into wrecking balls ready to smash her attacker in the face. She took him in, and then gasped.

Her racing mind screeched to a halt. "Isaiah?"

"You? You bit me!" He stumbled back. "What the hell are you doing in my sister's dress?"

She could feel the blood rising to her face, sweat oozing around her hairline, her pulse beating furiously in her neck. Keeping her fists up, she pulled in another breath.

Then, suddenly, his shoulders dropped, making him seem a lot less menacing.

She knew she should run, get away from him as fast as she could, but this was Isaiah, Celeste's brother, and her heart would not allow her to turn away. She dropped her fists, trying to think rationally. "You grabbed me. You're the one who needs to explain yourself." Without warning, her legs went limp, and she collapsed onto a padded bench. "But do it from over there."

"I thought you were her." He pushed a hand through disheveled hair. His tailored shirt had come untucked. A dark streak of dirt or maybe blood smeared a ruddy cheek.

"Her who? What could you possibly be thinking that would make it okay to drag me in here like that? You must've known how terrifying that would be for me—for anyone."

"I-I… When I saw you standing there, something seemed so familiar. From the back, I thought you were Celeste. That looks like the dress she was wearing the last time…" His voice trailed off.

It was true she and Celeste were about the same size and build, their hair similarly cut, though hers was mousy brown and Celeste's was auburn and somewhat longer. But the club was dimly lit, and Isaiah was probably drunk. He *might* be telling the truth. "But why grab her—I mean why grab me?"

"I didn't want her to get away."

Mia's heart rate was slowing down, but her defenses remained on high alert. "Why would Celeste run from her own brother?"

"You're right. She wouldn't. I just acted on impulse. I wanted to get Celeste to safety."

An image of Celeste cowering in the corner of a dirty cellar, a shackle cutting into a bloodied ankle flashed into Mia's head. She shivered. This creepy room with its three black walls and curtained doorway, the only light emanating from a skeletal lamp with a torn indigo scarf draped over the shade, was, in truth, safer than any of the places she imagined Celeste might be.

If Celeste was still alive.

Mia drew in a long, shaky breath.

"I'm sorry I scared you," Isaiah said.

"You should be sorry."

"I am." He sounded remorseful, and for Celeste's sake, Mia wanted to believe him. Still, only yesterday, he'd seemed almost cavalier about his sister's disappearance. Her pounding pulse warned her to not to trust him, but what if, like he said, he'd really thought he'd found Celeste?

And who was she to judge him when her own impulsive act had done so much damage? Would the Coopers forgive her if the truth about Celeste's missing keys came to light?

Suddenly needing to flee—from her own crimes as much as from Isaiah—she got to her feet. Besides, she really wanted to get out of this place before the bouncer discovered them.

Right on cue, the curtain whooshed open.

"Fancy, is that you? Are you okay?" Galen appeared, and in one swift motion hoisted Isaiah over his shoulder.

Isaiah froze, arms and legs extended.

"I'm fine," she said. "Please, put him down."

Still paralyzed, Isaiah said, "Let me go. Unless you want a lawsuit on your hands."

"Shut up," Galen said. "I'm talking to Fancy."

"This is a simple misunderstanding. I'm not hurt." Mia pushed on Galen's biceps, and he dropped Isaiah, who smacked his back against the wall but managed to keep his feet under him.

Then Isaiah's bloodshot eyes met hers, and she was torn between rebuking him and shielding him from Galen. Right now, in this moment, she felt like she was the stronger person, and it was up to her to make things turn out right—the same way she used to feel when she had to make sure the stove was off and cover up her mother, who was passed out on the couch. "He didn't hurt me."

Galen looked her over once and then again. "You sure?"

"Positive."

"Okay. But this area is off limits. Maybe you didn't know better, Fancy—" Galen turned and pointed his finger at Isaiah "—but this is your second offense. You're officially banned from the club." He paused. "As for you, sweetheart, you seem more interested in poking around than in procuring employment, so on behalf of

Lacy's management team, I regret to inform you the waitress gig isn't gonna work out."

"I understand. No hard feelings." She stretched out her hand.

Galen scowled. "I'm gonna count slow, and if you two aren't gone by the time I get to three…"

She rushed past Galen, heading out the back with Isaiah on her heels.

"One one thousand, two one thousand…"

A heavy metal door creaked shut behind them, and she found herself in a deserted alley with a half-drunk man who'd just yanked her into the sordid back room of a strip club. Had he really had a vulnerable look in his eye, or had that been her imagination?

And what was on his cheek? She squinted at the mysterious mark.

That was no dirt smear. It was a scratch, and she couldn't tell if it was fresh or old.

Cringing, she pressed her back against a brick wall.

Isaiah lifted his brow. "Fancy, huh? Nosing around? Waitress gig?"

"Second offense?" she fired back.

"It's complicated. Can I buy you a coffee? I'm supposed to be on the wagon, but I seem to have gone under the wheels."

That vulnerable look appeared again, coming dangerously close to sucking her in against her better judgment. "Sorry, I really have to get going."

Was Isaiah a sheep in wolf's clothing, in need of a guiding hand to bring him back to the fold, or a dangerous animal on the prowl?

CHAPTER 8

Wednesday

Feeling a tug of guilt for ditching her lesson planning yet again, Mia rushed out the door of the academy the moment her last class ended. Normally she was the first one in and the last one out, but what she was doing today was more important. Besides, she had plenty of activities prepared for her pupils to get her through the rest of the week—she could catch up over the weekend if need be.

In the parking lot, she waved a quick goodbye to Jane, who looked like she wanted to stop and chat, and slipped behind the wheel of her Jetta.

She arrived at Horton Plaza, parked, and then headed out on foot to drop off Celeste's dress at the dry cleaners. Next, she stopped by a copy shop—she was nearly out of the flyers with Celeste's photo and the tip-line number. She made 500 additional copies and then, beginning at First Street, systematically covered the Gaslamp Quarter, plastering lamp posts and trees, entering shops to inquire whether they'd seen Celeste, and cajoling staff into allowing her to leave stacks of flyers near the cash register.

She'd just completed Fifth Street when her phone chimed.

It was only Aunt Misty. She let it go to voicemail and repositioned the shoulder straps of her heavy tote with a newfound appreciation for the roomy old bag she'd purchased freshman year at San Diego State. The tote's once brightly colored floral pattern was faded to pastel, but the thick cotton fabric had held up to periodic washings. Big enough to hold a few books and a laptop back in the day, it was roomy enough now for flyers, tape, a hammer and nails, and even a thermos. Really, it was the perfect purse, and she no longer coveted another.

No Michael Kors snakeskin tote for Mia.

She had all she needed right here on her shoulder.

With a sense of purpose, she hurried toward a bench up ahead, fog swirling around her ankles—another balmy San Diego day was turning into a nippy evening.

But Mia had come prepared.

Positioning her bag beside her on the bench, she settled in, her heart beating fast in anticipation.

The tip of her nose was cold, and a cup of hot tea from her thermos would warm her up nicely, but she'd rather hold off. In just a few more minutes, according to its website, the board of Haven Foundation would convene in its Dream Hub building across the street.

The old, four-story red-brick structure, once a hotel, now housed the charity's office space, as well as a gymnasium, salon, and rooms for girls awaiting placement. Some had lost parents through death or imprisonment, many were street kids, and others had been rescued from trafficking rings.

Alma, one of the organization's founding members, had given a Dream Hub online tour, proudly showing off the girls' rooms. No dormitory-style accommodations would do. Instead, Haven girls were treated to bedrooms decked out in designer style, with personalized accessories and fresh flowers. The idea was that surrounding the girls with beauty would reinforce the idea they were worthy of all good things and bolster their self-esteem.

Mia checked the time on her phone.

If Alma was going to show, it would be soon.

She cupped her hands over her cheeks to block the wind and noticed a gray Range Rover pulling to the curb across the street.

She held her breath.

The car pulled away, and a petite woman, her back to Mia, drew a scarf over short, auburn hair. The woman ascended the stairs, one by one, as if every step cost her dearly. When she arrived at the landing and reached for the handle of the tall glass door, she turned her head long enough for Mia to confirm, from her profile, the woman was indeed, Alma.

Mia let out her breath.

5:56 p.m.

She'd have that cup of tea now.

*

At 6:50 p.m., Mia packed up her thermos, slung her purse over her shoulder and crossed the street. She'd had her eye on a magnolia tree on the front lawn of Haven's Dream Hub. Its thick trunk made a perfect spot to affix a flyer of Celeste. Taking her time, she pulled a hammer and two nails from her bag, and, being careful not to pound her thumb, fixed the top of the flyer to the tree trunk. Then she stopped, keeping her back turned. Around ten minutes later, she heard voices and the bustle of people exiting the building. She lifted her hammer and began pounding the flyer's bottom nail into the tree.

The nail was soon fully embedded in the bark, but she kept hammering. Her arm buzzed, and her heart banged in time to the steady blows until, at last, Alma's voice traveled to her on the wind.

"You ladies go on without me. I think I see someone I know." And then: "Mia? Is that you?"

Mia whirled to face Alma, doing her best to seem surprised. "Oh, hi!"

"What are you doing here?"

"I was just finishing up with a batch of these. I've covered what was left of the Gaslamp Quarter, and I'm planning to start on Little Italy tomorrow." Mia wrestled the hammer back into her purse and then tucked a lock of hair behind her ear.

"How many do you think you've done?" Alma asked.

"Since Monday? Around five hundred."

Alma drew in a sharp breath. "How do you find the time?"

"I start right after school and keep going until it gets dark." She wished she'd been old enough to search for her own mother back in the day, but perhaps it wasn't too late—if only she had something to go on. She'd set up a meeting with Samuels to talk about Shoshanna so that might be a good opportunity to bring up the subject of her mother's case with him. Unfortunately, that all had to wait until Friday—Samuels was busy with other leads and couldn't fit her in sooner.

Alma put her finger to her lips, then touched that finger to Celeste's image on the poster, which was hammered so deep it'd now become part of the tree's DNA. "I don't know how to begin to thank you for this."

"It's the least I can do." Alma's praise warmed her even more than the hot tea. It also lessened the sting, just a little, of a growing awareness, with every flyer she handed out for Celeste, that *no one* had looked for her mother.

"Well, it's very generous of you."

It *had* been a lot of hard work. And was it so terrible to want Alma to witness how much she cared? "This is such a coincidence. I thought you'd be home resting."

"The Haven Foundation is a project of mine that's near and dear to my heart. This is our Dream Hub." Alma whipped out her scarf, arranged it over her hair and tied it under her chin. "We do what we can for little girls and young women who've had a rough go of things. Baxter didn't want me to come to the board meeting tonight, but I've been so miserable these past few days, I thought focusing on doing some good for someone else might make me feel better."

"Is it working?" Mia understood the sentiment.

"Actually, it is. And seeing a friend of Celeste's, seeing *you*, is good for me, too. You know you still have her dress—"

"I'm going to return it. I promise. I just wanted to have it cleaned before giving it back."

"No, no, no. I don't mean anything like that. I was only thinking, if you were going to bring it by anyway, maybe you'd like to join us for dinner tomorrow night. Angelica will be there. Isaiah owes you a big apology, and—" her mouth quirked into a sad, half-smile "—I'd love for you to meet my husband, Baxter. I think it would be good for him to see what you've been up to, working so hard to get the word out about Celeste."

"I don't want to intrude," Mia said, praying her faint protest wouldn't result in the invitation's withdrawal.

"Not at all, we'd love to have you."

Mia tried to keep her voice calm. "What time? And I don't know your address." That was true enough. She'd seen photos of the luxury home in a local magazine, but the article hadn't provided an actual street number.

A gray Range Rover pulled to the curb.

"That's my ride." Alma turned, and then called over her shoulder as she hurried off, "I'll have Angelica text you."

Dinner with the family.

This was everything Mia hoped for.

CHAPTER 9

Thursday

The Coopers' private road stretched long enough to wind, bending its way up a steep hill through a tumult of glorious jacaranda trees, their lavender petals dropping onto Mia's windshield, carpeting the way.

A flurry of bright white flashes in the rearview mirror made her shoulders tense. San Diego's chief of police had topped this morning's news with an announcement that the FBI was looking into a possible connection between Celeste's disappearance and that of two other women in nearby states—the body of one had been found in a shallow grave, the other was still missing. Reporters, armed with cameras and crew, were camped at the foot of the private road, and not until they faded out of sight did Mia exhale a long slow breath.

Celeste had been gone nearly a week, now, and the sin of snatching her keys seemed more unforgivable by the hour.

After carefully parking her Jetta in the circular drive in front of the house, Mia retrieved Celeste's dress, now encased in a transparent dry-cleaning bag, then climbed the front porch steps, grasped the door's brass knocker and announced her presence.

Baxter Cooper himself welcomed her inside. "You must be Mia. Good to meet you."

Mia recognized him immediately. Though she'd never watched him on television—the reality TV show featuring his pawnbroker business, *Once a Pawn a Time*, had been off the air for more than a decade—she'd seen plenty of pictures online and in the society pages.

In person, he was even more handsome. His thick, silver hair gleamed beneath the brilliant entryway chandelier. Hardly a wrinkle marred his high forehead, causing her to speculate he might indulge in Botox. He looked far younger than a man approaching fifty and bore a strong resemblance to Isaiah with his deep-blue eyes, aristocratic nose, and square chin.

"Thank you so much for having me," Mia said.

"Our pleasure." His perfectly even tone offered no clue as to how he really felt about Alma asking a stranger to dinner at a time like this, but his posture was stiff enough to give her back sympathy pains. A resigned sigh followed his words, suggesting she wasn't the first stray his wife had brought home.

Footsteps sounded, and Mia watched the stairs hopefully, waiting for Alma to appear and save her from having to carry on an extended solo conversation with Baxter.

Instead, it was Isaiah who descended the staircase.

"I'll take that." Baxter suddenly grabbed Celeste's dress from Mia without asking or giving an explanation. Apparently, Alma had already filled him in on how it came to be in Mia's possession. He slowly smoothed one hand over the plastic dry-cleaning bag, and then cleared his throat and looked away, obviously choked up over the dress. "You and Isaiah go ahead. I'll join you in a moment."

Isaiah offered her his arm and whispered in her ear, "Not to worry. I'm sober."

As formal dining rooms went, this one was everything. An arched entry led into a large space with hardwood floors softened by a plush creamy rug. A rich-green ficus tree in the corner provided contrast to the room's muted tones and perfectly complemented the natural wood furniture. Golden light, from a multitude of fixtures embedded in the ceiling like stars, shone down onto a silver box of white hydrangeas centered on the teakwood dining table. Like Alma, the room was beautiful and elegant without being showy.

It'd taken a moment for Mia to catch her breath.

Here she was occupying the seat next to Isaiah, which was normally, she presumed, reserved for Celeste. It was hard to imagine a more bittersweet moment.

Baxter raised a forkful of air, then laid it down. "Celeste seemed excited about your book club, Mia. She had me pick up a copy of *Jane Eyre* for her."

The irony of that chased away any satisfaction Mia might have otherwise felt. If only she hadn't behaved like a jealous schoolgirl, she and Celeste might've become real friends. Then Celeste would have been here with her family where she belonged, instead of Mia, who didn't. "Really, sir?"

"Yes, really. Tell you what, though, how about you stop calling me 'sir' and 'Mr. Cooper' and that way I won't have to call you 'miss'."

"Agreed." Still, she couldn't deny she enjoyed being treated as if she *did* belong. Even Baxter seemed to be warming to her. And to be on a first-name basis with someone like him—a self-made man who'd started with one lowly pawnshop and then had gone on to become one of San Diego's most prominent businessmen—it was like a dream.

The Coopers' standing in San Diego society was one reason Celeste had seemed unapproachable. But now it was clear Mia hadn't given Celeste the credit she deserved. After all, Celeste wasn't too stuck up to work as a preschool teacher or to join Mia's book club. And she'd complimented Mia's work with Tennyson to her family. Being glamorous and carrying a designer purse didn't make her a snob. Just like being a minor celebrity didn't make her father one.

On the contrary, Baxter had managed to be a good host despite his obvious grief and probable reluctance. His eyes were rimmed red, no doubt from crying. All evening, he'd been going through the motions of eating without actually consuming any food. Now, he pierced a piece of roast, shoved it around on his plate, ringed carrots around the potatoes and stared at the new configuration of edibles.

"Honey, you need to eat." Alma squeezed her husband's arm. "For me."

"Don't know what you're talking about. It's delicious."

Alma lifted an eyebrow and exchanged a glance with Angelica.

"Leave him be, Mom," Isaiah said. "He probably filled up on that caviar he's got stashed in his office bar."

"Boy's right. I did fill up on snacks before dinner—but not caviar. I broke out the Chips Ahoy, I'm afraid." Alma faked a laugh.

But, Mia didn't read her as phony. Rather she thought of Alma as brave, putting on a front for the benefit of her family, and so what if there was a bit of tension in the air? Mia would adore having a sibling to bicker with, a father to discipline her, a mother...

She held back a sigh. Here sat four members of a close-knit tribe—where there should've been five. "Thank you for having me," she said for the umpteenth time that evening.

"I'm so glad you came." Alma extended her hand toward a decanter of red wine and Angelica moved it out of her reach. "But I'm sure you understand if we're not on our A game. I assume you've heard the news about the FBI."

Mia's heart took a long pause in her chest. "Yes, a little. Something about a possible connection with two other missing women. I didn't quite understand why."

"One in Colorado and another in Arizona." Baxter sat forward in his chair. "I phoned Samuels as soon as I heard."

"Would've been nice if the police had given us a heads up so we didn't have to hear it on the news. Detective Samuels has been about as transparent as a brick wall," Angelica said. "The way he's treating us you'd think our family was under suspicion. How many times does he need to interrogate *me?*"

"I guess two less times than he's come after me." Isaiah scoffed.

"He's just doing his job. Anyway, when I pressed him, he explained the concerns about the other women," Baxter spoke in a composed voice, seemingly trying to lower the rapidly rising temperature in the room. "First, there's both geographic and temporal proximity—both those young women disappeared in the past thirty days. And second, both women are in their mid-twenties and are believed to have been abducted off the street from well-known tourist areas after a night out. The young woman in Colorado was out drinking at the Pearl Street Mall, and the woman in Arizona was partying in Old Town Scottsdale."

And Celeste disappeared on a Friday night from the Gaslamp Quarter.

Mia took a sip of water, swallowing her thoughts. She didn't want to voice them and upset Alma, but it was plain enough where the investigation was headed. Had Mia taking Celeste's keys put her in the cross hairs of a serial killer?

"Mia, have the police interviewed you yet?" Alma asked, her voice weak and shaky compared to just moments ago.

Mia did have a meeting with Detective Samuels tomorrow, but she'd set it up herself to tell him about Shoshanna. At Pocket Park, he'd given her his card and asked her to call if she thought of anything that might be of use. Now Alma's use of the word *interview* seemed awfully close to *interrogate*, making Mia uneasy. Her mind flashed to the morning she'd woken up in her room, fully dressed and wearing wet tennis shoes.

The morning after the night Celeste disappeared.

Absurdly, her stomach flipped over—she'd never done anything remotely criminal in her life. Except for taking Celeste's keys, of course. "Why would they want to interview me?"

"You saw Celeste on Friday before she disappeared." Alma reached for the wine again, and this time Angelica didn't block her. "In fact, would you mind telling us about that night? I didn't want to press you for details right after you'd fainted, but maybe you're up to it by now."

"Of course. I'm perfectly fine," she said, though in truth she was feeling rather queasy.

"Go on then, please," Alma said. "I want to know it all. Tell me every detail you remember from the Piano Man. No matter how small. You never know what might be important so please don't leave anything out."

Mia looked helplessly at Angelica. Hadn't she explained to her mother that Mia didn't know anything? This was the moment where Baxter or Isaiah or Angelica should say something to Alma like: *Don't upset yourself. Leave the investigating to the police.*

But no one did.

Four pairs of inquisitive eyes turned on her.

Bile burned its way up her throat. She choked down a sip of cool water. This family deserved the truth. But no one suspected her of taking Celeste's keys, and coming clean now wouldn't help at all. Nor had Mia decided how to best handle the information about Shoshanna spotting Celeste at the strip club. She didn't know if that was connected to Celeste's disappearance or not, and she hated to tarnish the family's image of Celeste without good cause.

Still, Alma had said not to leave anything out and Mia was no liar.

Or at least she hadn't been up until now.

If lies of omission counted, she was definitely building a resume. "I wasn't with the group of teachers that night. I was supposed to meet one of the parents for dinner but she couldn't make it, and then on the way out I bumped into Jane and Celeste." She paused for air, trying not to hyperventilate. "I only wish I knew more."

"Which parent were you supposed to meet?" Angelica asked.

"Ruth Hudson."

"Tennyson's mom? That's interesting. Why couldn't Ruth make it?"

"She texted that something came up. Interesting that Ruth invited me out, or that she couldn't make it?"

"Both." Angelica leaned forward and rested her elbows on the table. "Celeste had an appointment with Mrs. Hudson penciled in the day planner we gave to Detective Samuels."

"But Tennyson is in my class, not Celeste's. I don't see why Ruth would need a conference with her."

"I don't think it was to talk about Tennyson. The entry specified *drinks*. It's a coincidence, I guess, but coincidences should be looked into."

"Let's leave the topic of Ruth for now, shall we?" Baxter jumped in. "Mia, did Celeste say anything to you about her plans for the evening? Where she might be headed after dinner? Was she going straight home? Why she didn't catch a ride with one of her friends?"

"I was just leaving the Piano Man when I bumped into her and some of the other teachers, so I don't know what happened after that. I wish I had the answers for you, but I'm afraid I don't know anything more."

"You're absolutely sure she didn't say anything else about her plans?" Baxter looked like he wanted to reach across the table and shake his daughter's whereabouts out of Mia.

"Not to me. Like I said, I only spoke to her for a moment. The other women are the ones you should ask about that."

Alma wobbled to her feet and, with trembling hands, reached for Angelica's plate.

"Sit down," Baxter commanded. "This dinner was too much for you. I don't want you lifting another finger tonight."

Alma thudded into her seat like his words had physically pushed her down.

Mia jumped up, regretting the strain she'd put on Alma. "I'll clear. It's the least I can do."

She began gathering up dishes.

"I'll help." Isaiah rose and started pulling plates. "Angelica, Mom, Dad, you all stay put. Mia and I have got it under control."

As Mia and Isaiah worked, Alma reached for Angelica's wrist. "Are we still on for church tomorrow afternoon?"

"Oh, Mom, I can't. I haven't been into the office all week, and I have to check in with my team. I don't know how late I'll be. Maybe Dad or Isaiah could take you."

Dead silence. Then Isaiah laughed. "C'mon, Mom. You know Dad and I are 'spiritual but not religious'. I wouldn't want Father Clifford to faint seeing one of us in a house of worship."

Mia, on the other hand, very much wanted to light a candle and say a prayer for Celeste. She wasn't Catholic, but surely that didn't matter in a situation like this. "I get off at three o'clock tomorrow. If that's not too late, I can take you."

Alma looked at her with watery eyes. "Would you? I'm not supposed to drive. I'm afraid the doctor has me medicated."

"I'd really love to. And Alma, if there's anything else I can do for you or the family, I'd be honored."

Alma sighed. "You truly are lovely, dear. Yes, let's light a candle for Celeste. I'll be ready at, say, three thirty?"

"Perfect." Suddenly realizing how precariously the plates were balanced on her arms, Mia sent a *where-is-it?* look to Isaiah.

He bent his neck indicating the way, and she followed him into a large kitchen with white cabinets, marble countertops, gleaming appliances and every gadget known to man. Loads of fresh flowers, probably from well-wishers, filled the room with a pungent fragrance that reminded her of a hospital.

Isaiah let his dishes clatter, willy-nilly, onto the countertop as she stacked hers ever-so-gently in the farmhouse sink.

He snuck up behind her, and she spun around, her heart beating only a little too fast. She wasn't scared of him—not as much as before, anyway.

He touched her shoulder, lightly, not in a threatening way. "Thanks for keeping our unfortunate meeting at Lacy's a secret."

"There was no reason to mention it."

"Still, some girls—women—would have loved to tell my family what an ass I am. I did say I was sorry, right? Because I'm absolutely repentant."

"Yes, you've apologized multiple times. And why would I want to hurt your family… or you?" She sidestepped his grasp.

"You wouldn't, would you? Because you're a nice person."

"Well, anyway, I would never."

"Good, because you're right, it would devastate my family. Mom can hardly sleep despite the way her doctor is loading her up with tranquilizers, and Dad doesn't eat. Angelica puts on a brave face, but I've caught her crying more than once. The last thing they need is to find out their black sheep—" he pointed at his chest "— is acting the fool at a strip club."

"I figured."

"But since you bring up the club…"

"I didn't," Mia said.

"What were you doing at Lacy's? You weren't really applying for the waitress job."

She wanted to tell him all about the matchbook she'd found in Celeste's pocket, and about Shoshanna, but she worried he might not keep Celeste's secrets as well as he kept his own. He claimed he wanted to protect his mother, but how could she be sure he wasn't merely looking out for himself? And if Isaiah did tell Alma her daughter was spotted at a gentlemen's club, there's no telling what it would do to her in her fragile state. Better to fill Detective Samuels in on things and then let him decide how to handle it. "What I was doing at Lacy's is a long story. And what about you? The bouncer said this wasn't your first offense. What did he mean by that?"

"Also a long story. I'd have told you over coffee, but you didn't have time. Now I'm the one who doesn't." He turned up his palms as if to say he knew she didn't trust him, and she hadn't earned his trust yet either.

Fair enough. Leaning against the counter, she almost crumpled from the weight of her misdeeds, her lies, the horrible thought of what Celeste might be going through. And then there was the uncertainty of her own mother's fate—something she'd compartmentalized as best she could until Celeste's disappearance had brought the past roaring back to mind.

"You okay?" Isaiah's voice sounded low and concerned.

She snapped to attention. "Perfect. But I should probably call it a night."

"Yeah, you seem tired." Something about the way he pushed his hair off his forehead reminded her of a little boy—a very sad little boy.

After a round of goodbyes, Isaiah walked her out like a gentleman. Approaching her Jetta, she looked down and dug in her purse for her keys. When she looked up again, Isaiah was frowning at her—waving a piece of notebook paper.

"What's this?" he asked.

"No idea. Where did you get it?"

"Off your windshield."

A sickening feeling of dread came over her as she grabbed the note from his hand.

Isaiah aimed his phone light onto the printed words and read them aloud:

Stay away from the Coopers.
I'm warning you.

CHAPTER 10

Friday

Detective Samuels had filled Mia's cup to the brim and, when she checked her watch, water splashed onto the front of her white blouse. Though her mouth was still dry, she set the cup down on the laminated table beside her, not wanting to chance another spill—this was awkward enough already.

"It's okay to be nervous. This your first time in a police interview room?" Detective Samuels offered no napkin.

"It is." She pulled her damp blouse away from her hot skin.

While he might call this walk-in-closet-sized space an interview room, she knew it was designed to intimidate. Who wouldn't feel anxious in a bolted-down chair, cornered between the door and the detective, with stark white walls staring you down? Reluctantly, she inhaled, and disinfectant fumes set cold fire to her lungs.

Behind her, she heard a clock. It hung out of her sight, but in ready view of the detective and the observation mirror. She shouldn't have agreed to meet over her lunch break—she was definitely going to be late getting back to the academy, and if she didn't forge ahead she might even miss her 3:30 appointment with Alma. The seconds ticked by loudly, the noise amplified, reminding her that even though she couldn't see a microphone, the room was wired for sound. In the beginning, she'd agreed to allow her interview to be video recorded, but she hadn't asked about the logistics. Now, she wondered where the unseen camera was.

"Shall we get started?" Detective Samuels was the type who could intimidate without raising his voice or pounding his fist. All he had to do was look at you with those knowing eyes of his.

"Sure." Despite the frigid temperature of the room, a tiny bead of sweat dripped off her nose. She could really do with a tissue. "I'm afraid I'm short on time, though."

The detective folded his arms.

She stared, longingly, at the cup of water. Was he going to ask her a question or should she just start talking?

He leaned forward. "You called me, remember? What's on your mind?"

"I-I saw Celeste at the Piano Man on Friday night." That wasn't what she wanted to talk about, but Alma said the police would have questions about what happened at the restaurant so she might as well get that part out of the way.

He kicked back in his seat and put his hands behind his head.

"At the Piano Man, I spoke with Celeste briefly on my way out the door. I simply stopped to say hello to her and to Jane Glasgow, another teacher."

"Did you notice anything out of the ordinary with either Celeste or Jane?"

Like finding Celeste's keys on the floor?

"You mean their moods?"

"Anything."

Stop worrying about yourself and think about Celeste. Answer the question.

"Celeste seemed happy. Normal. And Jane, too." She frowned, concentrating, trying to think of something that might actually be of use. "Oh, but earlier that day at school, not at the restaurant, but at work, I do remember Celeste seemed a little off."

"In what way?"

"On Friday, around noon, I went into the teachers' lounge, and Celeste was sitting there, staring at her phone. I don't know why, but she seemed distracted, worried. Her eyes were puffy and watery, although, I suppose, that could've been allergies."

"Did you ask her if anything was wrong?"

"We're not close, I'm afraid."

"So you noticed something was off but you didn't go to the trouble to ask what was going on. Did she volunteer anything to you?"

Of course he was right. She should've asked if Celeste was okay. She'd wanted to, but she'd been too self-conscious to say anything, too worried Celeste would act like it was none of her business. "No. She got up, rather quickly, and left the room, like she didn't want to be sad or mad or whatever in front of me. I didn't try to stop her because I assumed she wanted to avoid me."

"Why would she want to avoid you?"

"She wouldn't. At least not me, specifically. Sometimes I think irrational thoughts like that, and I need to stop." She also needed to guard her words more. This wasn't a therapy session, and Detective Samuels wasn't Dr. Baquero. He might be a cop, but that didn't mean she could trust him.

"So, Mia, if you didn't notice anything unusual that happened at the Piano Man, and you've only just now remembered, when I asked you, that Celeste seemed off at school on Friday, why did you call me? You said you had information about the case."

"I said I *might* have information." She didn't like being misquoted, even if it was only a small deviation from her words, especially when she was being recorded.

"So do you or don't you?"

She studied her nails, wondering if he'd noticed they were chewed to the quick. Next, she became aware of the rise and fall of Samuels' chest—the way it seemed to match her own breathing. Was that some kind of interrogation trick or had it just happened naturally? Regardless, it was time to tell him the real reason she'd come here. It would be a relief to leave the whole matter in his hands and never have to worry about what happened at Lacy's again. "I found a matchbook from a strip club. You remember I fainted."

This wasn't coming out clearly, but he'd been there when she passed out, so surely she didn't need to explain what happened at Pocket Park.

"After you fainted, Angelica took you to Celeste's apartment to lie down. I remember."

"Yes. At the apartment, I changed into one of Celeste's dresses."

He didn't balk at that like Aunt Misty had—he'd witnessed the tearing of her blouse.

"And I found a matchbook in her pocket."

"From a strip club."

"Lacy's Gentlemen's Club. I went there to ask around, and one of the dancers told me she had seen Celeste."

"When?"

"I don't know. But the dancer's name is Shoshanna, and I thought it might be a good idea for the police to talk to her. That's why I called you. Do you think Celeste's going to the club has something to do with her disappearance? She could've met someone dangerous at Lacy's." She hated the way her voice was wobbling, but this was one of the main reasons she'd shoved down all her nerves and come here: to bring the police information that could help them find Celeste. Possibly to help them find a serial killer.

"I think it's worth interviewing Shoshanna. Could be nothing, or could be an important lead. Won't know until I look into it. Does Celeste frequent a lot of clubs?"

"She has a lot friends, an active social life. Plenty of men interested in her, I think. But I've never gotten the impression she was wild. Not that I'm saying going to a strip club is wild, but it isn't typical for Celeste. At least not that I've heard."

"And what about you? What were you doing at Lacy's?"

Why was he asking something she'd already explained? She was trying to help, and he was turning things around on her, like she'd done something wrong. Or maybe she was being paranoid, and he was simply doing his job, trying to tease out any inconsistencies in her story. "Like I said, I found the matches, and I went to the club to ask about Celeste. I was door-knocking. Just like I volunteered to do at the park. I want to help."

"I can see that."

"What?"

"That you really, really want to help. And quite frankly…" He leaned in close. He'd apparently already had his lunch, because she smelled garlic on his breath. "I'm wondering why this investigation is so important to you."

She rubbed the back of her neck. "Celeste is my friend."

"You just said you weren't close."

"We work together, and I like her very much. I admire her. *Naturally*, I want to help."

He pinned her with his gaze, and she started to wriggle like a mounted insect coming back to life. Could he tell she'd not only admired Celeste, but envied her as well?

"I'm getting a strange vibe from you, Mia."

"Maybe you should stop worrying about my vibe and focus on the facts so you can find Celeste." If she could dig herself out of a shed with a tin can, she could stand up to Detective Samuels. Only Mia no longer felt like that version of herself—what happened to that brave little girl? Was she still there, inside her, somewhere?

"I'm all about the facts," Samuels said, "but following my instincts, paying attention to the vibes people give off, has taken me a long way. And I'm getting the distinct impression you aren't telling me everything." He stretched his legs in front of him until his shoes nearly touched hers. "What are you hiding?"

His *instincts* unnerved her. If it would help, Mia would confess to taking Celeste's keys—but it wouldn't. On the contrary, he might waste precious time looking at *her* as a potential suspect. "I'm not hiding anything."

She followed his gaze to her clenched fists. It would be easier to walk out now. Leave it at that, but there was another very important reason she'd come here today. "But I would like to ask you something for me. Nothing to do with Celeste."

"I'm listening."

She closed her eyes, and then opened them. "When I was six years old, my mother, Emily Thornton, went missing. We lived—I suppose 'squatted' would be a more accurate term—in an abandoned cabin within San Diego County. I don't know if that falls under your jurisdiction, but if it doesn't, surely you know people." She paused, though not long enough to lose her nerve. "I'd like to see my mother's case files. Can you help me with that?"

He pulled a hand over his face, as if to wipe away any clues to his reaction. "Depends."

"On what?"

"Has your mother's case been adjudicated?"

"It was never solved, if that's what you're asking."

"No body was ever found? No one was convicted of any wrongdoing?"

"No. Which is why I'd like to see the files. I want to find out what happened to her. People don't just disappear. Whether she's living or-or… not living. She's out there, somewhere, and I want to find her. I *need* to find her."

"And you think there's something in the records that might help you. I get it. But I have to say, first, it's unlikely that you can solve a mystery the police couldn't. And second, you're not entitled to the files. If the case had been adjudicated, tried in court, all records would be available to the public and you could request access via FOIA."

"What's that?" she asked, her chest tightening with disappointment.

"The freedom of information act, but in your situation that doesn't apply. Even if the case is not being actively investigated, it's still out there, potentially prosecutable. You can't get the records because someday it might be reopened."

"Okay then, I'd like to get it reopened. How do I do that?"

"You can't. Not without good reason. It'd be a waste of scarce resources." He puffed out his lips. "I'll tell you what, though."

She held her breath, daring to hope Detective Samuels actually cared that a woman had gone missing and no one had ever bothered to search for her.

"I'll ask around. See if I can get a look at the case files, and if I think there's something viable in them, I'll get back to you."

"Thank you." She was glad her voice sounded calm, and though she was grateful—incredibly grateful—she refused to gush like he was doing her a favor. Because it wasn't a favor: finding her mother was the job of the police.

A job at which they'd failed miserably.

Besides, his appraising look made her wonder if he had some ulterior motive for agreeing so quickly. Perhaps he was interested in finding out more about her because he didn't fully trust her.

"You're welcome." He angled his head. "Is there anything else? You look like you're not quite done."

Tell him about the note Isaiah found on your windshield.

That would be a mistake. No one except Aunt Misty had known she was dining at the Coopers' home. And it was probably Aunt Misty who'd left that note—after all, she'd done worse things, like the time she'd deleted all the emails sent by Mia's school friend because she'd thought he was a "dangerous boy".

"That's all, Detective, but if I think of anything else that could help you find Celeste, I promise I'll be in touch."

CHAPTER 11

Arms locked, Mia and Alma rushed inside St Michael's church with a volley of frenzied questions flying over their heads: *Has there been a ransom note? Your son's been interviewed multiple times. Is he a suspect? Do the police think it was a serial killer?*

Looking back over her shoulder, Mia wished she could barricade the doors, but after a few deep breaths she realized there was no need. Apparently, the reporters were going to respect the sanctity of the church and give Alma a chance to say a prayer for her daughter in peace.

"I think they'll leave us alone now." Breathless, Mia pressed a hand to her chest.

The reporters had been camped at the bottom of the Coopers' private road, but up until now they'd been reasonably respectful.

"I think that brunette is a bad influence. When she jumped in her van, the others climbed in theirs. This is the first time they've followed me."

Mia knew exactly who Alma meant. A pretty brunette with stick-straight locks and over-filled cheeks, perpetually blushed up and camera ready. Already tall, her height was increased to star level by stilettos. "I don't know how she can move that fast in those shoes. I hope she twists an ankle."

"I was thinking exactly the same thing." Alma's eyes locked with hers, and for the first time since she'd met her, Mia detected a spark of fun in them.

Mia smiled. "Not very Christian of us, is it?"

"I won't tell if you won't." Alma's mouth twitched, and then without warning her shoulders started to shake.

In unison, as if they'd both caught the same contagious disease at the exact same moment, they could contain themselves no longer and peals of laughter rang through the church vestibule, echoing off the gilded walls and high arched ceilings.

When she finally regained control, Mia said, "Nice acoustics."

Alma swallowed a few times before responding, "I bet the choir sounds great."

"Please, can you show some respect?" A woman with a teenager in tow pushed past them on her way out.

"We're so sorry," Mia whispered.

"Really sorry," Alma said, her tone and her face sagging back into their previous state of despair.

At least, Mia thought, as they ushered each other from the vestibule into the sanctuary, Alma had gotten some relief. For one minute, she'd been able to think of something other than her daughter's disappearance. And Mia knew from experience how few and far between those moments came in the beginning. "It gets better. I promise," she said, without considering what her words revealed.

Alma looked at her with a question in her eyes, then simply nodded and said in a low voice, "I hope so."

Taking in the beauty around her, sunlight pouring through stained glass, towering gladiolas atop elaborately carved altars; Mia noticed she and Alma were the only people left in the sanctuary. Aunt Misty wasn't organized religion's biggest fan, and Mia had never been inside a Catholic church, though she'd seen pictures, of course. St Michael's did not disappoint with its stunningly high ceilings, rich tapestries and everywhere-you-looked statues. Alma stopped in front of a wrought-iron table, filled with ascending rows of red votive candles. Some were burning, emitting a pungent, waxy odor. Mia hung back as Alma placed a bill in the collection box and lifted a match from a side holder.

"Excuse me," she whispered, wanting to get her questions in before Alma began to pray, "but are there rules?"

"You're not Catholic?"

"No." She'd been praying and hoping, in her own way, for as long as she could remember, though. Trying to keep the faith that good was stronger than evil.

"They aren't rules so much as guidelines. The candle is for whatever prayer you want to offer. For the dead or for the living. The flame continues to burn, signifying your prayer continues after you're no longer present. Anyone can light a candle, Catholic or not, and usually we place a small donation to cover the cost."

"Is it okay if I light two candles?"

"Of course." Alma's look asked the question that remained unspoken.

"One for Celeste and one for my mother," Mia volunteered.

"What's your mother's name, dear?"

"Emily," she said, unable to keep the tremor from her voice.

"I'll light a candle and say a prayer for Emily, too," Alma said. "Has she passed?"

"I-I don't know. She went missing when I was six years old." She shouldn't be burdening Alma, who was carrying the weight of her own loss, with this information, but somehow in this moment, Mia felt closer to Alma than she had to anyone in a long time, including her aunt. "We don't know for sure, but the police think she ran off with her boyfriend. No one has seen or heard from her in twenty years."

Alma touched her heart, and then held the match in her hand to an already flaming candle, lit two others with it, and bowed her head. After placing a five-dollar bill in the collection box, Mia lit two candles as well, and then closed her eyes, picturing her mother's face, remembered mostly from photographs. Next she called up an image of Celeste, as she prayed for their safe return.

At last, Mia opened her eyes and smiled at Alma. "Thank you."

"Thank *you* for coming with me," Alma said, her face unguarded, open.

The two shared a hug, and then wandered toward the vestibule.

When Mia turned to again admire the magnificent artwork on display, she heard Alma's quiet footfalls behind her, and then, the discordant, rapid-fire clicks of heels on marble. She spun around, just in time to see the tall brunette reporter thrust a microphone in Alma's face.

"Have you heard from a kidnapper? Do the police have any leads?"

Alma shot a pleading look at Mia.

"Can you please give Mrs. Cooper some privacy? We're in church. I'd really appreciate it," Mia tried.

"Are you the family spokesperson? What's your name? Do the police think Celeste is dead?"

"Please! Leave us alone!" Alma cowered, and then took a few shaky steps to the side.

"Just a few more questions." The reporter lunged, jamming her mic in Alma's face, simultaneously grabbing her by the sleeve.

Alma stumbled back.

Mia rushed toward Alma, and at that very moment, the reporter careened forward and banged her shoulder into Alma's chest, toppling her straight into Mia's outstretched arms.

"Are you okay?" Mia whispered, making sure Alma was on steady feet before releasing her. Then she glared at the reporter. "You pushed her."

"I'm sorry. It was an accident—my heel slipped. But why is she stumbling around? Is she drunk—like the son?" Next, the woman jammed the mic in Mia's face, all the while body blocking Alma, who was trying to skirt her and make an escape.

Mia's head started to spin. Voices reverberated around her, echoing off the walls, and then, suddenly, everything went silent, as if someone had hit the mute button.

The reporter launched herself, yet again, toward Alma.

It must've happened fast, but for Mia, time slowed to a crawl. She wrapped her arms around the reporter and locked them tight when she struggled to get free.

They tumbled onto one of the pews, and Mia's head thunked painfully against wood. The screech of a microphone in her ear sent shock waves through her body. Her blurred vision sharpened until, at last, the contorted, furious face beneath her came into focus.

"Get off me! Somebody help!"

The world jolted back to real time.

Mia had the leggy brunette reporter pinned beneath her on a church pew. Something had snapped inside, and Mia hadn't been able to stop herself. "You want me to let you go?" she said between wheezy breaths. "Stay away from the Coopers."

"I promise! Now get the hell off me!"

Trembling from the adrenaline jetting through her body, and more than a little shaken by her utter loss of control, Mia climbed off the reporter and looked up—straight into the lens of a camera.

CHAPTER 12

Mia kicked off her shoes and lay down on the living room sofa. Its old, thin cushions offered little protection from the hard surface beneath, but after battling that reporter, she didn't have the will to walk the extra steps to her bedroom. Besides, she wanted to catch Aunt Misty as soon as she came in the door.

She'd been avoiding Mia, and they needed to talk.

If her aunt had, indeed, left that menacing note on Mia's car, it was imperative she own up to it. When Isaiah first shined his light on that note, for a split second, Mia's pulse had gone haywire and a thousand terrifying possibilities had flooded her mind.

Even now, a tiny voice in her head kept asking, *what if it wasn't Aunt Misty?*

And not knowing for certain had forced her to play defense with Detective Samuels. Bad enough to conceal the information about Celeste's keys—now, she was keeping *two* secrets from him. No matter how disappointed she was in her aunt's behavior, she didn't want the police breathing down her neck.

The door opened, and Aunt Misty entered the foyer that opened onto the living room. After tossing her purse onto a stand by the door, she came straight over, dropped a kiss on top of Mia's head, pushed Mia's feet aside and turned on the television.

Mia sat up, tugged the remote out of her aunt's hand and hit the mute button. "We need to talk."

Her aunt smiled. "First, can I just say I've had a crazy day? Aileen called in sick, and I had to take over an early meeting for her, then I had to show three houses and handle the closing documents on another. Tonight, though, is going to be all about you, starting with a special dinner. I've got all the fixings for your favorite German chocolate cake. I just need to know if you want me to make my famous chicken casserole, or that Salisbury steak you like so much?"

"Salisbury steak." She'd skipped lunch to go down to the station today, and the thought of Aunt Misty's cooking made her stomach rumble, but she didn't intend to let her aunt distract her with all this chatter. A special dinner sounded like someone was trying to make up for something—leaving an intimidating note, for example.

"I was hoping you'd pick steak."

Mia turned to square her gaze with Aunt Misty's. "I need to ask you about something that happened last night."

Her aunt's face paled. "Something happened at the Coopers? It's nothing bad, I hope."

"Nothing good, that's for sure." She took a deep breath. Suspecting her own aunt, the only family she had left, made her uneasy. Even if Aunt Misty thought she was looking out for Mia, scaring her like that had been cruel. "Last night, while I was at the Coopers, someone put a note on my car. It's very important that you don't lie to me about this."

"I don't understand. What did the note say? Are you... Are you suggesting *I* left it?"

"With everything that's going on, with a possible serial killer out there, I have to know the truth. Did you—" Her words were interrupted by a knock at the door.

Aunt Misty's eyes widened.

Mia got to her feet. "I'll find out who it is."

"Be sure to check through the peephole before—"

"I open the door. I will. Contrary to popular opinion, I do exercise reasonable caution in my daily life." She pressed her eye to the peephole, and her stomach dropped. It was far too soon for Samuels to bring news about her mother, and none of the other reasons that came to mind for his visit were positive. "It's Detective Samuels—one of the police assigned to Celeste's case. I had an interview with him earlier today, down at the station."

"The police interviewed you?" The alarm in her aunt's voice was apparent.

"I'll explain later." She opened the door and ushered the detective inside.

Samuels took a seat in an armchair across from the united front she'd formed with Aunt Misty on the couch. After the requisite offered and refused cup of tea, and a silence long enough for Mia to come up with a number of catastrophic scenarios in her head, Detective Samuels announced the reason for his visit. "I'm here about the note you found on your car last night. You should've reported it."

How did he know? She'd parked her Jetta in the Coopers' drive, and the reporters were supposed to stay off the private road—but what if one of them snuck up to the house? Might they have seen her aunt leaving the note? Would they be able to identify her? She cast a cautionary glance at Aunt Misty. "There's nothing illegal about a note on someone's car."

"If the note contains a threat, then yes, it's illegal."

"So you already know what's in it?" If Mia had believed for a moment that her frustration with her aunt outweighed her desire to protect her, she'd been wrong.

Detective Samuels pulled out a plastic bag and a glove from his pocket. "I assume you didn't throw away evidence."

"Evidence?" He didn't realize that the note probably wasn't connected to Celeste's case because he didn't know her aunt like she did. He didn't understand how deep Aunt Misty's fears ran, what she was capable of doing to keep Mia "safe".

"Yes, evidence. Where is it—the note?"

Beside her, Aunt Misty seemed to be shrinking in size. Mia longed to reach for her hand to reassure her, but she didn't want to draw attention to her aunt's discomfort, and Samuels had already implied Mia was concealing evidence.

It was one thing to keep quiet about the note until she could question Aunt Misty, however, now that the police were aware of its existence, she couldn't pretend she'd gotten rid of it. Especially because there was a possibility her aunt hadn't done it. If only she'd had a chance to get this sorted before the detective had turned up. "It's in my room. I'll get it."

She hurried to retrieve the note. She'd hidden it inside the hope chest along with her other dirty little secret, and now Detective Samuels might burst through her bedroom door while the chest was open.

The thought sent her pulse skyrocketing.

As she dug around, Celeste's keys gleamed at her, but this wasn't the time or place for self-recriminations. She didn't dare leave Detective Samuels alone with Aunt Misty for long. Continuing her search, she came upon the old photograph of herself as a child, and a deep sense of loss welled up inside her, not because of what she remembered, but because of what she didn't. Fighting back a barrage of emotions she kept digging until, at last, she spied the note. In case there really were serial killer fingerprints to be had, she used her fingernails to lift it by the corner, and then slammed the lid of the chest.

Back in the living room, she held the note out for Samuels who took it in a gloved hand.

The frown lines on his forehead deepened, and then he read aloud, in an ominous tone:

"'Stay away from the Coopers. I'm warning you.' You didn't feel threatened by this?"

"I was going to tell you." She rested her chin atop steepled fingers. "I just wanted to think about it."

"You wanted to find out if your aunt wrote it."

"Yes. I wanted to speak to my aunt first." Mia felt her jaw tighten. "Earlier today, you said you were getting 'a vibe' that I was holding back information, but apparently you already knew about the note. So now it feels like *you're* the one not being straight with me. Where did you get your information?"

"I didn't know at the time, and for the record, I don't have to disclose my source to you. *I'm* the cop. But in the interest of mutual cooperation, I don't mind telling you. About half an hour after you left the station, I got a call from Isaiah Cooper."

Isaiah? She could understand why he might feel the need to inform the police, but she'd explained to him last night it was only her aunt, nothing to worry about, and he'd seemed to accept that. Though she hadn't specifically asked him not to tell anyone, she thought it was understood. She barely knew him but, considering she'd kept his secrets, this felt like a betrayal.

"I can see you're surprised, but I don't know why. Isaiah thought, and rightly so, that this was a matter for the police. The threatening tone alone—'I'm warning you'." He wove a heavy thread of malice into his voice.

"That's *not* a threat. There's no negative consequence mentioned."

"It's implied."

"Not really. It doesn't say stay away from the Coopers *or else*. It could simply mean 'I'm warning you' in the same way you'd counsel a child not to dive into the shallow end of a pool. That would be the opposite of a threat. Instead of meaning harm, the intent would be to protect."

"So who are *you* protecting?"

"You're making too much of this. You have the note. I've said I thought Aunt Misty might've written it, and if she did, it's not relevant to the case. She meant no harm, and that's that."

"I'll be the judge of what's relevant, and whether or not it's illegal."

"Are you saying I could be charged with some sort of crime?" Aunt Misty gripped the arm of the couch like it was coming in for a crash landing.

"That would be at my discretion, ma'am. *Are* you the author of this letter?"

"I'm not." But the way Aunt Misty's eyes were darting around made her look guilty—and she probably was.

The wheels in Mia's head were spinning, but taking her nowhere. "If someone did threaten me—and I'm not saying I find this note threatening in any way—wouldn't it be up to me to press charges?"

"Not your call," Detective Samuels said flatly.

"I didn't write it!" Aunt Misty found her voice again.

"Then you won't mind printing out the words for me so I can compare your hand to that of the note."

Could he really analyze a printed note the same way he could compare a longhand sample? "Aunt Misty, please. Just tell the truth. Because if you didn't write this, then that means…"

Actually, she wasn't sure what it would signify. Maybe it could've been a reporter. But why would a journalist warn her to keep away from the family? Maybe it could've been the same person who took Celeste but that seemed far-fetched, paranoid. "Detective Samuels, have you considered that Isaiah Cooper might have planted this? I didn't actually see it on my windshield. He was the one who said he found it, and then he showed it to me."

"Why would he?"

"I don't know, but we didn't get off on the right foot."

"Seems like a weak motive to me, but I'm happy to collect a sample of his handwriting for comparison as well. While we're at it, in the spirit of inclusiveness, might as well get one from you, too."

She felt blood rushing to her face. "That makes no sense."

"I don't mind looking foolish if it helps me solve a case." He handed her a paper and pen.

CHAPTER 13

Saturday

Strange how the sudden absence of sound can be just as startling as an alarm. Mia rubbed her arms until the feeling came back to them. Between rushing out the door after school all week to put up flyers, interviewing with Samuels and taking Alma to church, Mia had fallen behind, and thus found herself at the academy, late on a Saturday afternoon, slugging away on next week's lesson plans. At some point, she'd put her head down for a moment, fallen dead asleep, and then suddenly awakened to an eerie silence.

Taking in her empty classroom, now shrouded in twilight, shadows transforming the walls into Rorschach cards, she shivered.

How long had she been out? She shouldn't have put her head down, but it'd felt so heavy. She hadn't been sleeping well lately, but she was glad she'd thrown away her old sleeping pills, because, as far as she knew, she hadn't had another sleepwalking event since the night Celeste went missing.

Suddenly, a pang of anxiety stabbed her in the chest, but she soon dispelled it with a few deep breaths, along with some rational thinking. Yes, she'd awakened dressed the morning after, and her shoes had been damp, indicating she'd been outside at some point, and no, she wasn't certain the gas gauge in her car hadn't changed a tiny bit, and okay, she had been mad at Celeste for excluding her—but she had never physically harmed anyone in her life, and she never would. It wasn't like she'd awakened covered in blood with a knife in her hand.

The accusing voice in her head whispering *what if* was nonsense.

Worse than nonsense—it was self-destructive. Her thoughts, like the room, were growing uncomfortably dark, and the cleaning crew would've gone home by now.

She was probably the only one left in the building. Time to pull it together and get out of here.

She checked her phone. Three missed calls, all from her aunt.

She clicked the ringer off vibrate, dumped it in her purse, and made her way to the door, then froze with her hand on the knob.

On the other side of the door, she sensed a presence.

Maybe a floorboard had creaked or maybe there'd been another, almost imperceptible, sound, but somehow, some way, she *knew* someone was out there.

Stay quiet.

Holding her breath, she eased her hand away from the door.

Then watched, pulse pounding in her ears, as the knob slowly turned on its own. The door creaked open and her hand went to her throat.

"Mia."

"Baxter." Her breath came out in a rush. "You scared me."

"Sorry. I heard someone moving around in here, and I thought I'd check it out. What are you doing here on a Saturday evening?"

"Lesson plans." For some reason, she was embarrassed to admit she'd fallen asleep at her desk. "What about you?"

"Pinkerman okayed it, and the janitor let me in."

"He's still here?"

"Luckily, yes. Alma wanted me to bring home the family photo Celeste keeps on her desk and that cardigan she always wears."

Mia stared at him, noticing for the first time that he had Celeste's favorite sweater draped over his arm and a framed photo in his hand.

She pictured Celeste grabbing her red cardigan, making a big show of putting it on and chattering her teeth every time Pinkerman fired up the air conditioning.

A complete waste of energy. Doesn't she know this is San Diego? She's going to freeze us to death!

The memory, braided together with Mia's fatigue, left her drained; a hollowed out feeling started taking hold in her chest. It'd been more than a week. There had been speculation about a serial killer, but *this* seemed premature.

Baxter reached out and put his hand on her shoulder, and then, seemingly reading her mind, said, "I know, right? We're not giving up. And frankly this wasn't my idea. But her mother…"

Mia watched as Baxter's eyes moistened, waited for him to collect himself.

"Her mother wants them. She's says it will help her feel closer to Celeste. So here I am. I worry it will do more harm than good, but I'm doing all I can to keep Alma's spirits up." His voice was low and tense with emotion.

It was obvious how much he cared.

Mia nodded. "This must be so difficult for you both. I want you to know I'm thinking of your family every day."

"Thank you," he said. "Alma and I appreciate everything you've done."

"I haven't done much." Not nearly enough.

"But you have—putting up all those flyers—more than five hundred is what I heard." He offered his arm. "May I walk you to your car? It's getting dark, and I'd like to make sure you get out of here safely."

Her throat tightened.

Good fathers were plentiful. Loads of people had them, but what would it be like to have one of her own?

In the parking lot, she unlocked the car with her key fob, and as Baxter opened her door for her, impossible as it seemed, she felt a pang of envy toward Celeste.

CHAPTER 14

Monday

Mia arrived at 8:15 a.m. at Harbor Youth Academy, a good forty-five minutes before her first class was scheduled. It was her habit to arrive half an hour early, but today she'd allowed additional time. Over the weekend, a spate of news stories had aired regarding Celeste's disappearance and its possible connection to the murder of an Arizona woman and the disappearance of a Colorado coed. Unfortunately, one channel also ran footage of Mia's scuffle with that reporter at St Michael's.

If she'd seen it, Pinkerman would surely want to discuss it.

The edited video from inside the sanctuary made Mia look deranged. Channel Four News had failed to air the portion in which the reporter accidentally shoved Alma. Instead, they'd shown, out-of-context, Mia lunging for the reporter and tumbling on top of her onto a pew with the following voice over:

Cooper family spokesperson, Mia Thornton, attacks local reporter. Pins her down and threatens her with bodily harm.

Some of which was a distortion of the truth, and some of which—the threatening with bodily harm bit—was a bald-face lie.

Nor had Mia claimed to be the family spokesperson.

That false report had caused Mia problems with Aunt Misty, who was already paranoid about the Coopers, and who, after watching the report, broke open her *for-dire-circumstances-only* bottle of tequila.

Mia pressed her palms to her temples to mitigate the throbbing in her head. The way things were going, she saw zero chance that Pinkerman wouldn't be mad. With downcast eyes, she passed the teachers' lounge, then turned the corner into the long hallway that led to the classrooms and to the director's office. The thud of a heavy door closing, followed by the slap of shoes on tile, made her raise her gaze. And there, posed with her back to Mia's classroom, lurked Ruth Hudson.

Mia had been too lost in thought to see exactly where Ruth had come from. Was she looking for Mia? She forced her best *Miss Mia* smile into place for Tennyson, but he wasn't trailing timidly behind his mother like usual. She raised a hand in greeting, but Ruth didn't make eye contact.

She rushed past so closely Mia could smell her gardenia-scented body lotion.

She wanted to believe Ruth must be in a terrible hurry, but she couldn't quite reassure herself. Ruth had obviously seen her, and Mia would've hoped for at least a smile as a show of support—a sign that Ruth understood there must be more to the story than what she'd seen on TV.

"Mia…" Pinkerman poked her head out of her office and motioned. "May I see you for a moment?"

Once inside Pinkerman's office, seated across from the stern-faced director of Harbor Youth Academy, Mia felt sweat dampen the back of her neck. She clasped her hands, waiting, wondering, as she often did, what prompted Pinkerman to wear her beautiful, thick black hair slicked into a topknot that had long since gone out of fashion, even for schoolmarms. Her cold appearance didn't jive with the welcoming tone of her office, with its walls covered in children's drawings and posters of kittens. Mia sometimes thought that the director of Harbor Youth Academy's stark style might be overcompensating for a soft heart. Or maybe it was simply that it was harder for a woman in a position of authority to be taken seriously.

"Mia, I've known you a long time—" Pinkerman tapped some papers on her desk to align the edges "—and I've never observed you to be violent or confrontational in any way."

The nervous fluttering in Mia's stomach settled.

"But what I saw on the news shocked me."

"I can explain." Mia's voice cracked, making it seem as though she was guilty of something.

"Good. Because we've had a complaint."

So soon? "From whom?"

"If you don't mind, I prefer to begin with your explanation. You did say you have one."

Mia nodded. "Alma Cooper needed a ride to church, so I gave her one."

"That was good of you. But I was surprised to learn you were the family spokesperson. Pardon my saying so, but I didn't think you and Celeste were close."

"I'm not the spokesperson, and Celeste and I aren't close." She shut her eyes, grasping for something both positive and true to say about her relationship with Celeste. "She was going to join my book club."

When she opened her eyes, Pinkerman lifted an eyebrow in challenge.

"No, really, she asked her father to pick up a copy of *Jane Eyre*. But as I was saying, Alma and I—"

Pinkerman's other eyebrow went up.

"I mean *Mrs. Cooper* and I went to light a candle for Celeste, and a group of reporters tailed us. One reporter followed us inside and later shoved Mrs. Cooper. She said it was an accident, but Alma would've fallen if I hadn't been there to catch her. So when the reporter reached for Alma a second time, I stepped in."

"You knocked the reporter down."

"No. I put my arms around her to stop her, and I'm not exactly sure what happened after that. One of us stumbled, I think. Then, the next thing I knew, she was underneath me on the pew."

"Why didn't you get off right away?"

"I should have, but honestly, I was angry, and I wanted her to promise to leave the Coopers alone."

"I believe you." Pinkerman rubbed her jaw. "But the problem is the complaint came from Ruth Hudson, so I can't ignore it."

"Ruth?" Mia should've known when she'd seen her in the hallway.

"I don't know why you're so surprised. Her husband is on the board. The Hudsons have a vested interest in preserving Harbor Youth Academy's outstanding reputation—as do we all. It isn't seemly for one of our teachers to be wrestling around with a reporter. It makes you look unhinged."

"I understand." Mia had thought Ruth would've given her the benefit of the doubt. "And I promise nothing like this will ever happen again. I'll apologize to the board and to Ruth."

"I'm not sure that's good enough. Mrs. Hudson has requested Tennyson be transferred to Jane's class."

"But…" Mia didn't finish her thought. Jane had a way with all the kids, and Mia would never raise a concern over her competence. It was only that Tennyson had his challenges, and he and Mia had forged a special bond. Everyone, especially Ruth, knew that. "What do you mean that's not good enough? Am I being let go?"

Pinkerman picked up a teddy bear snow globe she used as a paperweight, then put it down again. "No, not yet. I don't think it would be good for morale at a time like this. The other teachers, the students, need stability. Change is hard, and you've never done anything remotely like this before, so I'm going to give you another chance."

Not to mention the school was short-staffed without Celeste, but again, Mia didn't speak her thoughts aloud. Instead, she sat.

Silent.

Deflated.

"You're on probation. I'll look in on your class often, and I'll be keeping a close eye out for any untoward behavior." She met Mia's eyes. "I don't know what got into you. You're not a troublemaker."

"No, I'm not. I promise you have nothing to worry about."

Pinkerman nodded toward the door. "I'll pop in on you before your noon break."

Mia closed the door behind her, and then jumped when she felt a hand on her shoulder.

"Are you doing okay?" Jane's voice had never held more empathy.

Her concern nearly brought Mia to tears. She was unaccustomed to anyone, especially one of the other teachers, behaving as if her feelings mattered.

Taking her off guard yet again, Jane hooked her elbow through Mia's, guided her into Mia's empty classroom and shut the door. "I'm proud of you for giving hell to that reporter. Celeste would hate someone hounding her mother."

Mia wanted to hug Jane. She'd surmised the truth of things without any explanation. "Thank you for not believing the worst of me."

"Of course. I know you. You wouldn't hurt a fly." She lowered her voice to a whisper. "But I'm not so sure about Ruth Hudson. I cannot believe she had the nerve to complain about you."

"How did you know?"

"Pinkerman told me. She said Tennyson's moving to my group, which is ridiculous because everyone knows that fragile boy of hers is blossoming under your tender care."

What a nice surprise to find an ally in Jane. "I think so, too. But I understand why she's uncomfortable. That news report made me look like a crazy person."

"Anyone who knows you should've realized it wasn't the whole story."

"Still, I understand Ruth's concern."

"You're being generous, Mia, as usual. But Ruth should focus her attention where it belongs—on the home front."

A frisson of unease traveled up Mia's back. "You mean the divorce?"

"I saw her holding hands with Paul at Pocket Park last Monday. I think she's taking the jerk back."

The consensus at school was that Paul was at fault, but… "I don't know the story. Was he cheating on her?"

"Probably." Jane continued to keep her voice low. "He was sure trying his damnedest to get with Celeste."

Mia's fingertips began to tingle. *If* that was true, that made Paul Hudson a suspect of sorts, at least someone the police should look into. She wasn't one to buy into gossip, but it wasn't gossip coming from Jane. Jane and Celeste were close confidantes. "Really?"

Even though the door was shut and they were already whispering, Jane cupped her hands around her mouth. "He wouldn't leave Celeste alone. Kept showing up everywhere she went, leaving little gifts and notes. She told him he better stop or she was going to tell his wife. Celeste was supposed to meet Ruth for drinks on Saturday, and she was all set to fill her in on what a creep her husband was. She didn't get the chance, of course, but I think Ruth already suspected something, the way she kept dropping hints to me, trying to get me to admit something about Paul and Celeste. It wouldn't surprise me if Ruth asked you to dinner to find out if *you* knew anything. Not that she wouldn't want to have dinner with you anyway."

"It's all right." Mia shoulders sagged. "It does seem odd that she invited me out. But I thought, maybe…" A sudden thought occurred. "Jane, what did the police say when you told them about Paul Hudson stalking Celeste?"

"I never used the word *stalking*."

"You said he kept turning up places, that he wouldn't leave her alone. That's stalking. So what did they say?"

"I haven't told them yet."

"Why not?" She was in no position to call out Jane, but she could hardly believe she'd kept such important information to herself. Unlike the keys, this was potentially important evidence.

"You don't think Paul Hudson would hurt Celeste, do you? The news is saying this looks like a crime of opportunity, that a serial killer probably followed her into the alley."

Hearing those words made Mia's heart hurt all the more, but she didn't have the luxury of wallowing in her guilt right now. "It *was* a stranger, right?" But then why had the police interviewed family members so many times. At dinner, Angelica had said she felt under suspicion.

"If you believe the news, yes," Jane answered. "Still, I've been worrying myself sick over Hudson."

"If you're worried, why haven't you told the police?" she asked again, in a tone she hoped wasn't judgmental. She just wanted to understand Jane's motive for keeping it under wraps.

"I'm scared," Jane said.

"Of Paul?"

"Hudson's on the board. He could make Pinkerman fire me, and I *cannot* lose my health insurance. I have diabetes. How would I afford my insulin?" She started to tear up.

Mia put an arm around her. "It's okay. You don't need to explain it to me. I understand."

"You do?"

"Completely, but the police need to know about Paul and Celeste. If you can't tell them, then I will."

"But you're already in trouble with Pinkerman. You'll definitely get fired."

"If I'm a dead woman walking, it might as well be me. I'll phone Detective Samuels right after work."

"You'd do that for me? But how can you? You don't know the details."

"I'll just say I overheard some of the teachers. I'll say I don't even remember who was there or what day it was—just a vague memory. Then the police will do their job, interview everyone and find out the truth. Some of the others might know about this too, and if they confirm that Paul was bothering Celeste, then no one person, except maybe me, will have a target on her back. What do you think?" Mia thought it was a viable plan, but Jane didn't respond.

As the color drained from Jane's face, Mia turned toward her desk.

There, spotlighted by sunlight streaming in from a high window, sat a big, white, fluffy ball.

Celeste's pom-pom keychain.

CHAPTER 15

Detective Samuels' voice boomed as he spoke with the crime scene techs who were dusting for prints in Harbor Youth Academy's four-year-olds' classroom. He'd ordered Jane, Mia and Alma (who'd been called to the school to identify the keyring) not to leave, and now the three of them huddled on wooden ladder-back kiddie chairs placed out of the way of the police, directly beneath a vent blowing the pungent odor of piney floor cleaner up their noses. If not for the bone-crushing grip Alma had on her hand, Mia would be tempted to bolt out of her chair and make a run for it.

"If that's not Celeste's keyring, I don't see the purpose of turning Mia's classroom upside down, or of questioning us." Jane crossed her arms.

"From what I gather, Samuels wants to get what he needs before the place is overrun with children, just in case I'm wrong." Alma's lips quivered as she spoke. "He compared it to finding a possible murder weapon."

"What does he mean by that?" Mia's heart climbed to her throat, but she deliberately infused her voice with calm, both for Alma's sake and because she didn't want Samuels to sniff out her fear with his killer instincts.

"He said when he's on a case and he finds a smoking gun, he doesn't wait until he knows for sure it's the murder weapon before collecting evidence from the scene, and in this situation, he won't wait until after he determines if these are the actual keys Celeste had with her when she arrived at the Piano Man on Friday night."

"But you told him they're not hers," Jane said.

"He wants to try the keys in Celeste's door and her car, just to make sure. I don't think he thinks I'm lying, but you know he has to show due diligence. I'm not insulted. I want him to consider every possible angle—document everything. I want him to find my daughter."

Mia wanted him to find Celeste, too. But she wasn't as keen on him considering every possible angle.

Not if it meant putting *her* under a microscope.

When she'd spied that giant, white, fluffy ball on her desktop, her first thought had been that Aunt Misty had found Celeste's keyring and had put it there to teach her some sort of lesson. But that theory didn't hold water because Aunt Misty wouldn't have known the keyring belonged to Celeste. Even if she had, she wouldn't have done anything that could potentially get Mia in trouble.

And when, on closer inspection, Mia had realized that the keyring on her desk did not belong to Celeste—Celeste's was inscribed with the designer's name and had a charm dangling from its chain—she could only stand silently by while Jane got weepy and Pinkerman called the police.

Pom-pom keyrings weren't uncommon, and therefore, this one was probably left by a parent or older sibling—an unfortunate coincidence, nothing more.

Except… every bone in Mia's body was ringing with alarm.

She couldn't entirely discount the idea that someone had snuck into her classroom and deliberately planted a look-a-like keyring, showcasing it on her desk, to let her know they knew what she'd done.

To let her know they were *watching*.

An involuntary shudder drew sympathetic looks from both Alma and Jane.

"What a mess!" Jane said. "This is definitely creepy, but I don't think it should be allowed to disrupt the entire school. Pinkerman overreacted canceling classes for the day. And she should've waited before she called the police. I'm so, so sorry, Alma, that we got you all worked up over a coincidence."

"Not to worry," Alma said bravely. "I want to be in the loop, and I'm glad Samuels is so conscientious."

Mia nodded, but as she watched Samuels collecting evidence, she couldn't help wishing he would be a little less thorough. She snaked her hand out of Alma's grasp, and her fingers brushed against the cool rungs of a gold charm bracelet Alma wore. Mia sent her a shaky smile. The idea of this wonderful woman finding out what she'd done and hating her was too much to bear.

She simply couldn't confess to stealing Celeste's keys.

But, assuming Samuels would interview them each privately, there was still something she needed to tell him.

Paul Hudson had been stalking Celeste.

When Mia saw the detective headed their way, she decided to volunteer to let him question her first.

"Ladies." He eyed an empty kiddie chair and wisely chose not to sit. "I'm sorry to keep you cooling your heels and then run out on you, but I'm afraid something's come up. I'll be in touch later, though, to take your statements, hopefully by tomorrow or the following day."

"What came up?" Alma asked.

"We'll talk soon." Samuels clicked his tongue as if that put an end to the conversation.

"If this has anything to do with my daughter's case, I'd like to know. You promised me, Detective, that you would keep my family informed of any new developments."

He lifted one shoulder. "Is it all right if I talk freely in front of everyone here?"

"Certainly." Alma nodded. "Please don't make me wait."

"There's no break in the case or anything of that nature. I promise I wouldn't keep anything that important from the family," he said.

"I'd like to judge for myself what's important or not," Alma said.

"It's just something I've got to deal with regarding the footage from the security cameras at the Piano Man."

"Security footage?" Mia's stomach clenched. She hadn't noticed any cameras at the restaurant, but then again, she hadn't been looking for any.

As she tightened her grip on the chair, her phone, which had been resting in her lap, began to vibrate.

She picked it up and looked down at the message.

It was from Ruth Hudson.

CHAPTER 16

Since Alma was on medication that made it unsafe for her to drive, Mia dropped her at her home before heading to the Piano Man for a noontime lunch with Ruth Hudson.

Unlike earlier at the preschool, now, when Mia raised her hand in greeting, Ruth smiled back at her from a sidewalk table. Ruth had changed out of the jeans she'd been wearing this morning into a bright, summery dress printed with birds and butterflies. It was one of those fifties throwback styles with a close-fitting top and flared skirt, and she'd brushed her shoulder-length hair into a bouncy style—a fun look only peppy people like Reese Witherspoon and Ruth could pull off.

Mia entered the restaurant's patio gate, and then got a close-up look at her lunch date. Dark rings under Ruth's eyes belied the cheery message her outfit attempted to convey.

Mia tugged self-consciously at her plain blue shift and took a seat across from Ruth at the outdoor table, set with a white cloth and a vase containing a single giant sunflower. The air was heavy with a mix of freshly brewed coffee, cinnamon and well-loved mutt—the Piano Man was one of San Diego's many dog friendly venues. "Sorry if I kept you waiting," Mia said.

"No worries. I just got here, and considering I cancelled on you Friday it would serve me right. Thanks for meeting me," Ruth said, her soft voice as pleasant as always.

You'd never know that just hours ago she'd filed a complaint against Mia. Her shoulders stiffened at the thought, and she eyed her surroundings, noting a camera on the storefront directly across the way. Why couldn't Ruth have asked to be seated *inside* the Piano Man so Mia could check out the location of the indoor security cameras? No matter, she could scout them easily enough on a trip to the ladies' room. "I'm glad you got in touch."

"Sorry I couldn't make it the other night, but my goodness, who could've predicted what a turn things would take with Celeste?"

True enough, but Celeste going missing didn't serve as an excuse for Ruth's behavior. She had yet to explain why she'd left Mia in the lurch. "Why couldn't you make it on Friday?"

"Oh, something came up." Ruth leaned in, and the look in her eyes told Mia the subject was closed. They were moving on. "Let me get straight to the point. I'm sure you're wondering why I asked to meet you today. I'm sorry about complaining to Pinkerman—the old battle axe."

That knocked Mia back. The last thing she'd been expecting from Ruth was an apology. "Pinkerman's not so bad. She has a job to do as director, just like you have a job to do as a mother." Mia decided against pussyfooting around. "I understand why you're concerned after what you saw on the news. I get why you requested a change for Tennyson. But if I'm being honest, I think he's better off in my class. It's taken some time for us to establish a bond but we've forged a good one. He's making friends more easily than he did in the beginning, talking more, participating. Jane is a terrific teacher, but this means he's going to have to start over again with a new group—and he'll be at a disadvantage with the five-year-olds."

Ruth nodded. "You're right. Tenny did have a rough start, and it will be hard for him to be smaller and younger than the other kids in class. As you know, things haven't been easy at home lately. You've been great for my son. I really mean it, and that's another reason I asked you to lunch. I need to say sorry, and also to thank you for taking such good care of him."

"Then why move him?" She wanted to shake Ruth. "And why didn't you ask me about what happened with that reporter before complaining to Pinkerman? I thought… I thought we were friends. Or that we could be, anyway."

"I did, too. But I'm sure you understand that's no longer possible."

"Why not? Don't you want to hear my side of the story?"

"There's no need. I'm sure you were only trying to keep that reporter away from poor Alma Cooper." Ruth cleared her throat.

Mia had the ironic feeling she was being gaslighted in the Gaslamp Quarter. Everything Ruth professed was a contradiction. She said she wanted to be friends but declared it impossible. She said she understood that Mia hadn't done anything wrong, yet she'd complained to Pinkerman. She said she appreciated Mia's care of Tennyson, but she was moving him out of her classroom.

Mia shoved her menu aside and waved off the approaching server.

Whatever game Ruth was playing, she didn't want any part of it.

After the server retreated, Mia said, "What is it you want from me?"

"I told you. To say thank you, and I'm sorry we can't be friends."

"Because?"

"Paul won't allow it. He's adamant after what happened between you and that reporter. I tried to tell him we weren't getting the whole picture, but he says cameras don't lie. So you see the position I'm in."

"Not really. I thought you were separating."

She raised an eyebrow. "If I were, he'd still have every right, as Tenny's father, to ask me to move him out of your class. But no, I'm not leaving my husband. Paul and I have reconciled."

The server approached again, far too soon, and this time, to placate him, they both ordered iced tea.

"What about the sea of electrified eels?" Mia asked dryly.

Ruth looked mystified for a moment, then a look of understanding crossed her face. "Oh, *that*. That's just something one says when they're angry. Funny you remember."

"Funny you don't. It sounded like he'd done something terrible." She tried to catch Ruth's eye but couldn't.

Tea arrived.

Ruth stirred Stevia into hers and took a few sips, clanked her spoon around again, sipped some more. "At one time or another, we've all done things we're not proud of. Like the rest of us, Paul isn't perfect. But, I think, Mia, when one has a family, one has to think of what's best for them—especially those who have no blame or say so."

Okay. Ruth was taking Paul back for Tennyson's sake. Plenty of spouses had forgiven an indiscretion for the sake of a child, but what if Paul's indiscretion amounted to something more. Did Ruth really know all about Celeste, like Jane assumed she did?

Or was she in the dark?

If Ruth did know her husband had been harassing Celeste, it would be better not to bring it up, in case Ruth tried to warn Paul before Detective Samuels could question him. But if she *didn't* know, and Paul had something to do with Celeste's disappearance, then Ruth and Tennyson might be in danger, too, and that was a chance Mia was absolutely unwilling to take. "I'm sorry to have to tell you this, but I heard a rumor Paul had been romantically pursuing Celeste."

Ruth's hand slipped, knocking over her tea, spilling what little remained in the glass. "That's a lie."

"I don't know anything first-hand, but it's not a lie that I heard the rumor. Are you sure you haven't heard it, too? Why were you going to leave him?"

"That's none of your damn business." Ruth narrowed her eyes at Mia. "And I don't know where you get your nerve all of a sudden. I've heard *nothing* about my husband and Celeste Cooper, but if

I had, I wouldn't put stock in it, and I certainly wouldn't repeat it. A horrible story like that could destroy my family."

Mia gave her a minute. It was a lot to take in, and Ruth's reaction was understandable. Her face looked like she'd developed an instant sunburn.

"Don't you dare mention this to the police. You haven't already, have you?" That nice, sweet tone of Ruth's had completely changed. In the course of a minute she'd gone from a genteel socialite hosting a luncheon with her underling to a prosecuting attorney, grilling a hostile witness.

Which made it easier to let any remaining niceties fall to the wayside. "Tomorrow, Detective Samuels will be taking my statement regarding an incident that happened at school. You were notified, weren't you, that school was closed for today? That's how you knew I'd be free for lunch?" Mia asked.

"Yes, but the notice didn't say *why* classes were cancelled. I just assumed it had something to do with Celeste. Perhaps you'll be kind enough to tell me what's happened."

Mia took a sip of tea to soothe her dry throat. *Someone* had left those keys on her desk. It might've been coincidence, or it might've been something much more nefarious. She couldn't imagine how Ruth would know she had taken Celeste's keys, but Ruth had been in the right place at the right time to have planted the look-a-like keyring on Mia's desk. "Were you coming out of my classroom when I saw you this morning?"

"I didn't go near your classroom."

"You were standing right outside my door."

"I was coming from a meeting with Mrs. Pinkerman. You know that."

"Yes, but after that, did you go inside my classroom?"

"I said no. What are you implying?"

"Someone put a pom-pom keyring like the one Celeste carried on my desk. Pinkerman called the police to check it out."

"Was it hers?"

"No."

"Well, then…" Ruth tapped her fingers impatiently, but didn't drop her gaze. She was all eye contact now, like a kid in a staring match. "You've got nothing to worry about, do you?"

CHAPTER 17

Checking over her shoulder, Mia took note of a black sedan creeping behind her. It had been idling at the curb, and then pulled away as she left the Piano Man on foot. Moments ago, she'd said her goodbyes to Ruth and after scouting the indoor security cameras, exited out the front, heading for her Jetta, parked in a lot near Horton Plaza.

On a trip to the ladies' room, she'd verified that cameras were aimed at the exact spot where Celeste had dropped her keys. The same spot where Mia had scooped up those keys and put them in her own purse. And, as if that weren't alarming enough, she thought she'd detected a threatening tone when Ruth leveled her gaze and asked: *You've got nothing to worry about, do you?*

Maybe Mia was getting as paranoid as her aunt, seeing danger in an innocent set of keys, imagining a menacing subtext behind Ruth's words—but that black sedan…

She quickened her pace to a near run.

Because of the bumper-to-bumper traffic in the Gaslamp Quarter, she was making more headway on foot than the drivers on the road.

She glanced over her shoulder again.

That suspicious sedan was still behind her.

Which, under the current traffic conditions, wasn't unusual.

Don't let your imagination drive you crazy.

Behind her, an engine revved—so did her heart rate.

Be logical. No one is out to get you.

Tempted as she was to break into a full-blown run, she slowed down instead.

If someone was playing mind games with her, she wasn't going to let them get the better of her.

Steps ahead, she spied her baby blue Jetta parked at Horton Plaza. She also noted the entry to the alley where the police had found Celeste's purse.

Just get in your car and go home.

Mia turned and marched into the alley.

Her throat closed, and she shivered in spite of the temperate weather. If the reporters were right about a serial killer, Celeste was probably taken from this very passage. There was something familiar about the dank smell, the walls crowding in on her as she moved forward. Her pulse began pounding in her ears like a tactile alarm. She *recognized* that green dumpster. Well, of *course* she recognized it. It was the same as every other dumpster in every other alley in the country. It didn't mean she'd been here before. That sleepwalking episode made it easy to doubt herself, but therapy had taught her not to descend into irrational thinking. She refused to continue to *what-if?* herself.

Hugging her body, Mia did a three-sixty, looking for anything out of the ordinary.

The black sedan inched by the alley's entrance, signaled a turn onto another street, and relief washed over her.

Save for the dumpster, overflowing with refuse, there was nothing to speak of in this alley. No people, no trees, only the backs of buildings with grimy, peeling paint and smeared graffiti. The narrow passageway connected two trendy, well-trafficked streets, and there was a clear view of the entrance and exit. She could see why Celeste might cut through. For an alley, it seemed safe, and would no doubt shave a good half-mile off the route between Celeste's house and the Piano Man.

But why had Celeste chosen to walk home in the first place when she could've simply called a Lyft, or better yet, accepted the ride Jane had offered? Mia estimated that Celeste's Gaslamp adjacent home, even shortcutting through here, was around two miles from the Piano Man—perfect for a morning jog, but quite a trek in heels.

And something was bothering her about the whole "empty purse in the alley" scenario. It occurred to Mia, as she studied her surroundings, that Celeste hadn't *necessarily* been through here. Mightn't an assailant have attacked Celeste elsewhere and tossed the purse later?

A chill ran up her back, but she ignored it and kept moving, deciding to retrace the route leading to Celeste's house.

How would Celeste have gotten in, if she'd made it home?

A spare key hidden under a stoop, maybe.

The hollow echo of Mia's pumps on the pavement reassured her that if anyone approached from behind, she'd get plenty of notice. Keeping her eyes peeled, she finally emerged triumphantly onto the street.

Down the block, she spotted Celeste's house and stopped short.

What did she hope to accomplish with all this?

What if the police were staking out the place?

It would look suspicious if someone recognized her lurking about. Then again, turning around would look worse. Deliberately, she lowered her shoulders and let her arms swing freely at her side. She even managed to whistle a tune.

Nothing wrong with walking down a public street.

And, if pressed, she could invent a reason for being here—though nothing came to mind right this second.

Except that all-night doughnut shop down the way.

The thought of their delicious, maple-iced long johns made her mouth water. She could legitimately pass by Celeste's house on her way to Sugar Tooth, and Aunt Misty would love it if she brought home treats.

Now that she had her reason for being in the neighborhood, she felt comfortable enough to approach Celeste's home.

At the window, a curtain moved, and Mia's breath caught in her throat.

For a single, optimistic heartbeat, she thought it was Celeste.

But then she recognized Angelica's white Mercedes parked on the street.

If Angelica had peeked out from behind that curtain, she'd likely have seen Mia—so better to be bold than try to hide.

She climbed the steps, all the while mentally rehearsing her speech: *I was on my way to Sugar Tooth and I saw your car so I decided to take a chance you were here. Just wanted to say hello.*

Mia lifted her fist, hesitated, then knocked loudly, as if she had nothing to hide.

Angelica opened the door, and Mia took a step back—coughing and choking on the smell of bleach.

CHAPTER 18

"Can I get you anything? Coffee, water… a good stiff drink?" Angelica infused her tone with camaraderie, as if they shared a secret just between them.

"I'm all right." Mia appreciated Angelica's inclusiveness; though, if there was a secret, Angelica had yet to let her in on it. Eyeing the open, half-empty bottle of Chivas and the lone red solo cup on Celeste's coffee table she added, "But don't let me stop you."

"Don't mind if I do." Angelica lifted the cup, then chugged its contents with disquieting fervor.

To be fair, Mia didn't know how full the cup had been, or if the Scotch had been diluted with soda, and in any event, be it early afternoon or no, Angelica had every right. Still, Mia didn't think Angelica had her brother's weakness for drink, and she couldn't help wondering what was going on. When she'd dropped Alma off at her home this morning, Alma mentioned Angelica had gone into the office for an important meeting.

Yet here Angelica was, day drinking, in Celeste's house—which currently reeked of bleach.

It was strange, but Mia was okay with strange.

In truth, she was grateful Angelica had opened the door to her. With Dr. Baquero no longer on speed dial, Mia needed someone to talk to, and though she couldn't confide her troubles to Angelica, it was nice to *pretend* they were the kind of friends who could tell each other anything.

Gazing around, Mia mentally inserted herself into the room's history, imagining that she'd helped Celeste pick out that modern, arched lamp and the Monet poster softening the room with its wonderful pastel colors; and that she and Angelica had often sat together on this suede sofa. Best of all, she imagined that, any minute, Celeste would burst through the front door, bearing a takeout pizza she'd purchased for their confab. Naturally, she'd have gotten their usual—deluxe vegetarian on a thin crust, extra cheese, hold the onions.

"Guess you're wondering what I'm doing here." Oblivious to Mia's daydream, Angelica poured more Scotch into her cup and set it on a coaster.

Funny… she thought she owed Mia an explanation for being in her own sister's house. Surely it was the other way around.

"I told Mother I was going to the office." Angelica took another gulp. "You were with her earlier, so I wanted to mention that you shouldn't say a word about this. It's just between us."

"What is?"

"That I'm here, not at the office. Promise you won't tell."

Mia sighed. There was certainly no shortage of secrets to keep. "If that's what you want, I promise I won't say a word. It's none of my business anyway."

"Oh, but it is. You're entitled to know what you're covering up, right?"

A cover up? If she didn't have to walk back to her car and then drive herself home, she'd take Angelica up on that drink.

"Operation clean up."

"Oh, you've been cleaning. I couldn't help noticing how… fresh… the place smells." She leaned in. "But is that okay? What if the police need to check for blood spatter or prints or…" The desolate look on Angelica's face made her regret her big mouth. Blood spatter? What a horrible thing to say. "I mean, I know the police think Celeste never made it home, but what if she did?"

"Third post cap from the right on the front porch railing is hollow. That's where Celeste keeps her spare key—and it was still there when the cops searched this place."

"Couldn't Celeste have put the key back after she went inside?"

"I guess, but then how did her purse get in the alley? Besides, the police were here from dawn to dusk on Sunday. They had special lights and sprays and fingerprint powder. A team of them came through, took a ton of photos, and then gave us the all-clear to reoccupy if we wanted—that's why I'm here."

"To reoccupy?"

"To get it ready for *Celeste* to reoccupy. She's coming home. I feel it in my bones, and I want things to be nice for her. All those people traipsing in and out, even if they did have shoe covers on." Her brows drew together. "They dusted fingerprint powder everywhere. And Celeste obviously wasn't expecting to be gone long, because she left dirty dishes in the sink. You were here last week. I'd put the nuts and bolts back together by then, but surely you noticed it needed a deep clean."

"Well, I… No, I didn't notice the place being dirty." Her heart ached for Angelica—the younger sister clinging to hope… and yet, if the situation were reversed, Mia would be more worried about preserving evidence than tidying up. Even if the cops had cleared the place, a new clue might come in that would make them want to take a second look, and… "Why keep this a secret from Alma?"

"Because if I tell my mother that I have to get the place ready for Celeste then it's going to trigger the thought of another possibility—what if Celeste doesn't come home again, ever?" Angelica poured more Scotch. "Celeste is going to have a spit-shined house and a warm bed with clean sheets when she gets home. I've seen to that. But my mother and father, and especially my brother, don't need to know I've been over here. I don't want them voicing the question 'will she or won't she come home?'; and I'm sure Isaiah would make a big thing out of it, and say we shouldn't get our hopes up. Well, to hell with him." She covered a belch with her hand. "Pardon me."

"Nothing wrong with hope," Mia said softly. She was no psychiatrist but she'd sat on Dr. Baquero's couch long enough to recognize magical thinking when she saw it. Angelica believed that if she cleaned up Celeste's house *as if* she were coming home, that meant Celeste *had* to come home. "I really do understand. And I give you my word I won't mention seeing you here today."

Angelica smiled in seeming relief. "Thanks Mia. You're the best."

"I'm not." Mia didn't feel worthy of Angelica's trust.

In that moment, she decided.

She was going to tell her about the keys.

"Angelica?"

"Sure you don't want a drink?"

"Maybe a small one wouldn't hurt," Mia said.

Angelica wobbled to the kitchen and a minute later returned with another red solo cup, which she half-filled with liquor before giving it to Mia. "Neat okay?"

"Neat's great." In the space of time it'd taken for Angelica to get the drink, Mia had lost her nerve. She swilled the booze before carefully setting the cup on a coaster. Perhaps she just needed some Dutch courage.

Angelica sat down on the couch, her body angled toward Mia, shoulders back, spine straight, eyes expectant.

Mia took another gulp of Chivas that burned on its way down but did little to bolster her nerve. She simply couldn't bring herself to confess—but she could tell Angelica something else instead. "I've been meaning to tell you. I found something in Celeste's pocket the day I borrowed her dress."

Angelica leaned forward, mouth slightly agape while Mia unloaded the whole story about the matchbook, the strip club, Shoshanna and the run-in with Isaiah.

When Mia finished, Angelica snapped her jaw shut and said, "Why didn't you tell us before?"

"I didn't want to upset your mother."

Angelica frowned. "At least you told the police. Has Samuels checked out that dancer yet—Shoshanna?"

"I don't know. He doesn't share a lot. He's not exactly a fan of mine."

"You think not?"

Mia shrugged. "Listen, I promised your brother I wouldn't mention seeing him at Lacy's. I don't want to put you in a bind, though. If you think you have to tell him I told you, I'll understand."

"So you'll keep my secret, but I don't have to keep yours? That's my kind of bargain, but, in this case, I happen to agree. It's best not to mention *any* of this to my family unless the police think it's related to Celeste's disappearance. Mother's very fragile right now." Suddenly, Angelica looked away. "You said Isaiah dragged you into a back room?"

"Yes, but it was just a case of mistaken identity. After all, I was wearing your sister's dress." Suddenly aware of how strange that sounded, she hurried to gloss over her admission. "Besides the club, I was hitting some of the swankier restaurants that day, and I thought dressing with class might maximize my chances of getting people to talk to me." The quizzical look in Angelica's eyes was fleeting, unfocused, a little too drunk to care. "And, of course, he'd been drinking."

Angelica picked up a cap and screwed it on the Chivas bottle. "You'd think *I'd* know better than to get wasted like this."

"You're not going to be perfect. None of us are," she quoted Dr. Baquero. "It's okay to make a mistake, as long as you recognize it and learn from it. And it's no crime to have one too many once in a blue moon." She'd seen it with Aunt Misty. Never touching a drop, and then binging on the anniversary of her mother's disappearance. If getting bombed once a year helped her aunt cope, who was Mia to judge?

Angelica shook her head. "It's not okay. I have to set a better example. Isaiah's an alcoholic."

"You're not responsible for his sobriety." That much she knew for sure. Dr. Baquero had hammered it into her head hard enough when she talked about her own mother.

"Maybe not, but my family has enough to handle without Isaiah going into a full relapse, and you can bet he'd use me as his excuse. He'd claim my drinking triggered his. He'd say it was my fault—and my mother would take his side like she always does, his and Celeste's. *Everyone's* but mine." Angelica got up, stumbled a little on her way to the mantel for a tissue.

"I'm sure that's not true." How many drinks had Angelica had before Mia arrived?

"Oh, but it is. Celeste is her firstborn, Isaiah's the baby, and don't even get me started on the Haven girls. Do you have any idea what it's like to take a back seat to a charity case?" She blew her nose. "No, I don't suppose you do, since you seem to be Mother's latest project—no offense."

"None taken." She tried to ignore the knot forming in her chest, tried to put herself in Angelica's shoes. Angelica wasn't in a good state of mind. She didn't really mean the things she was saying—it was the liquor talking.

"Don't repeat this. But, off the record, Isaiah's a screw up. Celeste and my father have been round and round with him about his drinking for years."

"Celeste had a problem with Isaiah?" Every brother and sister had conflicts. That didn't mean…

"She read a lot of books about addiction, and she latched onto this concept called *tough love*. She was always pushing Dad to set stricter limits with Isaiah—for his own good. Then it got out of hand."

Mia reached out to still her bouncing knee. "What do you mean?"

"Celeste wanted our father to cut Isaiah out of his will. I was against it, but I couldn't talk her out of floating the idea with Dad."

"That is harsh."

"But it sort of worked. Isaiah checked himself into rehab at this luxury place in Arizona. And he's been sober, or at least he had been sober, for months—until Celeste disappeared." Angelica caught her eye. "Isaiah's my brother, and I do love him, but if I'm being honest, I don't always like him. He's made a lot of bad decisions, and when he's drunk, he can be a real shit."

Mia could feel his hand clamped over her mouth, her feet dragging the ground as he hauled her into a back room at Lacy's. Her hand climbed to her throat.

"Be careful around him—I'd hate for anything to happen to you."

CHAPTER 19

Tuesday

After a long afternoon with the kids at the preschool, Mia could've used a freshening up, but if she'd taken the time, she would've been late for her interview with Detective Samuels. Pushing a recalcitrant lock of hair behind her ears, she smiled at him.

No reciprocation.

The skin around Samuels' eyes rested placidly, like a lake on a windless day, showing not a ripple of movement. But his calm visage didn't set Mia at ease—quite the contrary. The very stillness of his expression, his ability to sit for long periods without moving a muscle, made her squirm in her chair.

She knew she couldn't win the game she was playing with him. Eventually, he would get the truth out of her.

All he had to do was wait her out.

To keep her hands from shaking, she clasped them tightly in her lap. Her eyes stung from not blinking, but she'd be darned if she would be the first to break. Samuels tilted his head, and she sucked in a breath. Why was he looking at her like that?

Had he seen the security tapes from the Piano Man?

Did they show her making off with Celeste's keys?

She cleared her throat.

He continued his torture by silence routine.

He was supposed to be interviewing her, yet it seemed she always had to get the ball rolling.

That clock behind her was damnably loud. "Is this room wired for sound?"

"Uh-huh."

"Where's the camera?"

"Doesn't matter. Let's get down to business."

"Fine. Because I've got something to tell you."

"More breaking news to report? Really, Mia, after yesterday, I'm on pins and needles."

"You don't seem like it." She'd learned that when a person's behavior doesn't match his words, the best way to deal with it is to bring it out into the open. "Maybe you're a good detective, but you make me uncomfortable. I came here to be helpful, and you're putting me off with your manner. You said you wanted to interview me about the incident yesterday, but you haven't asked me a single question."

"Well, this isn't a southern social. We're not here to make small talk and sip mint juleps."

"No. You're supposed to take my statement, so how about doing that?"

"I'm listening. I have been all along, but if you're looking for structure, you can start at the beginning of your day yesterday. What were you doing from the time you got up until the time you found those keys on your desk at school and called the police?"

She took a sip of water, nodded, and began. Fifteen minutes later, she folded her arms across her chest. "And that's everything. I noticed Jane looking all pale, and when I looked where she was looking, I saw the keys. We both thought, at first, the keyring was Celeste's, and we'd already told Pinkerman before I realized…"

He leaned forward. "Before you realized it wasn't?"

"Yes." There was that suspicious look again. She wanted the neutral expression back. "Alma came and checked the keys and said she didn't think they were Celeste's, but Mrs. Pinkerman had already called you."

"Huh. Because the way you said 'I realized' made me think that you came to the conclusion, on your own, that those were the wrong keys. Did you somehow recognize them as different *before* Alma arrived?" He tapped his chin. "To be frank, I'm surprised how much you ladies know about each other's keyrings."

She tugged at her collar. "Alma said that Celeste's keys had a charm on the keyring and the designer's name engraved—"

"Yes. *Alma said*. But I'm asking did you realize, before Alma told you, that the keys did not belong to Celeste?"

"Gosh. I guess, yes, maybe, possibly. In hindsight, it seems so obvious. Why? Is that important?"

"Sometimes little things matter." The man was a human lie detector—no electrodes required. She'd bet a year's supply of glue sticks he knew she'd recognized that the keys were different. But she was beginning to get the feeling he hadn't seen her taking the keys on the security footage. If he had, he would've confronted her by now. Maybe, somehow, she'd gotten lucky. Maybe the camera hadn't been aimed as perfectly as she'd thought.

"How do you think those keys wound up on your desk?" he asked.

"I wish I knew." He had no idea how badly. "Do you think it means something? Since the keys don't belong to Celeste, I wasn't sure it mattered."

It mattered very much to her, but she could hardly explain why to him.

"What's your other news?"

Typical of him to stonewall when she asked the questions, though she ought to be glad they were changing topics, moving on to matters that might actually lead them somewhere important. Still, she hesitated, remembering the way Ruth's face had screwed up when Mia brought up Paul and Celeste, like she was either going to burst into tears or spit in Mia's eye. "I feel terrible mentioning this, but I have some information. There's a rumor going around. I don't know how it got started, or if it's true, but the word at school is that one of the dads was interested in Celeste."

"Who?"

"Paul Hudson."

"Interested how? Were they dating?"

"He's married, I'm afraid."

"So they were having an affair."

"No. Supposedly it was one-sided. Paul kept turning up the same places as Celeste, putting the moves on and so forth."

"And you heard this from whom?"

"I *overheard* it a while back. I'm not sure who was talking. I was in the teachers' lounge. But I'm not in on the gossip so I didn't hang around and join in."

"And you and Celeste weren't close, so she didn't confide in you. Have I got that right?"

She didn't love his tone. "Right."

He straightened. "Do you think that's what upset Celeste?"

"When?"

"During our last interview, you said you saw Celeste in the teachers' lounge on Friday morning, and she'd seemed like she'd been crying. You also said you didn't know why. So I'm wondering if, upon further consideration, you think she might've been upset over this problem with Paul Hudson."

She hadn't put that together but… "Maybe that was it. That would make sense."

"Uh-huh." He rapped his knuckle on the desk.

Was that a signal?

Would someone burst in and start playing bad cop?

Not that Samuels had been playing good cop.

A beat passed and no one showed up.

Samuels got to his feet. "That'll be all."

He was dismissing her without pressing her. She'd said she'd overheard a rumor about Paul Hudson, but she didn't know where, and Samuels had simply accepted that lame answer. "Are you taking this seriously? Are you going to look into what I just told you?"

"I will. Just like I looked into the Shoshanna story."

She lifted half out of her seat. "You talked to her? What did she say?"

He picked up his jacket and tossed it over his shoulder, looking like a movie detective lounging there with such panache.

"Please. I would really appreciate it if you'd tell me what she said about Celeste, unless it would compromise the case, of course. I'm the one who told you about the club. I think it's a fair question."

"It won't harm the case. So, all right, no reason for me not to disclose. Shoshanna said she saw someone who looked like Celeste, but she's not sure. That 'sighting' happened around two weeks ago, and she doesn't know anything else. Doesn't remember anything out of the ordinary about the woman who may or may not have been Celeste Cooper. She was keyed up when you came in with the missing person posters, and thought, just in case, she should say something."

"Are you going to follow it up? I told Angelica, and she agrees it's out of character for Celeste to go to a strip club."

"There's not much to follow up on. When did you speak with Angelica about this? I thought you hadn't told anyone else."

"I was with Angelica yesterday…"

He dropped back into his chair and sent her a look that made her shrink back into hers. "Uh-huh. And you had dinner with the Coopers the other night, went to church with Alma—that was quite a show you put on for the cameras."

"It wasn't a show." She didn't care what he thought of her, but she did care whether or not he planned to take action. "Will you or won't you check out Paul Hudson?"

"I'm leaving no stone unturned." His tone had finality to it, and he did his "conversation-over" tongue click. She'd heard him say the same words and do the same thing before—that day when Alma had pressed him in the classroom.

Perhaps he'd gotten all he needed from this interview, but she hadn't.

And she didn't intend to leave this room until she did. "I guess you police have that no-stone-unturned thing on auto-responder."

"What are you talking about?"

"I'm talking about a married man stalking a woman who's now missing." She took a deep breath. "And I'm talking about my mother's case. The detectives told my aunt they left no stone unturned, but I don't believe that's true. You said you'd check out the files. You said you'd see about reopening my mother's case."

He held up his hand. "You know I never promised any such thing. I said I'd try to look into it."

"And?"

"There's nothing to report." He dragged a hand through his hair. "I'll be straight with you. Right now, there are around forty thousand unsolved murders in the United States, and that's not counting missing person cases like your mother's. We don't have the resources to reopen dead-end cold cases."

"So you did or did not look into it?"

"I looked. Like I told you I would. But the news isn't good. Most of the time, Mia, when I pull a cold case, I've got boxes and boxes of evidence, hundreds, often times thousands, of pieces of paper to go through." He shook his head. "Your mother's case was different. I found one evidence box."

She scooted to the edge of her chair. "So there was something. What was in the box?"

"You're missing the point. It was only the *one* box. The officers on the scene took photos and lifted prints from the cabin and from the shed you dug yourself out of." He paused, like he was waiting for a reaction.

If he thought she was going to break down and cry just because he brought up the shed, he was in for a disappointment. "Go on."

"Cell phones were uncommon back then. There were no Facebook accounts to check out. The detectives took statements from your aunt, from a couple of waitresses who'd worked with your mother, and the hunter who found you in the woods. But there was no one else to question. The only person who might have known anything of value was you, and child services had you locked down tight. The detectives got one shot at you with a social worker present. You said you didn't remember anything—not even digging your way out of that shed. It seemed likely your mother had run away and abandoned you. And that was that."

"So, you're telling me no one even tried. They didn't conduct a real investigation. That should be reason enough to reopen the case."

"Just the opposite. I've got no cause to delve into a twenty-year-old crime with no clues. Unless you've got something new to say, unless you suddenly remember key facts that will generate more leads, there's nothing I can do." He lowered his voice. "I am sorry."

"I can't tell what you're thinking, or if you mean what you say."

"I do mean it. Nothing sticks in my craw like lazy police work. But let me say this…"

She braced for the worst.

"Now that I know how much you suffered as a child, I can't help seeing you in a different light. Especially after the way you've had me chasing my tail these past couple of days."

"I'm not asking for your pity."

"Good, because I'm not offering any up. I've got a job to do, and I can't let my emotions get in the way. I'm looking at you, Mia, and I'm thinking that your baggage makes you interesting."

"I take it you don't mean *interesting* in a good way."

"Correct. The last thing you want is to pique the interest of a major crimes detective. But that's what you keep doing. First, you faint, or pretend to faint, in the park in front of Angelica Cooper and get her to take you to Celeste's house and let you borrow Celeste's clothes. Then, you come up with this story about a matchbook—"

"I did faint. And going to the house, borrowing Celeste's clothes, none of that was my idea. I didn't come up with a *story*. I found the matches, and I gave them to you. They're real. You put them in an evidence bag."

"You could've gotten them from the club yourself."

"Shoshanna, the dancer, told your guys she saw Celeste."

"Shoshanna doesn't know who she saw. You went to the club looking for Celeste and that made Shoshanna think perhaps someone who looked a little like Celeste might have been there at some point in the past. That's not the same as seeing her."

"I'm not lying about the matches."

"You made up a story about applying for a waitress job at the club, so who knows what else you've invented. As for your snooping around, I might find it humorous if this were a game, but it's not."

"No. It isn't. Celeste's life is at stake."

His brow rose. "I'm well aware. You did say you want to know what I'm thinking. Shall I continue?"

Please don't. "Yes."

"The list goes on. After fainting and bringing up the matches, you find a mysteriously vague, yet threatening, note on your car."

"I'm not the one who told you about the note."

"And why not? But my point, really, is that such a mysterious note exists."

She wanted to ask if the handwriting analysis had come back, but his upheld hand warned her not to interrupt.

"Next, you summon me to the school to investigate a set of keys that look like Celeste's but turn out not to be, and *now* you say you remember some gossip about Celeste having an unwanted admirer, which, if true, should've been the first thing out of your mouth when Celeste went missing. If there's really a rumor going around the school, I wonder why no one else has mentioned it."

His implication wasn't lost on her. "I don't know why no one else said anything. You should absolutely ask the other teachers. I'm only trying to help."

"But see, Mia, I wonder if you are. You're a complicated young lady with a tragic past. A woman who has been largely overlooked, and, I'm thinking, underestimated by her peers. It would be a mistake for me to do the same. I wonder if all these things you're bringing to my attention are real, or if you're engineering drama in order to shift the spotlight away from Celeste Cooper and onto Mia Thornton. I can see how a young woman, starved for attention, might do such a thing. I can understand it. I can even sympathize. But if that is what you're doing, it's *far* from helpful."

Her fists balled up, her eyes stung, but she wasn't going to give him the satisfaction of seeing her break down. Gritting her teeth, she got to her feet and looked him dead in the eye. "I don't want a spotlight on me. I find that accusation both unfair and unkind."

He rose, and then extended his arm toward the door. "Don't misunderstand me, Mia. The picture I just painted of you, as a mixed-up misfit and an attention seeker, is not unkind in the least. That is, I'm afraid, my *best*-case hypothesis."

CHAPTER 20

Mia removed her clenched hand from the steering wheel and rubbed away the tightness in her jaw. She glanced at the speedometer.

Sixty in a forty-five.

She let up on the gas.

A mixed-up misfit in need of attention.

If that was Detective Samuels' best-case scenario, what was his worst? The answer was obvious: he thought she had something to do with Celeste's disappearance.

She could hardly blame him, considering all those weird occurrences—and he didn't even know about the keys.

But everything she'd told him about was real. She didn't imagine anything. She wasn't manufacturing drama. More drama was the last thing she needed in her life.

Still, what did these strange events amount to?

Taken individually, there was nothing she couldn't explain away.

A horn honked, and she checked her rearview to find a gray-haired woman barely peeking above the dashboard. She'd just cut off somebody's dear old grandma.

She slowed to thirty, turning her head just enough to mouth sorry, and then she saw it, two cars back—a black sedan. She signaled a lane change and moved to the right, let up on the gas until she was crawling along at what had to be an aggravating speed for the drivers behind her. But in the slow lane, she had every right to hold steady below the speed limit. In her side mirror, she kept an eye on the sedan. Instead of gaining on her, or passing her from the other lane, it slowed, too.

Click click click.

She'd forgotten her turn signal.

She tapped it off, taking note of the emblem on the sedan. She'd never owned a Lexus, but she recognized their logo. If only the sedan would pass, she could memorize the plate. Her speedometer read twenty-five. The Jeep behind her was climbing her tail, but the black sedan—the Lexus—still kept pace in the next lane over, while car after car switched to the far-left lane to get by. Between the two of them, they were creating a blockade. She sipped from a water bottle and forced herself to concentrate. If this really was the same car she'd seen following her yesterday in the Gaslamp Quarter, she needed to do something about it.

She could drive back to the police station, but the thought of facing Samuels with yet another vaguely ominous circumstance dissuaded her. Without proof this car was tailing her, he couldn't do a thing to help. And it would only reinforce his theory that she was some mixed-up misfit looking for attention.

The on ramp to the interstate was coming up, but she didn't dare go home. If this person—she couldn't tell if it was a man or woman beneath that baseball cap—didn't already know where she lived, she didn't want to lead them there.

Not signaling her intentions, she turned into a residential area. The Lexus followed suit.

Her hands relaxed on the wheel, and her thinking sharpened.

Aunt Misty always insisted Mia was better under pressure—and she might be right.

Time to pull over.

Either the sedan would find a way to wait—confirming her suspicions, or pass by, giving her an opportunity to glimpse its license plate.

Or… the Lexus could turn down another street before she had the chance to pull to the curb—like it just did.

She blew out a breath.

She had already been worked up from the week's events, and then Detective Samuels had put his big fat *you're-a-basket-case* cherry on top. She was just on edge—the number of black Lexus on the streets of San Diego might be shy of infinity, but not by much.

Mark down one more *probably nothing* on the list.

If she let her paranoia get out of control, she'd only prove Samuels right.

She hit the Bluetooth on her steering wheel. "Call Dr. Baquero."

"Calling Dr. Baquero, work," came the reply.

"Cancel! Cancel!" She disconnected.

It was enough to know her psychiatrist was still there if she needed her. But Dr. Baquero wasn't a detective. She wouldn't have the answers to Mia's questions about Celeste.

Only she might be able to help with something else.

Mia was about to repeat her command to call Dr. Baquero when the phone rang.

Bluetooth caller ID popped up.

Right away, Mia hit the answer button. "Alma, hi. How are you feeling?"

"Could you stop by, dear? I was hoping to speak to you in person."

"Of course, I'm not that far away. Is now good?"

*

Alma returned from the kitchen to the Cooper family living room with a bouquet and a brave smile on her face. Not wanting to arrive empty-handed, Mia had stopped to buy a bunch of purple Pacific Coast iris, dotted with lacy white yarrow. Now, the flowers towered majestically, as iris are meant to do, from an etched crystal vase.

"So thoughtful," Alma said, placing the arrangement in a prominent position on the fireplace's mantel. "They brighten the room, don't you think?"

"I do," Mia replied, but the room hardly needed brightening with its pale hardwood floors and reams of light pouring in. The French doors led to a stone patio surrounded by the greenest grass Mia had seen this side of a golf course, and the place was overflowing with floral offerings from well-wishers.

"I adore these," Alma said, following Mia's gaze, and perhaps reading her thoughts. "These iris are native, so natural, and unlike some—" she swept out an arm "—not in the least funereal."

Mia couldn't agree more. One, no doubt well-intended, person had actually sent a wreath.

"Celeste isn't dead. I wish people would stop sending these—and all the food."

"I'm sorry," Mia said. "I should've realized the last thing you need is more flowers."

"Oh no!" Alma rushed over to join Mia on the couch. "I meant it when I said I adore these. Iris is my favorite flower—next to the California poppy—nothing can beat those. It just came out wrong. And I'm grateful for every arrangement. But between you and me, the outpouring of support can be overwhelming."

"Ah, Mia. I didn't realize you were here." Baxter Cooper strode into the room, kissed his wife and took a seat in the wingback chair opposite Mia. "I'm not interrupting, I hope," he said, looking like a man who had no intention of clearing out no matter the reply.

And why should he? This was his home. The other evening at the academy, when he'd walked her to her car, she'd felt so safe with him. She liked being around him, but still, she'd rather spend time with Alma alone.

"I asked Mia over." Alma smoothed her hair, and her gold charm bracelet jangled pleasantly.

"I can see that," Baxter said.

"To thank her, again, for fending off that horrible reporter."

"I've been meaning to call you myself, Mia." Baxter caught her eye.

"Me?"

"Yes. I've been thinking quite a lot about what happened at St Michael's. My understanding is the reporter accidentally pushed Alma."

"But I would've hit the floor if Mia hadn't caught me. I was rickety from my medication, and she was too aggressive."

He shifted onto one hip, rummaging in his pocket. "I think we owe you more than gratitude, Mia. I'd like to compensate you for your trouble. And… while I don't mean to be critical, I wouldn't be looking out for my wife if I failed to mention that there's been quite a bit of negative press about the incident."

"Oh no!" Mia fanned her warm face. "I never meant to make a scene."

"I'm hoping we can avoid any unseemly public displays in the future." Baxter pulled out a money clip and peeled off a thick offering of crisp bills.

"We know it's not your fault," Alma rushed in. "You were only trying to protect me. Just let us compensate you for your trouble."

"I can't take money from a friend—if that's not too presumptuous of me to say."

"Of course not. I *am* your friend." Alma waved Baxter off, and he tossed the bills onto a side table. "Please don't take offense."

What just happened? One minute everything was fine, and the next Baxter seemed to be blaming Mia for the publicity. It was almost as if he wanted her to stay away from Alma. Hopefully she was reading him wrong, but, if not, she was sure she could change his mind. He was looking out for his wife and so was she. She just needed to make him see how good she'd be for Alma.

"How have you been sleeping?" To Mia, Alma's complexion seemed sallow, her arms too thin.

"Oh, perfectly. With all the mother's little helpers how could I not?"

"Are you eating?"

"I'm trying," Alma said.

"You look run down. And you mentioned feeling overwhelmed. Maybe there's something I can do to help out."

"I have to admit, if you're sure you wouldn't mind, that I could use help sorting through all of these." Alma rose, made her way to a sideboard and opened a door to reveal stack upon stack of envelopes. "But I'd *insist* on compensating you."

"Letters from the public," Baxter said. "Honey, no one expects you to reply to every one of those."

"But they've taken the trouble to send their prayers for Celeste. I can't ignore them."

"Roseanne can help you," Baxter said.

"Darling, no. You've forgotten she's reduced her hours to three mornings a week." Alma cut her gaze to Mia. "Our housekeeper. I think you met her, or maybe not, but her sister's come down with some mysterious illness and Roseanne has become a second mother to her nieces and a nurse all at the same time."

"Then I'll hire you a proper secretary," Baxter replied.

A look passed between Alma and him that Mia didn't know how to interpret. "But why not, if Mia has the time?"

"It's too much to ask." He shook his head, firmly. "We've offended her once already. She said she doesn't want our money, and it would be a terrible imposition otherwise."

Mia eyed the mountain of letters. Clearly Alma needed to give up on the idea of answering all of them. And likely some would be ghoulish, not fit for Alma's eyes. There were a lot of crazies out there. "What if I come by after work every day and help sort through them—just until you find someone official. I don't mind at all."

"Absolutely not. We won't take advantage," Baxter said, rising to his feet, towering above both her and Alma. "Unless we pay you, and you've already made quite clear how you feel about that, so it wouldn't be fair."

Alma reached for her husband's hand, and he pulled her up.

"I'm right, and you know it." He kissed her hand, and Alma's bracelet tinkled melodically.

Suddenly, inexplicably, Mia couldn't catch her breath.

"Mia." Alma reached an arm around her. "Are you all right? Don't worry at all about this mess. Baxter will get me a secretary. That'll be just fine. I shouldn't have mentioned anything. I can see we've upset you."

"You haven't." She hesitated and looked from Baxter to Alma. "I-I was just admiring your bracelet, and I lost my train of thought."

But that wasn't the whole of it. Alma's bracelet, with its melodic sound, had triggered something—a memory.

Mia could see her mother's delicate wrist, a silver bracelet encircling it—hear the soft tinkling of charms.

"This?" Alma held up her arm for Mia's inspection.

Reaching out, Mia touched the charms, three golden ovals with miniature photos of Celeste, Angelica, and Isaiah as children. "It's beautiful. It just reminded me of a bracelet my mother had. Hers was silver, not gold, and it had three charms. I can see them—a star, a heart and a cross. I'd forgotten until just now."

Alma turned to Baxter. "You remember what I mentioned about Mia's mother."

"Of course, my condolences." Baxter's sympathetic look appeared genuine.

"You must miss her terribly," Alma said.

"I guess I mostly try to put it out of my mind. But her bracelet is a nice memory. Thank you for bringing it back to me."

Alma patted Mia's shoulder, then dropped her arm from around her. "Thank you for the gorgeous bouquet."

Baxter cleared his throat. "We don't want to keep you from your aunt. Misty, isn't it?"

"I should get home. She gets worried if I don't check in. A bit of a helicopter auntie."

"I don't blame her," Alma said, as she and Baxter escorted Mia to the door.

After a quick round of "see you soons" and more hugs from Alma, Mia exited the Coopers' home. She worried she might've lingered too long over the goodbyes, but at least she felt less shaky. For a moment, she'd been quite disoriented.

A flash of wind whipped her hair in her face, and now, fully aware of her surroundings, she descended the porch steps.

And gasped.

It was Paul Hudson.

There, in the circular driveway—lounging against the hood of a black Lexus.

CHAPTER 21

The setting sun bounced off the black sedan. Was it really him? Shielding her eyes from the glare, Mia verified the truth—it was indeed Paul Hudson. Should she rush to her car and speed away, like Aunt Misty would counsel, or stand her ground?

Her heartbeats counted down the seconds until she realized that, by remaining motionless, she'd defaulted into a decision. She pulled up her chin, rolled her shoulders back, stretched her spine to reach her full height and marched straight for him.

"Hello, Mia."

Look him in the eye.

"Stop following me," she said.

An unlit cigarette dangled from his lips. That didn't fit the image he liked to portray. She wondered if Ruth knew he smoked. She wondered if Ruth knew a lot of things about her husband.

"I'm not following you," he said.

"And let's add *stop lying* to the list."

Still lounging against the hood of his car, he pulled the cigarette from his mouth and bounced it between two fingers. "Trying to quit. I haven't smoked in years but these past few months have been a lot. And now I've got you to deal with. I always thought you were a nice kid, Mia. But at the moment, I'm not so sure."

"I'm not a kid, and I've no reason to be nice to you. I've seen this car multiple times. You've been following me for days."

"You sound paranoid. I'm not the only person in San Diego who drives a black Lexus."

"But you are the only one who tailed me here."

He flicked the cigarette away and turned his palms up. "Talk like that is exactly the kind of thing that makes me doubt your mental stability. I came to give the Coopers my sympathies. Celeste was a lovely young woman, and this is a terrible tragedy."

"Celeste *is* a lovely young woman. You're talking like you know she's dead."

"Naturally, I'm hoping for the best. But I'd be lying if I said I haven't considered the possibility that this may not end well. At some point, we're all going to have to start facing facts."

She was glad, now, not to have to see him at school anymore when he picked up his son. Whether he'd followed her here or not, the guy was toxic. "You're not here to offer condolences. Let's cut through the BS. I assume Ruth told you that I know you've been stalking Celeste."

"She did, and I'd appreciate it if you'd stop spreading gossip." He sighed. "I'm a married man. I've got a reputation to protect, and what would you know about Celeste's private life unless *you're* the stalker? You weren't friends. I don't believe for a minute she'd confide her private affairs to you. You think my showing up here is strange; well, I can say the same thing about you. Maybe you followed me."

"Alma asked me over."

"Why would she do that? And what's this about you being the family spokesperson? None of it makes sense unless you've grossly misrepresented yourself to the family. Now you're lying about me to my wife. What's your game?"

She jabbed her index finger at him, all but touching his chest. "I don't have to explain myself to you, and I'm not afraid of you. I've already told the police everything. Detective Samuels knows you were hounding Celeste. Turning up places you shouldn't have."

"Like I'm doing now, with you? Try spewing that nonsense to him—that I'm following you around town. He'll see right through that." Paul stepped closer.

She wanted to run, put as much distance between them as possible. Holding his gaze, she leaned in. His breath reeked of stale nicotine. "He's a good detective. Sooner or later he'll figure it out."

"Time will tell whether or not Samuels is worth his salt. But you've done damage, repeating terrible things to my wife and the police—things that could ruin my marriage and cost me my job. And as I said before, I know you didn't hear any of it from Celeste. So where, exactly, did this despicable rumor come from?"

"You just admitted that there is a rumor, that I'm not making it up."

He fell back, smiling, as if they were having a friendly chat, and her chest loosened. "Maybe someone got the wrong impression from something Celeste said. Who was it, Mia? Who's been talking about me?"

"If it's not true, what are you worried about? All you have to do is tell the truth."

"Unlike you, that's what I'm doing. But how am I supposed to handle a situation like this one? What am I supposed to do about you, Mia? I guess I'll have to figure that out on my own. Meanwhile, I'm warning you." He slowly raised a closed fist, then opened it and pushed his hand through his hair. "Stay away from my family."

*

Still reeling from her encounter with Paul Hudson, Mia pulled into the nearest gas station and killed the engine. Her tank was nearly full but she was shaking hard—whether from anger or fear she wasn't sure, but she needed to take a minute to compose herself before getting back on the road. Looking for her gas card, she rifled through her console and came up with a handful of receipts. One was sticky and left her fingers smelling like maple. She closed her eyes, willing herself to relax, think pleasant thoughts, think about anything except that jerk, Hudson.

Her breathing began to slow, and then, without warning, an image flashed into her mind. She was standing in Sugar Tooth— that all-night doughnut shop on Celeste's street. A young woman, her pink hair pulled into a ponytail, was slipping a maple-iced long john into a bag.

The big, digital clock on the wall was flashing *2:30 a.m.*

Mia opened her eyes and grabbed the receipt. Frantically, she scanned it for a date, praying it was from yesterday. But she knew it wouldn't be. After she'd visited Angelica at Celeste's place, she *had* gone to the doughnut shop, but she'd taken the bag of doughnuts, with the receipt tucked inside, home to Aunt Misty. It was hard to focus her eyes, but finally, she located the date, smudged but still legible, on the bottom of the receipt.

This is a coincidence—nothing more.

Still, a cold, clammy feeling crawled up her back. The night Celeste disappeared, Mia was at that doughnut shop just down the block from Celeste's house. She must've driven there in an altered state, while she was sleepwalking, because, other than that clock blinking on the wall, she couldn't remember a damn thing about it.

Just like she barely remembered the shed.

Post-traumatic amnesia was what Dr. Baquero called that.

She heard her breath rasping, felt her chest tightening.

What had really happened the night Celeste went missing? Had Mia gone back, gotten into some kind of altercation with her? Was her mind protecting her from something too terrible to bear?

Is that why she remembered only flashes?

No.

She might've been near Celeste's house that night, but she didn't have a scratch on her. If she'd gotten into some kind of fight there would've been evidence of it: a cut, a bruise, a scraped fist.

And memory loss was a side-effect of that damn sleeping pill. There was even a warning on the package insert. These thoughts she was having were irrational, and she wasn't going to give them space in her brain.

Paul Hudson was following her—he'd practically threatened her. She had enough *real* problems to deal with.

She didn't need to invent any more.

CHAPTER 22

Wednesday

The steep descent into the bowels of Torrey Pines State Reserve sent shock waves up Mia's legs and jabbed needles into her knees each time a boot pounded a rocky step. Parry Grove Trail's 118 stone stairs deterred many a hiker, even on a sunny Sunday morning, so on this dreary, overcast, late Wednesday afternoon, Mia knew she'd find what she sought.

Solitude.

Evidence of nature's brute strength—and beauty—surrounded her as she wound her way through sage scrub and sandstone bluffs. Mangled by wind and time, the sculpted cliffs resembled pleated washboards. Ahead, the bare arms of a Torrey pine stretched out, their ends hooking like skeleton fingers, near an overlook where a weathered bench awaited.

From that bench, a favorite spot of Celeste's, Mia peered out across the Pacific, watching the waves crash against the cliffs and wondering what it would be like to fly—to fall, while the clouds thickened, hiding the sun.

After a few minutes of contemplation, she slung her pack off her shoulders and dug for the trowel and paper bag she'd stowed. Opening the sack, she peeked inside. *Wrong bag.* It contained the ham sandwich she hadn't eaten at lunch.

She removed her jacket, thrust her arm deeper into her pack and grasped a second paper bag—the one with Celeste's keyring inside.

As she tapped the rubber handle of her trowel on the bench, her resolve steeled.

Where were her gloves?

Once located, she put them on, shouldered her pack, scurried off the trail and took cover behind a massive clump of scrubs.

*

Her appetite had been missing in action since the night Celeste disappeared, but this evening's hike and a job well done—she'd successfully buried the brown bag containing Celeste's keyring—had resurrected Mia's hunger.

She waited impatiently while a group of hikers and one straggler made their way past the overlook, and then emerged from the bushes to reclaim the overlook bench. There she choked down her dry ham sandwich, took out a tall steel tumbler filled with cold water and drank it in one go.

Her thirst quenched, she set the empty tumbler beside her.

Everyone was looking for Celeste.

If Mia went missing, how long would it take for anyone to notice?

And once they did, would they organize meetings in the park, door knocks and ground searches?

Or would they do what they'd done for her mother?

Nothing.

She pulled a manila envelope from her pack and scanned a yellowed newspaper clipping.

CALIFORNIA MOTHER ABANDONS CHILD IN SHED

San Diego County Sheriff's department spokesman says Mia Thornton, age six, was found unconscious in the woods last Saturday. She apparently tunneled her way out of a nearby storage shed where empty cans, a toddler toilet, and an animal water feeder were found. The girl was air-evacuated to a local hospital and released two days later, in stable condition, into the custody of her aunt. The whereabouts of the mother, Emily Thornton, age twenty-six, medium build, blond hair and brown eyes, are unknown. If anyone has any information regarding Emily Thornton, please contact the San Diego County Sheriff's office.

A grainy photo of her mother was included in the article. There was nothing more.

Mia carefully folded her mother's clipping. Next, she inspected around a dozen articles, just a small sampling from front pages of various newspapers since Celeste had gone missing twelve days ago.

According to the stories, FBI agents were reviewing Celeste's case, looking to connect it to the disappearance of women in Arizona and Colorado given the geographic and temporal proximities and similar age and background of the women. Speculation about a serial killer in the southwestern United States targeting young, attractive women was exploding on the air and in print.

Mia slipped the lone article about her mother back into the manila envelope, and set the others aside.

The wind slapped against her cheeks and shot grit into her eyes. She wiped them with the back of her hand.

There might be a serial killer snatching young women off the street, so of course the authorities would go all out to investigate Celeste's case. But there was no denying that who Celeste was also drove the aggressive response.

Beautiful. Girl next door. Daughter of prominent business owner.

These were the descriptors used over and over in the news.

All Emily Thornton got was a physical description. No matter what her mother had done to Mia, and no matter how lowly her station in life, Emily Thornton was a real person—and she deserved to be looked for.

A drop of rain fell on Mia's face. She'd better hurry. The sun would set soon, and then she'd have to rush to make it off the trail before dark.

But she wasn't yet done with her work.

She scanned a different article that she'd read and saved six months ago.

San Diego Star congratulates Alma Cooper. Mrs. Baxter Cooper receives San Diego Women's League service medal at the downtown convention center. She is being honored for her work with HAVEN, a charitable organization for young women.

A photo of the entire family—Alma, Celeste, Angelica, Isaiah and Baxter—showed Alma beaming as Celeste kissed her cheek.

Next, she came to her final clipping—this one from the "Harbor Youth Academy Buzz", the school's newsletter:

CELEBRATE GOOD TIMES AND GOOD TEACHERS

Last night's auction raised over sixty thousand dollars. The top donation of ten thousand dollars came from Mr. and Mrs. Paul Hudson. Thank you to the Hudsons and to all of our generous donors!

Sue Ellen Keck won the raffle basket including a first-class ticket to Cancun, Mexico. Congratulations Sue Ellen!

Mia's hand trembled when she came to the section where she'd scratched out Celeste's name and written in her own.

A one thousand dollar bonus and heartfelt congratulations goes to Harbor Youth Academy's Teacher of the Year:
~~*Celeste Cooper!*~~ *Mia Thornton!*

Harbor Youth Academy also wishes to congratulate this year's runner-up, ~~Mia Thornton.~~ Celeste Cooper.

Mia took a deep breath, rolled all the articles, save the one about her mother, into a tube and wedged it into the steel tumbler. She rummaged in her pocket for the doughnut shop receipt, stuffed it in the tumbler, too, then took out a lighter and flicked it on, holding it to the pages until the articles caught fire. Orange flames licked the sides of the silver tumbler, and when her envy had finally turned to ash, she dropped on the top, twisted tight, and cut off all its oxygen.

Just in time, too, because the crunch of gravel and the banging of boots told her she wouldn't be alone much longer. She started to pack up and had one palm curled around the tumbler when the sound of a familiar, male voice set her heart pounding.

"Is this seat taken?" Isaiah extended his hand toward the empty spot beside Mia.

More afraid of being caught than of him, uncanny as his timely arrival seemed, she smiled and patted the bench. "Wow. This is a surprise."

"Maybe it's fate." He raked a hand through tussled hair and plunked down beside her, showing no sign he'd witnessed her setting a fire in a travel mug.

"Then cheers to fate." Lifting the tumbler, she toasted him.

After a test-sniff of the air, her racing heart slowed. Luckily the smoke generated by her little fire had seamlessly blended with the earthy, humidity-heavy air surrounding them.

He closed his eyes and drew a long breath. "I love the way it smells before a rainstorm. This is one of Celeste's favorite places." Then he lifted one eyebrow, the weight of the coincidence seeming to hit him at once. "Did you know that?"

"No," she lied. It was why she'd chosen to come here. She'd seen a number of pictures and stories of this very spot on Celeste's Instagram, but admitting that to Isaiah would unquestionably raise her to stalker status. Good thing he'd stumbled upon her instead of vice versa. "I can't believe we bumped into each other like this."

"I know, right? I haven't been up here in a while. The last time was with Celeste—the day she talked me into checking myself into rehab."

"Celeste talked you into it?"

"Yeah. She and Angelica convinced my dad, get this, to cut me out of the will if I didn't get sober. I was in a rage, but then Celeste dragged me up here, and we sat on this bench and talked until the sun went down."

"And Angelica?" Angelica had told Mia she wasn't on board with Celeste's tough love plan. So which one of them was telling the truth—Isaiah or Angelica? The sibling rivalry subtext in this family was confusing.

"Angelica doesn't hike." He got quiet, and seemed to be focusing his gaze over the horizon where the sinking sun was turning the ocean to blood. "I'm oversharing, I think. Is that okay?"

She wasn't sure. She was still irritated that he'd told Samuels about the note.

"About that note," Isaiah said, as if reading her mind.

"What about it?"

"You understand I couldn't ignore something like that when my sister's gone. I'm not prepared to decide what's important and what's not. I know you said your aunt wrote it, but you could be wrong."

"I don't think I am."

"Then why ask Samuels to check a sample of my writing?"

She shrugged. "Getting even, maybe."

He turned, directing his attention fully to her, now. "We're not even, though, not yet. Listen, I know I really messed up that day at the park."

"And at the club."

"Yeah. That was worse. But we had a nice time at dinner, don't you think?"

She nodded.

"And this is even better." He sent her a sweet, *forgive-me?* look.

Angelica had warned her about her brother. He'd grabbed her at that club, and now, he'd conveniently happened upon her out in the wilderness—only it *was* a popular trail—and Celeste's "favorite thinking spot", according to her Instagram. And it was hard for Mia not to notice the vulnerable look in his eyes. Her head told her to wrap it up, but part of her wanted to linger and get to know him more. "I agree. This is nice. What are you doing here, again?"

"Just chasing a memory, I guess. And, don't laugh, but something happened today that I wanted to share with Celeste. She's not here, but you are. Would you mind if I show you something personal?" Not giving her a chance to respond, he stuck his hand in his pocket.

Her throat tightened. She couldn't outrun him, but she readied herself to punch him, knee him in the groin, and scream for help if necessary. How far away would those other hikers be by now?

While she held her breath, he worked a coin out of his pocket and held it up between two fingers, admiring it.

"Hold out your hand."

She opened her palm.

"I apologize for my past behavior toward you." He pressed the coin into her hand.

"What's this about?" She frowned, completely mystified.

"It's about me starting over. That, my friend, is a twenty-four-hour chip."

She smiled at him. "Good for you."

"I've got an entire day of sobriety under my belt." He took back the coin and pulled his phone out of his pocket. "To new beginnings?"

"New beginnings." She could use a clean slate herself.

"Say cheese." He raised his arm, leaned in close to her and smiled for a selfie.

CHAPTER 23

Thursday

"Thanks for seeing me on short notice." Since Mia was supposed to be spreading her wings and flying on her own, she'd hesitated to call, but Dr. Baquero had offered her booster sessions as needed.

"It's not a problem. I told you, I'm here if you need me, and frankly I've been expecting your call. When I heard the news about your friend, your fellow teacher, I realized you must be facing a barrage of emotions. Celeste Cooper is the woman we discussed at your last session, isn't she?"

Mia nodded.

"So tell me everything."

Where to begin? The last time she'd sat on this couch seemed like a lifetime ago. "I'm more numb than anything. It's hard to believe someone I know is missing, and with everything that's happened, I'm having a hard time keeping my head on straight."

"*Everything* that's happened. It sounds like more than Celeste's disappearance. Are there other things you need to discuss?"

That was Mia's cue to launch into a disjointed, stream of consciousness account of the events of the past week, with special emphasis on the mysterious keys that landed on her desk, Paul Hudson, and her interview with Detective Samuels. When she'd finished, she spread her arms and collapsed against the couch like she'd just run the Secret Stairs of La Mesa. "So what should I do?"

Dr. Baquero frowned. "I'm not a lawyer. I can't give legal advice."

"I'm not asking you to. But you'll have an opinion, and you're the only person I trust with this information. No one else knows what I've told you about Celeste's keys—or about Paul Hudson following me. Detective Samuels already thinks I'm a nutcase—sorry, I know you don't like me using that term—but anyway, I'm afraid if I accuse Hudson of threatening me, it'll only cement Samuels' opinion. Especially if he already knows I took Celeste's keys. Maybe he's just holding on to that information, waiting to spring it on me at the worst possible moment."

"You covered a lot of ground today. Remind me how the detective would know you took Celeste's keys."

"There are cameras in the restaurant where it happened. And the day I found those keys on my desk, Samuels got called away because of something to do with the restaurant security footage. Later, he let me know, in no uncertain terms, he thinks I'm a kook—and that's his best-case scenario."

"What do you think his worst case is?"

"That I had something to do with Celeste's disappearance."

Dr. Baquero leaned forward, holding Mia's gaze. "Did you have something to do with it?"

The question knocked the wind out of her. When she tried to inhale, she couldn't. Maybe if she exhaled, she could restart the breathing process. Closing her eyes, she concentrated on relaxing her chest until a long slow breath released, and then her lungs filled with air again.

She opened her eyes.

Dr. Baquero didn't seem to have moved a muscle. Her back was arched, her mouth half-open like she'd been in a state of suspended animation while Mia had been fighting for air.

How much time had passed?

Did she still want Mia to answer the question?

"No. I had nothing to do with Celeste's disappearance—not in the way you mean," she managed belatedly. It was a shock to the system to think her psychiatrist, someone who knew her better than almost anyone, could suspect her. There was absolutely no way she could bring up the sleepwalking incident now. If she admitted to being on Celeste's street the night she disappeared, her therapist might not believe she was innocent—and Mia couldn't blame her considering she had no idea what had transpired that night.

Her hands felt clammy and cold.

Was it possible she did have something more to do with it?

Her chest expanded, and her fists uncurled.

Mia might have been jealous, she might have been hurt, but she'd never wanted anything bad to happen to Celeste. She'd been over that night again and again in her head, but she was still coming up empty, and she had to believe if she'd really done something to Celeste, she'd know it. Even if she couldn't remember, deep in her heart, she'd *feel* it.

Dr. Baquero's hunched shoulders dropped. "I'm sorry but I had to ask. Please understand I don't think you'd lie to me, or that you'd intentionally harm your friend, but you do have gaps in your memory—not recently I know, but I need to be sure. You're absolutely certain? Because a woman's life may be at stake."

"I understand your point, but the answer is yes; I'm certain. And I remember everything—except most of what happened the year my mother went missing." *And while I was sleepwalking.* Mia tugged at a loose thread on her shirt. "I guess that's quite the blank spot."

"You said 'I had nothing to do with Celeste's disappearance— not in the way you mean'. So, in what way then?"

"If I hadn't taken Celeste's keys, she wouldn't have been in that alley for someone to grab her—or whatever happened."

"Celeste made her own decision to walk home. She had plenty of options. You told me one of the other teachers offered her a ride. Even if she didn't want to impose, she could've called Uber, Lyft or a cab. *You* didn't kidnap her. *You* didn't mug her, or hurt her in anyway. You're not responsible for what happened that night."

"I still feel terrible."

"Feelings aren't always rational, but they can be managed. Keep chipping away at those self-destructive thoughts, replace them with reason, and eventually your emotions will come into line. And, Mia, I will give you one piece of advice—let the police handle this situation with the parent from your work. Tell Detective Samuels about this Hudson fellow following you. He might be dangerous."

"Hudson will just deny it. And if Samuels has seen the tapes from the Piano Man and those tapes show me taking Celeste's keys…"

"Regardless of what went on with the keys, regardless of what Samuels does or doesn't know about them, you need to tell him about this Hudson character."

"You may be right about Paul. In a way, he threatened me—Samuels should hear about that."

"Good, so you'll fill Samuels in on Hudson. And, if you're so worried about the keys, why not just admit what you did? The anxiety over being found out is likely worse than suffering the consequences if the truth does come out."

Mia shook her head. "I disagree. The consequences are worse. You know me better than anyone, maybe even better than I know myself, and you just asked if I had something to do with Celeste's disappearance. If *you* questioned whether I might be capable of hurting her, think of the police. I don't want to send them down the wrong path. I don't want them wasting time investigating me when they could be hunting the real culprit."

"So then, you're being noble. You're not worried about what your new friends, the Coopers, will think of you?"

She ducked her chin. "You're right. I don't want Celeste's family to hate me—I can hardly stand to think of it, but it's also because of what I said about leading the police in the wrong direction."

"If it's going to come out eventually, don't you think it's better for you to be the one to bring it to light?"

"If I don't say anything, there's no reason it would be found out. Unless it's on CCTV, of course."

"All right. I'm done pressing. But think about getting this key caper off your chest and out into the open. I'm concerned about the sheer number of stressors you're juggling. I'd hate to see all the progress you've made over the past few years unravel. Are you sleeping well?"

Not at all—but she didn't dare come clean about the sleepwalking and the pills. "I'm okay. And in some ways I feel stronger than I did the last time we talked. In fact, that's one of the reasons I called. You remember, a while back, we talked about hypnosis."

"To help you recover childhood memories surrounding the trauma of losing your mother. You opted out—said you didn't see what was to gain by reliving a horrible event."

"I've changed my mind. I want you to put me under. When I asked Detective Samuels about reopening my mother's case, he told me that was a no-go—unless I remember something significant. Something that could generate a lead."

"This might not be a good time, Mia. With all the problems you're facing, I worry hypnotic regression could cause you to lose ground—after you've made such great progress—after all the work you put in to get where you are today. I'd suggest waiting a month or two and then seeing how you feel."

"You were in favor of hypnosis before."

"Circumstances were different."

She set her jaw. "No one ever really looked for my mother, not the way they're looking for Celeste. Samuels says I'm the only one who might know something that would justify reopening her case. I wasn't ready before, but I'm ready now. I have a reason to relive the pain. *Please*, Dr. Baquero, I'm the only one who might know something of use to the police, and you're the only one who can help me remember."

CHAPTER 24

Dr. Baquero reached for a remote, and the shades on the window behind her desk whirred down. A thin strip of light crept in beneath the shade, gently mediating the near blackness in the office. "All right then, I'll help with your recall. But only you decide."

Blood whooshed in Mia's ears. Apprehension seeped through the cracks in her resolve like water through a neglected roof. "What will I decide?"

"Everything. Are you comfortable?" Dr. Baquero lowered her voice, barely speaking above a whisper.

"Yes." Mia settled back against the couch, clutching the cushions. "But I'm confused. I don't know what to decide upon."

"Once we begin, you will know all you need. Paths will present themselves, and you will decide which ones to take, or whether to simply stand still."

"Okay. I understand." Though she really didn't. But she suspected, from the melodic tone, the change in rhythm of Dr. Baquero's voice, the hypnotherapy had already begun.

She *needed* to remember what happened with her mother.

She *had* to do this—leaky confidence or no. "Did we start already? Do I just close my eyes and give complete control to you?" As much as she trusted her therapist that sounded scary as hell when she said it aloud.

"See how perceptive you are, Mia. You're exactly right—we've already begun, but I won't ask you to give me the power. You'll be the one in control. I'm here if you need me, to act as your guide if you wish. Let your eyes focus on an object."

Her gaze flew straight to the coffee cup on Dr. Baquero's desk.

Keep calm and kick ass.

"Let your vision soften."

The lettering on the coffee cup grew less distinct, then changed into nothing more than a wash of color.

Her breathing slowed.

Her eyelids changed to stone.

This was too easy—she couldn't be going under so soon.

She squeezed her hand into a fist, fighting her descent into the unknown.

"If you're not ready, you can slow down. Take your time, Mia."

She heard the clock ticking in the background, her breathing growing louder.

"Only you decide," Dr. Baquero called from far away.

You decide. You decide.

The words echoed off the walls.

"When you're ready your eyes will close. Your body will seem heavy—your arm light, as if a helium balloon is tied to your hand."

You decide. You decide.

Her chin dropped to her chest. Her arm began rising, then suddenly plummeted to her side.

Words and sounds came from far away, bouncing off the walls of a long tunnel.

"Now then, Mia, you are free to dream, to search and find the things you wish to know. Don't be afraid. Anytime you want to come back, you don't need me at all. Just count backwards—or forwards. You can wake up anytime and keep only the memories you choose. You don't have to bring them all back with you. If something feels unsafe, simply discard it before you wake."

She pictured herself swaddled in a blanket and felt her own arms wrap her body. How old was she? She had questions, but she didn't know what they were.

"It's safe to dream, Mia."

A whisper of a kiss grazes my cheek.

A sweet, sweet voice is singing softly in my ear.

I love it when Mommy sings.

Mommy brushes my hair.

I like the tug on my scalp, even though it stings, because it means she is here with me. We are together. She drops a kiss on top of my head, and I see her face smiling back at me from the mirror.

I ask: Will we have dinner tonight?

Mommy frowns and says I'm making her lose count of the strokes—now she'll have to start over again.

One hundred more strokes to make my hair shine.

I'm glad, even though it means more pulling and burning. Glad for more time with Mommy. My stomach rumbles, and I look up at her, wanting to ask again about dinner, but this time I keep silent. Mommy will feed me when she can.

We're not starving; we're just hungry. Like Mommy says, it's not the same thing. We have to be careful, portion our food so we have something for the next day and the day after that. My stomach growls, very loudly this time.

Mommy tells me someday soon we'll have ice cream. She asks me what kind I want.

I say chocolate because I know that's her favorite, but I don't remember what ice cream tastes like.

Mommy finishes brushing my hair and gets up.

Come back!

I want her close to me, caring for me.

But she's at the hope chest, pulling out my pajamas.

I go to her, and she removes my shift and puts me in my nightclothes and drops my shoes and dress in the chest.

I look down at my feet and think how silly my toes look. I don't have slippers. The cement floor of the cabin is cold against the soles of my bare feet, but I like that better than the gritty dirt floor of the shed.

I'm crying now, big tears rolling down my cheeks.

Mommy shushes me and tells me to be a good little girl. Not to cry.

I hear drumming on the windows. Rain is coming down hard outside. I crawl onto the bed and draw my knees up and watch Mommy getting ready.

She's putting on her nightclothes, too. My PJs are an old T-shirt with holes and a pair of flannel pants Mommy got for me at the Salvation Army store. But Mommy's are pretty and bright.

Mommy's nightgown is red and lacey, and she pulls a shiny black robe over it. She goes into the bathroom, and when she comes out, the air around her smells sweet. She sees my tears and gives me a hug. She says she has a surprise for me and shows me a pretty glass bottle with a gold cap and sprays me with the most wonderful smell.

Her smell.

I tell her I love her and put my head on her shoulder.

I'm drifting off to sleep, and then I hear the grinding noise I've learned means there's a car coming up the dirt road.

Mommy jumps up.

She yanks me by the elbow.

She says he's early, and now we have to hurry.

Hurry!

He's coming!

Twenty. Nineteen. Eighteen.

I hear the tires grinding.

Seventeen. Sixteen. Fifteen.

No, Mommy, please. I don't want to go out in the rain.

Hurry, Mia! He's coming.

Fourteen. Thirteen. Twelve.

She says his name—I'm covering my ears now.

Eleven. Ten. Nine.

I don't want to go in the shed.

I don't want to remember the shed.

You decide. You decide what to bring back with you when you wake up.

Eight. Seven. Six.

Mommy shakes my shoulders. Tells me not to make a peep.

Five. Four.

She lifts her hand and brushes the hair from my eyes and tells me she loves me, always.

Three. Two. One.

Mia opened her eyes.

CHAPTER 25

Friday

Her hypnosis session with Dr. Baquero had left Mia drained, like she'd been lifting mental weights, with each set becoming progressively more difficult until at last, she'd reached the point where she could no longer bear up. Then last night, she'd fallen into bed, exhausted, and slept through the night for the first time in a long while. There had been no major breakthrough—nothing that would get Detective Samuels to reopen her mother's case, but at least she'd remembered *something* from that night.

In her heart, she knew it was *the* night—the last time she'd seen her mother.

She wished she'd been brave enough to go all the way—to face the shed, but Dr. Baquero said not to push, that moment would only come when Mia was ready.

Now, she closed the cover on the *The Little Engine That Could* and smiled at her pupils—minus Tennyson, who'd been moved to Jane's class per his mother's request. Mia tried not to think about him struggling to fit in with the new kids. Jane was a great teacher, and Tennyson would adjust over time.

Instead, she focused on how lucky she was to get paid for helping mold all these eager little minds, shape their first experiences with the outside world, nurture their self-esteem.

Like they always did at the end of the day, when they exited her classroom, each pupil stopped to give her a hug. She missed

Tennyson, but it was a relief not to have to face Paul and Ruth. She didn't want a scene at school, and the next time she saw that man, there was no way she'd grin and pretend nothing had happened.

I'm warning you, he'd said.

What a creep.

"Mia! Hurry up. Why are you still here? Everyone's waiting for you in the teachers' lounge." Jane poked her head inside Mia's classroom, her voice ringing with excitement.

"Waiting for what?" For the life of her, she had no idea.

Jane hooked her elbow through Mia's and marched her out the door and down the hall. "You're joking. Have you forgotten your own book club? The inaugural meeting?" Then she laughed. "I'm teasing a little. Honestly, I'm not surprised you forgot with all that's been going on. But the important thing is—the rest of us haven't."

Jane flung open the lounge door, and Mia covered her mouth. Sun poured in through a row of high windows, brightening the grass-green walls. The four-seater tables had been pushed together to form one long serving area, set with a checkered cloth, paper plates and cups and plastic utensils. Several bags of chips, as well as a platter of oversized cookies flanked Sue Ellen Keck's crystal punch bowl, and best of all, the same women who'd left her out of their monthly outings for over a year perched on chairs, arranged in a semi-circle, enthusiastically waving copies of *Jane Eyre* at her like flags for a soldier returning from war.

"Oh my goodness!" she said, unable to believe her eyes. "When did you do all of this? Jane, are you responsible?"

Jane shook her head. "It was my suggestion to go ahead with the meeting, but everyone pitched in."

Glancing around the group, comprised of Sue Ellen, Poppy, Easton, Taraji and Jane, Mia splayed her fingers over her heart. Maybe a few women showing up for a book club wouldn't seem like a big deal to others, but to her… "You guys, I'm overwhelmed. I didn't think anyone cared… about book club, I mean."

Though that wasn't all she'd meant.

She couldn't believe they'd done something so thoughtful for *her*.

"Of course we care," Sue Ellen said. "And I think I speak for everyone when I say we're really sorry we didn't tell you sooner about our monthly get-togethers. We didn't think you'd want to come along, but it was thoughtless, and frankly, shitty of us, not to invite you."

"We're sorry," Taraji said.

"Very sorry," Sue Ellen and Poppy added in unison.

"Celeste's mother told us what happened at the church with that reporter, and we all think you're a badass," Jane said.

A couple of the women applauded.

"I-I… it was nothing."

"No, it was something. *Really* something. I'm not sure I would've had the nerve to tackle that reporter, but you did. And with Celeste gone—" Jane suddenly stopped speaking and hid her eyes with the back of her arm.

"With Celeste gone," Taraji took over, "we've realized we *all* need to be there for each other. Plus, this book was something else. How did I not know about these Brontë chicks before now?"

"You actually read the book?"

"Some people didn't finish, but I did."

"It was short notice—we decided spur of the moment to make this happen," Poppy offered.

"Everyone gets an A triple plus for effort." Mia grabbed a couple of cookies and some punch and took her place among the gang. "Who read it? Who wants to talk?"

Sue Ellen held up her copy. "It was so, so sad. Poor Mr. Rochester. Why did he have to be blinded? That was cruel of the author. I wanted a happy ending."

"Not me." Taraji piped up. "He deserved worse. But the man I'm really wondering about is Isaiah."

"Are we talking about the book?" Sue Ellen asked. "I don't remember… oh. You mean—"

"This." Taraji flashed her phone, and then turned it back around and read. "'Mia and me at Parry Grove Trail overlook, Torrey Pines State Reserve'."

"What?" Jane asked sharply. "That's Celeste special spot. What is that?"

"Isaiah Cooper's Instagram. He posted a selfie of Mia and him." Poppy leaned forward. "Is he really as messed up as they say, Mia? I heard he's a falling down drunk, and that you've been chasing after him."

"I heard it's Paul Hudson she's after." Easton raised both eyebrows and gave a low, mean laugh.

It felt like someone had cut the cable on an elevator, that's how fast Mia's stomach plummeted. If only she could close her eyes and count to three and when she opened them, none of these women would be here, staring at her, laughing at her. Mia had foolishly believed their apologies when all they really wanted to do was to gossip—to humiliate her. This whole thing had been a set-up. Mia slowly set her plate on the floor, her hand shaking so hard one of the cookies fell off.

"Why would you think I was after Paul Hudson? Nothing could be farther from the truth." She could feel the tears welling behind her eyes, hear the quaver in her voice.

"Because Ruth said so." Easton smirked. "She told me you came on to Paul, heavy, at Pocket Park when everyone was out searching for Celeste. She said she invited you to lunch to ask you nicely to back off, and later, you trapped Paul by his car, outside the Coopers' house and tried to kiss him."

"Is that true, Mia, because if it is…" Jane's voice faded as the door creaked open.

All eyes turned to Pinkerman looming at the threshold.

Pinkerman's arms jerked at her side as she strode into the lounge. "I'm not sure what's going on in here, but whatever it is it's over."

"It's just the book club," Sue Ellen said quietly.

"It sounds more like the gossip club to me. How can you be so insensitive, Mia? I never, never would've believed it before today. But maybe it's a good thing. Seeing this behavior from you makes what I have to say a lot easier." She cleared her throat. "Everyone listen up. I've just had a phone call from Paul Hudson. He tells me that you, Mia, have made a number of false accusations against him because he rebuffed your advances."

"No. No, that's not true. I never—"

Pinkerman put up her hand in a stop sign. "Don't interrupt. He also says there's gossip going around the school, and I can hear for myself he's right." She shot a glare around the semi-circle. "I have no tolerance, *zero* tolerance, for this behavior. If I find any of you spreading rumors about the Hudsons, or anyone in the Cooper family, you have my word you'll suffer the same consequence as her." She pointed a stiff finger at Mia. "You've got an hour. And after that, you're not permitted on school grounds again."

CHAPTER 26

Saturday

Mia finished washing up and stuck her hands beneath the hot-air dryer in the ladies' room at the Piano Man, all the while studying her reflection. The makeupless, puffy-eyed image staring back at her would ordinarily have made her cringe, but today, at least in one respect, she found it satisfying—her red-rimmed gaze held not a trace of surrender.

Yesterday, unprepared to face her aunt with the news that she'd been fired, and taken off guard by the way the other teachers had turned on her, Mia had hidden out in her bedroom for the remainder of the day. Apparently sensing Mia's deep distress, Aunt Misty had uncharacteristically let her be, allowing Mia the space she'd needed. She'd cried it out, and then eventually fallen into a dreamless sleep. Or, perhaps, a sleep whose dreams she'd chosen to forget. Then, this morning, after twelve-plus hours rest, she'd awakened clear-headed; defiant, energized, and determined not to let the creeps of this world, like Paul Hudson, defeat her.

And while she disagreed, vehemently, with Dr. Baquero's reasoning that it would be best if Mia simply confessed to taking Celeste's keys, she was tired of waiting around for the worst to happen. Whatever was going on with the restaurant security footage, Mia could ferret it out.

She rolled her shoulders back, exited the restroom and headed for the hostess stand.

There, she struck up a conversation about Celeste with a smartly uniformed young woman whose name tag identified her as "Heather".

"I'm sorry about your friend, really sorry. And I was here the night she went missing. I probably talked to her. I probably took her back to her table. I feel awful I didn't pay more attention—" Heather pursed her lips "—but Fridays get busy."

"Thank you. But there was no way for any of us to predict something like this. If we'd known, I think we all would've done things differently."

"I wish I could help. But I've told the police everything I know." Heather dabbed the corner of her eye with a tissue she'd pulled from her pocket. "I apologize, but I'm afraid I don't remember you either."

That acted as balm to Mia's soul. The young woman didn't remember a thing about Mia. It was beginning to seem possible that her mean-spirited mistake might remain buried up at Torrey Pines forever.

It was Heather who'd been manning the hostess station the night Mia had bumped into Celeste and Jane. Mia was certain of it because Heather had a distinctive patch of white in her otherwise jet-black hair.

If Heather didn't remember Mia, then she either hadn't seen or hadn't taken note of Mia snatching up Celeste's keys. And Heather's much bemoaned feeble memory provided a perfect segue into Mia's next topic. "It's good you have security cameras. Even if you don't remember anything out of the ordinary, maybe the cops will find something when they check the CCTV."

"I guess." She shrugged. "I still feel bad."

"You shouldn't. But, um, do you know if the police have seen the CCTV footage? Has it been preserved?" She tried to make her voice sound casual, like the question had just occurred, instead of it being the reason she was here.

"I don't know."

"You don't know if they've seen it, or don't know if it's been preserved?"

Now Heather's eyes narrowed, her face taking on what Mia read as a hint of annoyance, possibly because they were no longer talking about Heather and her feelings. "Neither. I don't know anything about the security cameras."

The disappointment must've shown on Mia's face because Heather's expression rebounded into a sympathetic one. "But Keisha Sims will know. You can ask her."

"You think she'll talk to me?"

Heather scoffed. "She'll talk to anybody who'll listen. She's going to tell you she's the assistant manager, but she's not. She's just a hostess, same as me. But ever since Lanelle, that's the *real* assistant manager, went on maternity leave, and they started letting Keisha make the schedule and do a few other things, she's been on a power trip."

"Who's been on a power trip?" A petite blond, no older than Heather, approached.

"No one. If you wouldn't eavesdrop you wouldn't mishear," Heather said.

"I wasn't eavesdropping." The woman's face flushed. "And now that I'm assistant manager you can't talk to me like that."

Mia cleared her throat. "Are you Keisha? The assistant manager?"

"Guilty as charged. How may I help you?" Keisha switched to an exaggeratedly professional tone.

"*Acting* assistant manager," Heather put in.

"I'm Mia Thornton." Mia extended her hand. "A friend of Celeste Cooper and family, and I was wondering if I could have a moment of your time."

"She wants to know if the cops got the security tapes," Heather said.

Keisha tilted her chin at Mia. "There are no tapes. The footage is digital."

"But you can transfer the footage onto tape for the police, can't you?" Mia asked.

"That's right. If you'll step into my office, we can speak in private," Keisha replied.

"That's Lanelle's office, not yours." Heather seemed keen on making sure Keisha didn't take any extra credit.

"Please follow me." Keisha turned her back on her fellow staff member and led Mia through the kitchen and down a hallway.

Keisha unlocked the door to a small office.

Mia had gotten lucky. Keisha's need to show off her authority had distracted her to the point she hadn't asked herself if it was appropriate to be talking about the restaurant's security system with someone other than the police.

Once inside the office, Keisha indicated a Spanish-style dining chair that had obviously been pulled from one of the restaurant's tables, and Mia took a seat. Keisha balanced on the edge of a black desk that looked cheap, like it'd come from an office supply store. She rotated a computer toward Mia, revealing a screen divided into sections of live feed from both the interior and exterior of the Piano Man. "You were asking about CCTV?"

Mia nodded, hardly believing how easy this was turning out to be. "For the family. I was just wondering if there was video from a week ago Friday night, and if the police have asked for it."

Keisha folded her arms across her chest. "Uh-huh."

Something in Keisha's tone was making Mia's stomach churn. "So…"

"Unfortunately—" Keisha smiled… odd since she was reporting a misfortune "—the footage was deleted from the hard drive."

"Oh no." Mia pressed her hand to her gut. Until now, she'd been holding on to hope that the footage would somehow magically show nothing of her, and yet still provide clues for the police, possibly even reveal the culprit following Celeste out of the restaurant. Now that chance was gone—but at least Mia could rest easy about the keys.

Keisha was still smiling, still inappropriately. "Don't you want to know how the footage got deleted?"

"Sure." At this point it no longer mattered, but Keisha seemed to want to tell her.

"I received a complaint about one of my staff. Heather, to be precise."

Mia nodded, numbly. She needed to stop at the pharmacy for an antacid, and she was definitely beginning to understand Heather's resentment toward Keisha.

"So it fell to me, as *assistant manager*, to sort it out. I had to review the footage from Friday night—naturally this is before we'd heard a thing about Celeste Cooper going missing or I wouldn't have gone near it. Anyway, I checked out the encounter between Heather and our unhappy customer, and it turns out it wasn't Heather who'd seated her. It was Lola, and all she did was escort her to the table. It was the customer who knocked over a wineglass and ruined her own white dress, not Lola."

"That must've been a disappointment," Mia said dryly.

"Anyway, I noticed the hard drive was almost full, so I thought I'd delete the footage to free up space. Turns out that wasn't necessary because when the hard drive runs out of room it just records over the oldest footage automatically. Too bad I didn't know that. It was, as you say, disappointing not to be able to provide a recording for the police. But my manager understood completely. I was only trying to help, and it's actually his fault for not training me properly." Her lips curled. "But you know what isn't a disappointment?"

"No." Mia got to her feet.

"You showing up to inquire about the CCTV."

Keisha had reviewed the footage from Friday night.

Mia should've seen this coming.

She dropped back down into her chair, a molten rock in her gut. To distract from the blistering pain in her belly, Mia dug her nails into her palms.

"I know what you did," Keisha said in a stage whisper. "You stole *her* keys. I didn't recognize you right away because you look different today. That night, you cowered like you were a nothing, a nobody compared to those women. When they turned their backs on you, I thought you were going to dissolve into a puddle on the floor. But then, you surprised me. You walked away with her keys, and I said to myself: *You go, girl!*"

No antacid in the world could quiet the fire in Mia's stomach. Her throat filled up with bile.

"Don't get upset. I like you better for showing some spunk."

Where was Keisha headed with this? Mia pulled a small water bottle from her bag, took a sip. The acid drained from her throat. What was the worst thing that could happen?

Keisha would reveal her secret.

And her world, unlike Celeste's, would go on turning.

She screwed the cap back on the water bottle and put it away. "Is that all?"

"Not exactly. I'm afraid my car's in the shop. Needs a new transmission."

Mia rose to leave. "I honestly don't care."

"That's not very polite. You should be nicer to me. If you ask me, you need all the friends you can get."

Mia crossed the room.

Keisha jumped up and got ahead of her, backing against the door, blocking Mia's exit. "My new transmission costs one thousand dollars, and I'm afraid I don't have the cash. The shop guy says my car'll be ready in two days. I told him that isn't enough time for me to come up with the money, and he said if I don't, he won't release my car."

"Let me pass, please," Mia said.

Keisha didn't budge. "Here's my thought: I'm betting my new friend, Mia, can help me out. If I give you forty-eight hours, you can come up with one thousand dollars. Can't you, hon?"

CHAPTER 27

Mia's head was aching as she headed from the Piano Man toward her car, parked down the street, just past the alleyway. Keisha had given her forty-eight hours to deliver one thousand dollars. But Mia had absolutely no intention of paying Keisha Sims a single dime, and that meant she had to figure a different way to avoid disaster.

Ideas, though not necessarily good ones, began percolating.

The first option that occurred to her was, like Dr. Baquero suggested, to simply confess to taking Celeste's keys and deal with the fall out. But that fall out included the likelihood that Alma, and all her family, would want nothing more to do with Mia. And Detective Samuels had already flagged Mia as a person worth watching. If he found out about the "lost" keys, that just might bump her up to a full-blown suspect.

Her second option was to call Keisha's bluff. Maybe Keisha figured she'd give it a shot, seeing as how she didn't have the cash for her car, but wouldn't carry out her implied threat because she had nothing to gain, really, by doing so. And if she did, it would only emphasize to her boss her foolish mistake in deleting the footage.

A corollary of option two was to call Keisha's bluff *but* be prepared to deny everything if she did go to Samuels with her story. With no CCTV footage available, it would be Mia's word against Keisha's—but lying outright to the police was something Mia didn't have much of a stomach for, as was evident from the ongoing burning in her esophagus.

The third option was to sleep on it, and then return to the Piano Man to try to reason with Keisha. Keisha looked to be a twenty-something like her, struggling to carve out a career, not an expert in extortion. If Mia had to bet, she'd put her money on this blackmail attempt being something of an impulse buy. A scheme Keisha might already regret. Maybe all Mia needed to do was give her the opportunity to take it back. Mia would give anything for the chance to undo her own wrongs.

She liked the final idea best, especially because it didn't involve Mia cowering in a corner. She'd been fired from her job, her fellow teachers had turned on her, even Ruth and Paul Hudson had teamed up against her, but that didn't mean she had to take it without fighting back.

The way Keisha had called her *a nobody* really hurt—it was past time for Mia to stand up for herself.

"Mia! Wait up!" Detective Samuels came trotting down the alley toward her.

Half-heartedly, she waved. She did need to tell him about Paul Hudson following her, but must she do it today—right this minute?

She could use a breather, but the look on his face let her know he was flagging her down for a reason. Resigning herself to her fate, she sat down on a sidewalk bench in front of a gelato shop, mere steps from her Jetta—she'd almost made it—and waited.

"Mind if I join you?" he said as he arrived, dropping beside her and wiping his forehead with a handkerchief.

"You didn't have to kill yourself. I wasn't going to make a break for it."

"Just getting my exercise."

"Okay. Anything interesting in the alley?" she asked, not that she expected him to answer. He hadn't been exactly forthcoming about his investigation to date.

"Not really. Just wanted to have another look. You never know when some small detail will jump out at you and break a case wide open."

That seemed true enough. "Mind if I ask where they found Celeste's purse?"

He pointed. "Underneath that dumpster."

"So it was hidden from view?"

"What's your point?"

"You do know, don't you, that bag's expensive? Even used, someone could get hundreds for it on Craig's List."

"I'm aware—that is I was made aware by some of my colleagues, and it's an interesting observation. I suppose you're wondering, like my colleagues did, how that purse lasted in the alley from Friday night until Saturday afternoon when we recovered it."

She nodded.

"Apparently, we just caught a break. The purse was in a hard-to-spot space under the dumpster."

She didn't bother to point out, because Samuels undoubtedly knew, that a certain segment of the population in San Diego had perfected the art of dumpster diving—and that included any and all areas above, below, and around the dumpsters. "A really lucky break. Was there a reason you chased me down?"

His expression, which had been just this side of light-hearted, suddenly turned grave. "You and I need to have a serious talk, Mia."

"I agree. Do you want to go first, or should I?"

CHAPTER 28

"Ladies first," Samuels said.

He probably thought if she revealed her information first that would give him the upper hand, but Mia was okay with that. There was no changing the facts. Paul Hudson had been following her. He'd lurked outside the Coopers' house and given her a "warning" accompanied by a threatening gesture. And that's what she relayed to Samuels, as thoroughly as possible, providing all the details she could think of, including that at one point she'd thought she'd lost the Lexus tailing her, but later Hudson turned up at the Coopers' anyway. She wasn't quite sure how that happened, but it had happened, nonetheless. The black Lexus couldn't be a coincidence. It must've been Paul all along. She finished up with: "I think you should get a handwriting sample from Paul Hudson. I think he's the one who left that note on my car."

Detective Samuels, who'd been diligently jotting down what she told him, put away his pen and paper and met her gaze. "Paul Hudson didn't write that note."

"You got the handwriting analysis back already? I was hoping to hear soon, but I worried the FBI would take longer."

"If I'd handed the note off to the FBI they would've taken months, possibly more to get back to us, which is one reason I didn't send it to them."

"But the FBI is assisting your department, because of those other women—right?"

"They've provided input, and they're making their resources available. We've sent priority evidence to their labs, spoken to their behavioral analysts, and accessed their databases, but the note on your car is not necessarily vital to this case. We got a guy here, in homicide, who took a class in forensic handwriting examination. He's got a certificate, and I figured he'd be our fastest bet, and as reliable as any considering."

"Considering what?"

"This kind of thing is soft science to begin with. Not discounting it. Just taking it for what it's worth—informative, one slice of the pizza, but not the whole pie."

"But you just said Paul didn't write the note—that sounded conclusive to me."

"Taking multiple factors into consideration, not only the forensic examination of the note on your car, I don't believe he did."

"What multiple factors?"

He lifted his hands, and then lowered them, as if he'd wanted to put them on her shoulders but thought better of it. "Before we get into that, I'd like to say my piece."

"Okay."

He cleared his throat. "Mia, I'm not gonna lie. Knowing what you've been through tugs at my emotions. You may not believe this, but detectives have hearts. That's why some of us go into this crazy, terrible line of work in the first place. But we can't let anything get in the way of following the evidence and going after the bad guys. We can't let our feelings cloud our judgment. So I'm laying it on the line, and I hope you'll heed my warning."

She leaned in, her chest tight, not knowing what was coming next. "I'm not sure what you're trying to say."

"You gotta steer clear of this thing. Stop playing amateur detective. Stop bringing me leads that take me down the wrong path.

And, for your own sake, stop sounding off about Paul Hudson. You've already lost your job over him. It's time to back off."

"Paul told you he got me fired?"

"That you got yourself fired by gossiping about him. And the story you just told me, about him following you around town—according to him, it's the other way around. He's considering getting a restraining order."

"I can't believe this. He's twisting everything. He and his wife are gossiping about *me*. He told Ruth I came on to him, and Ruth told one of the teachers she warned me to stay away from Paul—neither of those things is true. The only thing Ruth Hudson told me was to keep my mouth shut about her husband. They're obviously trying to discredit me because they want to divert attention away from Paul."

"Or they don't interpret things the same way you do. And there's a lot of room for error when one person's telling another person who's telling another person, etc. Bottom line is I don't want to see you get yourself in trouble—you or your aunt either. I sympathize. I do. I know you're upset your mother's case was never solved, but you gotta walk away from the Hudsons. From all of this. It doesn't look good."

"This isn't about my mother's case, and Paul Hudson is the one who's following me—like he followed Celeste. Did you interview anyone else about that?"

"I did. Angelica Cooper says she heard about Hudson and Celeste, too—from *you*. We got one young lady from the school, whose name I won't mention because she's fearful of losing her job like you just did, who says she heard something along those lines from Celeste. But she doesn't know it first-hand. Never actually observed Hudson with Celeste, didn't see any texts he sent, etc."

"You're looking at him, though. You're checking him out."

"We did. And he came up clean. I thought about that note, too, and I even got a sample of his writing. But my document guy ruled him out with a high degree of certainty. Not only that, Hudson has an alibi for the night Celeste disappeared. Seems the reason Ruth Hudson stood you up for dinner is that's the same evening she reconciled with her husband. Ruth and Paul were together all night. Apparently, they were up talking until the wee hours and then fell asleep in each other's arms. He's not our guy."

"But he followed me and then *lied* about it."

"So you say. He's says different. His wife, who seems reliable, alibis him." Samuels cleared his throat. "You haven't asked me who my expert thinks wrote that note on your windshield. So I'm gonna tell you. My guy ruled out Isaiah Cooper—again, high degree of certainty. Who he can't rule out is you—or your aunt. At this point, it seems likely, I'm not saying one hundred percent certain, mind you, but likely, that either you or your aunt wrote that note, and you told me yourself, you thought it was her."

Mia nodded. She had been pretty positive it was Aunt Misty. But that was before Paul Hudson followed her to the Coopers. "But—"

"His alibi's a good one. Unless you think Ruth, who was ready to kick him out, would not only take him back but lie to cover up a crime as bad as this."

"I *hope* she wouldn't go that far. And whether or not you believe me, I didn't write that note." Her heart sank. "So, I guess, as far as the note goes, that just leaves Aunt Misty."

Samuels got to his feet and paced toward her Jetta. Walked around it twice, bending down, peering underneath. "You say a Lexus was tailing you, but then stopped. Then you saw Hudson in what you thought was the same vehicle parked outside the Coopers' residence. But Hudson had his own reasons to be there, he says. Nothing to do with you. He thinks you followed *him*."

She shook her head, feeling helpless and confused.

"Lots of black Lexus on the road, Mia."

Samuels was dragging his hand around the undercarriage of her car, when, abruptly, he stopped, let out a grunt, and squatted.

Then he held out a gray box no bigger than a cell phone. "Any idea how a GPS got on your car?"

She doubled over, like she'd been kicked in the stomach.

"Please tell me you didn't put a tracker on your own car, and then make up this whole story about Paul Hudson following you just to set me up to find this device."

The sun beat down ferociously. She fanned her face and took short, shallow breaths, trying to slow down her heart rate. It seemed an eternity before the dizziness passed, but at last, it did. "I didn't write the note and put it on my own car. I didn't plant a tracking device for you to find, either. My aunt *might* have. It's not inconceivable. She's very protective. But it's hard to believe Aunt Misty would do such a thing, and if she didn't, and Paul Hudson didn't…" Her breath was coming way too fast. It had been years since she'd hyperventilated, but she knew the warning signs.

Don't panic.

Digging in her purse, she found a paper bag from one of the shops she'd visited and breathed into it.

Her lungs relaxed, filling with much needed oxygen.

She waited a beat, for good measure, and then said, "What if this has nothing to do with Celeste? What if it's about my mother, instead? What if Aunt Misty's been right this whole time? Maybe all these years, someone *has* been watching, and that's who put a GPS on my car?"

Samuels walked over and sat down by her side. His eyes searched hers. "Doesn't add up. Odds are the person who put the note on your windshield is the same one who put the tracker on your car. This appears to me to be some sort of desperate strategy on your part, but it's not going to work. I will not reopen your mother's case based on manufactured evidence. So, calm down, get up, and dust yourself off. If you wrote that note and put a tracking device on your own car, either because you want attention, or because you hope it will get your mother's case off ice, then go home to your aunt and let her take care of you—get some therapy. But if you didn't, then my advice is go home and pack your bags. Because if your aunt did this, you need to get away from her as fast as you possibly can."

CHAPTER 29

It's hard to pack your bags and get away as fast as you possibly can when you have nowhere to go.

Mia's new apartment wouldn't be ready until the first of the month. Aunt Misty was the only family she had, and her friends were more like acquaintances than the kind whose couch you could crash on during a personal crisis. The closest thing she had to a love life were a few guys she'd been texting from that dating app she'd signed up for at Dr. Baquero's urging a few months ago, but she'd never met any of them in person. A hotel seemed a logical choice for tonight, but would be too pricey to stay in for more than two weeks until her apartment was ready. She snapped the latch on her suitcase closed, dragged it to the edge of her bed, sat down and let the tears flow.

When she heard the front door open, she grabbed a box of tissues from her nightstand, blew her nose, dried her eyes, and gathered her resolve. For twenty years she'd been huddled inside with her aunt, shades drawn to protect her from the outside world. But with everything that had happened, it was clear to Mia that safety couldn't be found within a set of walls, and that this house was more hideaway than home.

It was time for her to go.

Aunt Misty opened the door to Mia's room.

"Thanks for knocking." *And yes, you bet that's sarcasm in my tone.*

"I thought I heard crying." Aunt Misty hurried over, sidled up to Mia on the bed, and reached out to stroke her hair. "What's wrong, baby?"

Mia pushed her hand away.

"Talk to me, please. I let you be last night, because you seemed like you needed your space." Aunt Misty gave her the *and-you-know-how-hard-that-was-for-me* look.

Mia didn't care. Her aunt was not going to soften her up and get her to feel sorry for her. Not this time. Mia lobbed a handful of wadded up tissue at the trashcan. "Big of you to keep out of my business for one whole night."

"Did something happen at work? Or have I done something? This morning, I went to get coffee and croissants from that bakery you like, but when I came home you were gone. You didn't leave me a note or anything. I called three times, and you never picked up. I've been worried sick. Where have you been?"

"Like you don't know."

"How would I?"

"You tell me." Mia scoffed.

Aunt Misty scooted away from her, shaking her head. "I can see you're hurt about something. You'd never speak to me like this otherwise. You're too good a girl."

"I'm not a girl. I'm a grown woman, and I'm tired of you treating me like a child. I got fired yesterday, but that's not why I'm upset."

"Oh darling, I'm so sorry…" Aunt Misty stopped speaking mid-sentence. She was staring at Mia's suitcase. "You're-you're going somewhere?"

"Great detective work. I'm leaving."

"Leaving *me*?"

"I'm moving out." She waited, knowing the hysterics were coming, but Aunt Misty just gaped at her, seemingly stunned into temporary silence.

"Did you hear what I just said? Aren't you going to wail and moan? Beg me to stay? Don't bother, because I've found an apartment, and it'll be ready on the first of the month. But I'm leaving now. I can't stay here one more day. Not after what you've done."

Aunt Misty opened her mouth but, still, she didn't speak. Then, at last, she started to cry; big tears dripped down her cheeks, silent sobs wracked her body, air leaked out of her lungs in short, wheezy breaths.

Despite her earlier resolve, the sight of her aunt's heartache doused Mia's anger like a bucket of ash poured over a campfire. She put her arms around her aunt. "I'm not trying to hurt you. I do love you, and I'm grateful you took me in. Thank you—I mean that sincerely."

Aunt Misty pulled away and wiped her face on her sleeve. "You don't have to thank me, sweetheart. When you say I took you in, you make it sound like a sacrifice. Like I rescued some pitiful waif off the street."

"You did." That was the truth of it, and the thought of all her aunt had done for her made her heart crack open. "You gave up everything for me."

"You've got it all wrong, Mia. It wasn't a sacrifice. You're my family. Without you, I'd have nothing."

"Because you stopped living for yourself and started living for me the day they found me in the woods. If it weren't for me, you'd have a full life—a family of your own. I know your fiancé left you because he didn't want a ready-made family. I heard the argument from my bedroom that night. I'm the reason you never married. I'm the reason your social life is nonexistent. But you never complained. And you never so much as left me with a sitter on a Saturday night."

"I had to send you to daycare before and after school all week while I worked, so how could I possibly turn around and leave you with a babysitter on the weekends—just so I could go out and have fun?"

"It might've been better for both of us if you had. I can't be your whole life anymore, and I don't want you to be mine. It's well past time for me to get my own place."

Her aunt rubbed her eyes with her fists. "That's a lot to unpack, and I won't try to address it all now, but I will say this: you've given my life purpose. I don't regret a thing. If you want to get your own place, in time, I understand. But you just got fired. How will you pay for this new apartment of yours?"

"I've got savings. Not a lot, but enough to tide me over for a month or two until I can find another job."

"You're going to need those savings for a rainy day."

Her eyebrows went up. "This *is* a rainy day. In fact it's more like a hurricane."

"You say your new place—which I can't believe you selected without me—isn't ready. So why go today? I don't understand." Then Aunt Misty paused, and her eyes hardened. "Unless it's the Coopers. Are they behind this?"

Mia suddenly remembered why she'd been so angry with her aunt. "The Coopers have nothing to do with this. Why would you say that?"

"Because since they befriended you, you've been distant. It's not natural the way you've attached yourself to Alma and vice versa. You've got a missing mother, and she's got a missing daughter so, in a way, I can see the connection. But you've only known each other a short time and you already seem..." She snapped her fingers as if trying to recall. "What's that word Dr. Baquero loves so much...?"

"Co-dependent. You can't seriously be calling my relationship with *Alma* co-dependent?"

"I can and I am."

Mia released a long breath. "I'm giving you one last chance to tell the truth, and then I'm heading out. Did you or didn't you put that note on my car?"

Aunt Misty shook her head. "I'm so disappointed in you, Mia. You're accusing me of not only of leaving that note, but of lying to you about it. And that scares me."

"The expert compared your handwriting to the handwriting on the note, and he can't rule you out. He can't rule me out either, but I didn't write it."

"Nor did I!"

"There's more."

"How can there be more?"

"Detective Samuels found a tracking device on my car." The last thing Mia wanted was to leave on bad terms, but Aunt Misty had gone too far. This time, Mia couldn't give her a pass. "He says whoever wrote the note must be the one who put the tracking device on my car."

Her aunt's face cycled through every emotion in the book, and then she settled into a familiar, hyper-alert posture, her gaze darting continually about the room, as if expecting the boogieman to pop up from behind the hope chest or burst out of a closet. "That detective is off his gourd if he thinks either you or I wrote that note. I don't believe for one minute that you did, or that you put that GSP on your own car, and I sure as heck know I didn't do it."

"GPS not GSP."

"See, I don't even know what it's called. How could I put it on your car?"

That was a little too convenient. Her aunt might not be a techie, but she was smart and well read. She had to know what a GPS was.

Why exaggerate her technical ineptitude?

Though to be fair, Mia wasn't too familiar herself. She was going to need to do an online search for spy gadgets later tonight so she'd be prepared to spot something like this in the future. "Anyone can get them. All you have to do is stick it under the car."

"And then what? Don't you have to install an app to follow the movements?"

And there you had it. Aunt Misty knew enough—certainly more than Mia.

"I wouldn't know the first thing about how to get data off a tracker. But that's not the point. The point is I would never do something like that to you, and I didn't."

Mia shook her head. "Ever since I turned off *find my phone,* you've been complaining you don't know where I am. I know you worry about me. If you did this, you can tell me. It won't change my mind about leaving, but at least it will be a step toward rebuilding trust."

"I didn't write any note, and I didn't track your car. You've got to believe me." Aunt Misty's pupils darkened. "Don't you see what this means?"

"That no matter how much I love you, I can't trust you to tell me the truth, even when it's incredibly important."

"Mia," her aunt grabbed her hands, "don't you see? This is *proof* someone is creeping around."

"It doesn't prove anything of the kind." Mia climbed to her feet, shouldered her purse, and raised the handle on her suitcase.

Aunt Misty dropped to her knees. "I'm begging you, Mia, please, please, please don't go. Someone *dangerous* is out there. Someone is *watching.*"

Mia's phone buzzed in her pocket.

She pulled it out and saw a voicemail.

CHAPTER 30

It was late afternoon, and a sudden storm turned day to night. Because of the rain and fog, Mia drove the distance from her aunt's home to the Coopers' place with wipers and headlights on. San Diego's bright, summer foliage was now the same dark brown as the surrounding air. Even though she knew it was an optical illusion, that beneath all this grunge, the trees and flowers remained vibrant, patiently waiting for the sun to reveal their true colors, dreariness sank into her bones.

She shivered, and then pulled into the enormous circular driveway, gazing up at the expansive, three-story brick house. Twice before she'd visited and had been drawn to its stately elegance. But today, with dark clouds as a backdrop, and water streaming off the gables like tears, the house seemed ominous, like a mansion out of a gothic novel, shadowed and secretive.

Her chest tight with apprehension, she killed the ignition.

Alma's voicemail had been garbled from a bad connection, part of the message cut off, but Mia had gotten the gist: "Did she have a moment to stop by?" A simple request, but for some reason—probably Aunt Misty's insistence that someone was *watching*—a strong sense of foreboding had taken hold of Mia.

She eyed the umbrella on the passenger seat.

A lot had happened today, and none of it had been good.

Waiting for the rain to let up made a perfect excuse to sit in the car and pull herself together. As the staccato beats of drops against her windshield lessened, she rested one hand on her abdomen, practicing her relaxation breathing techniques, and by the time the rain stopped, Mia felt ready to meet the remainder of the day with calm and reason.

She climbed out, breathing in the sweet smell of wet grass, and walked around her car, testing the doors to be sure they were locked, as well as the trunk where she'd stored her suitcase. Next she inspected the tires and windshield, then ran her hand around the muddy undercarriage of the car like Samuels had done earlier. Satisfied that her vehicle was secure and free of surveillance equipment, she cleaned her hands with a wet wipe from her kitchen-sink purse and headed up the walkway to the house.

Angelica opened the front door even before Mia rang the bell, but then didn't step aside to let her in. "Hi, Mia."

Angelica was looking at her like she was a solicitor or census worker. She didn't seem to be expecting her. A clap of thunder sounded, and just that quickly, it started to rain, pour really, again. "It's cats and dogs out here, may I come in?"

"Now's not a good time, I'm afraid," Angelica responded, a tight smile on her face.

"Your mother asked me to stop by," Mia said, determined. Alma had invited her, after all.

"All right, then. At least you're not dripping wet. I'll take you to her."

"Is she okay?" Mia asked.

"I'll let you be the judge." Angelica ushered her inside with a neutrality that felt cold compared to Mia's prior interactions with her—she was a lot friendlier when she'd been drinking.

But Mia had said, more than once, she'd be available if the Coopers needed anything, and she was glad Alma had called. The Coopers were hurting, and a lot of people, especially the press, were trying to take advantage of them in their time of need. The Coopers needed a friend, and Mia planned on becoming a good one. She wasn't going to take Angelica's brusqueness personally, or read ulterior motives into her behavior. Her mind could easily take a suspicious turn if she weren't on guard against paranoia.

She followed Angelica to the second floor, where Angelica rapped gently at a door. When no response came, she opened it and motioned for Mia to come inside with her.

"Mia!" Alma looked up, wild-eyed, from where she sat cross-legged on a Persian rug, surrounded by papers. Her hair was uncombed, and, even though it was late afternoon, she was wearing black silk pajamas. A tray with an untouched meal rested on a nearby desk along with a set of car keys and a prescription bottle. "How are you, dear?"

The question would've seemed normal if only Alma hadn't spoken the words so rapidly, sounded so breathless.

Mia exchanged a glance with Angelica. "I'm well, Alma. How are you?"

"She hasn't slept," Angelica answered for her mother. "She hasn't eaten. She's hasn't come out of this room since yesterday, and now she says she's going to drive herself to the post office to mail thank you notes."

"Does the doctor say it's safe for you to drive?" Mia couldn't hide her surprise. Alma had been so conscientious about not getting behind the wheel up until now. The lack of sleep, the grief, *something* seemed to be clouding her judgment.

Alma twisted a lock of hair around her finger, yanked it free and winced, seeming surprisingly agitated compared to the calm woman Mia had previously observed.

"He's forbidden it," Angelica said.

Next, Alma licked an envelope, and then tried to balance it on a tall stack of letters that promptly toppled over. "Driving is only forbidden if I'm taking tranquilizers, and I'm not—not anymore. I can't get anything accomplished all doped up." She frowned at Angelica. "Sometimes I think the lot of you want to keep me sedated to get me out of the way."

"That's absolute nonsense—and hurtful." Angelica folded her arms.

Mia lowered herself next to Alma. "Do you need some help with all this? Is that why you called?"

"Yes, but then Angelica showed up. I meant to call you back and tell you not to come, but…" She shook her head. "I forgot. I'm so distracted I can't think straight."

"All the more reason not to drive, Mom. And I said I'd take them." Angelica raised an eyebrow.

"You also said you need to get back to the office, and I should just let all of this go or else hire an assistant."

"I can post these letters for you. And I can come by every day to help you. I've got plenty of time." Mia hesitated but then decided to come out with it. Chances were the Coopers would hear it from Jane or someone else anyway. "I lost my job."

Alma's eyes widened. "Not because of that reporter, I hope."

"Not entirely."

"But that was part of it? You were protecting me from that awful woman and now… I'm so, so sorry."

"It's no one's fault." Except maybe Paul Hudson's but she wasn't going to go into that. "The point is I'm free to help you, and you don't need to worry about taking up my time."

"But you seemed insulted the other day when we offered you money, and I can't have you doing all this for nothing—especially now that you've lost your job. I'm perfectly capable of handling everything myself." Alma waved her hand frenetically.

"I'd *enjoy* helping you," Mia said. "I'm sorry if I seemed overly sensitive before. I just don't feel right taking your money."

Angelica nodded. "Well, then, that's settled. No point going round and round. If Mia won't take money—"

If she wasn't careful, Angelica might spoil this for her. "I want to help," Mia jumped in. "And I have an idea—we could compromise."

Alma stopped fiddling with the letters.

"I'm afraid, in addition to losing my job, I've had something of a disagreement with my aunt." Did she dare suggest? "What if I drive you to your appointments and help with whatever else you need in exchange for a place to stay—just until my new apartment opens up?"

"That's not necessary," Angelica said. "I can take more time off. I don't think—"

"We have plenty of space," Alma broke in. "And it would be so convenient to have Mia here. Angelica, you can get back to work. Only, let's make it room *and* board."

"You drive a hard bargain, but I'm in." Mia got to her feet. "You won't believe this, but I actually have my suitcase in my car."

A crash sounded overhead, and they all jumped.

Angelica sent Mia a pointed look. "I should warn you: Isaiah lives on the third floor—he's got an entire bachelor pad up there and his bedroom is directly above the guest suite."

CHAPTER 31

I hope you'll be comfortable. That's what Alma had said when she'd ushered Mia to her room. This particular guest room had been chosen for her because of its en suite bath and its proximity to Alma's study. Baxter had his own separate office, which his wife warned Mia was strictly off-limits. As he was a wheeler-dealer, his confidential papers were not to be disturbed.

Comfortable.

That wasn't the word Mia would use to describe her new quarters. Sumptuous, elegant, classy—any of those would've been a more apt description. The room itself was the size of her bedroom and living room combined. A series of black-and-white photographs of San Diego adorned light-gray walls with contrasting white trim. A lovely antique writing desk faced a bay window with built-in perch. An ocean-blue cushion, covering the perch, and a vase of red roses provided the perfect pop of color.

As for the bedding, one sank into it rather than sat upon it. The pillows, she thought, were goose down, as was a white duvet, so pristine it might've never been used. A smile played across her lips as she let herself pretend, just for a moment, this room belonged to her; that she, not Celeste, had grown up in such luxury—with Alma as her doting mother.

Sweeping her hand over the softer-than-satin sheets she closed her eyes, and then, suddenly, she recalled the scratchy woolen blanket that covered the worn mattress in the bed she'd shared with her real mother as a girl.

She pulled in a shuddering breath.

A knock sounded at the door and her eyelids fluttered open.

"Mia, are you up? May I come in?"

At the sound of Baxter's voice, she hurried to her feet, and, in front of a framed mirror, quickly smoothed her hair and wiped smeared mascara from beneath her eyes.

She opened the door. "I'm up. Come in, please."

Baxter gave her a warm smile and entered, then settled himself on the perch in front of the bay window, looking even more handsome with a day's stubble on his jaw.

She took a seat at the desk facing him.

"I trust you're comfortable," he said. "Is there anything you're lacking? Anything you need?"

"Oh, no. This is so lovely. So much more than I…" She was about to say deserve, but stopped herself. Everyone deserves good things.

"Excellent." He eyed her small suitcase. "But surely this isn't everything. I'll send Isaiah with you if you want to bring over more from your aunt's house. You must have boxes and furniture. We have a storage shed for anything that won't fit in your room."

A memory of a cold dark space, filled with tattered boxes, suddenly surfaced.

"Mia?"

"I don't have any furniture." Aunt Misty would disagree. She'd insist Mia keep whatever she needed from the house, but Mia wanted her own things. She wanted a fresh start. "There's a photograph my grandfather gave me. I could put it on the desk, but I won't need Isaiah's help for that."

"Well, if you change your mind, I'm volunteering him. Alma said you're not speaking to your aunt, so I thought having Isaiah along might ease the tension between the two of you."

"We're speaking." No matter what Aunt Misty had or hadn't done, Mia would never freeze out the only family she had left. Of course there was a great aunt around somewhere, and second cousins, but no one who was part of her life. And even if Mia's world had been filled with relatives, Aunt Misty was the one who'd taken her in, loved her, changed her world into someplace safe.

"Excellent. I hate the idea of being on the outs with family—having gone through it myself." He paused and wrinkled his nose, and then he frowned. "Have you been drinking?"

What? After dinner she'd brushed her teeth and gargled and the very, very faint scent of Listerine still hung in the air from where she'd spilled some in the sink. He must have the nose of a bloodhound. She jumped up and closed the door to the en suite bath. "No. I think that's my mouthwash."

"I'm sorry. It's just that Isaiah, as I'm sure you've noticed, has a bit of a problem. He drinks too much, and then he tries to cover it up with mouthwash, so I'm conditioned to be suspicious. I love my son, but I hate that he's weak."

"My mother was an alcoholic." She pulled her chin up.

"I just keep putting my foot in it, don't I? Sorry again. I don't judge you by your mother."

Her shoulders stiffened. "Mr. Cooper—"

He lifted a hand. "We agreed, Mia. Remember?"

"Baxter, then. I can't tell you how much I appreciate the opportunity to be here—to help out. The room is beautiful." She stopped short of asking if there was something else he wanted. That would be rude. But she longed for sleep, and she'd promised Alma they'd get an early start on the thank you notes tomorrow.

"You're probably tired. I just stopped in to make sure you had everything, and to say a proper thank you for helping out. In fact, I can't help wondering if this is too much to ask. You shouldn't feel obligated. I'm sure you have better options."

"Not at the moment."

"Do you mind my asking why you fought with your aunt? I don't mean to intrude, but if I can help with anything, I'd be happy to."

"It's nothing. I'm sure we'll get past it." She wasn't about to tell him that her aunt put a tracking device on her car. Especially when she didn't know, with one hundred percent certainty, that her aunt was the culprit. "But thanks."

"All right." He got to his feet and went to the door, then turned and looked at her, his eyes glistening like he might cry.

"Is everything okay?" What a thing to say when his daughter was missing.

He looked down, as if to compose himself. "How old are you, Mia?"

"Twenty-six."

"Same age as Celeste," he said, his tone wistful.

"I thought we were similar in age."

"Similar in other ways, too." He sighed. "Good listeners. My wife likes you, Mia. She's been so depressed, so overwhelmed, and the only time I've seen her laugh since Celeste… what I'm getting at is that you make Alma smile, and Alma makes me smile." He reached his hand out and rested it on her shoulder. "Do you mind if I tell you something about Alma and me?"

"Please," she said.

"The first time I met her, she was wearing a cream-colored blouse with a round collar and blue slacks. Her shoes were brown—they didn't match her purse. It was red. Her hair was swept up on one side with a barrette. Ladies used to wear those back in the day. Anyway, I caught Alma's eye from across a crowded room—don't worry, I promise I'm not going to break into song—but the first time I saw her, I knew she'd be the love of my life." His voice was shaking, and he paused a few beats. "I've traveled the world, Mia, and I've been lost a time or two, but Alma is my compass. She's the one who makes my life worthwhile. Sometimes, in my business dealings, I can be ruthless, and I wonder if I even have a heart. But then I think of Alma, and I know that I do, because if I ever lost her, it would break into a million pieces. I want you to know I'll do anything to protect my wife—give anything."

Mia could hardly breathe from the way he'd just poured his heart out.

And then, his face flushed as if he thought he might have revealed too much. "You're sure you don't need Isaiah to help you move anything?"

"No…" She hesitated. All she had left of her mother was still at Aunt Misty's. "There is one thing he could help me bring over. Not for the storage shed, though. If you really don't mind, I think this room is large enough for my mother's hope chest."

CHAPTER 32

Sunday

To Mia, Alma seemed like a different person. Unlike yesterday, she'd combed and coiffed and dressed herself in a neatly pressed blouse and slacks, the satin slippers on her feet the only indication she wasn't headed for a luncheon with friends or a casual committee meeting. No more frenzied gestures. No more run-on sentences. The contrast was so great it made Mia consider that Alma's agitated demeanor the day before might've been due to more than an absence of sleep, though she wasn't sure what else it would've been.

Since 7 a.m., not bothering with breakfast, Mia and Alma had been cloistered in Alma's study, going through mail. Baxter had been right to insist that Mia prescreen. Most of the letters were supportive, sending thoughts and prayers for Celeste's safe return, offers of assistance, and in some cases, heart-wrenching tales of someone's personal tragedy and how she'd coped. But scattered among these were horrible, horrible notes. Some speculated family members had done Celeste in—Isaiah was a favorite suspect, but all the Coopers, including Alma, had their accusers. Some contained graphic descriptions of what predators do to their victims, suggesting Celeste might have been dismembered, buried alive, or held as a sex slave in a moldy dungeon. These latter missives, Mia handled with gloves and set aside for Detective Samuels to examine, not knowing if they might become relevant at some point in the investigation.

As for the well-wishers, Mia was supposed to sort them into stacks for generic thank yous, which she would take care of, and those warranting personal replies, which Alma, herself, would compose. The problem was Alma refused to relinquish any of the notes for generic responses, and so, eventually, Mia relented and took over the task of addressing and stamping all the envelopes instead.

Now, an excruciating spasm gripped her writing hand. She dropped her pen and massaged the tight ball of pain out of her palm. The spasm passed, and she checked her watch. They'd been working for nearly five hours without a break. "Are you hungry?" she asked.

Alma looked up. "If you are, we can take lunch."

In truth, Mia didn't have much of an appetite. And she'd had trouble falling asleep, thinking about her quarrel with Aunt Misty, not to mention ruminating about how to convince Keisha, the woman from the Piano Man, to drop her extortion plan. That was a nightmare of a problem she hadn't yet figured out how to handle. But today her focus was on Alma. She seemed to be growing thinner by the hour and it was important to get her to eat regularly. Mia had also been put in charge of reminding Alma to take her medication. According to Angelica, the doctor recommended a noontime pill and nap and that wouldn't sit well on an empty stomach. "Great! I'm starved."

They wandered into the kitchen where Mia prepared sandwiches from the chicken salad a neighbor had brought over the day before, and then went to retrieve Alma's pill from the medicine cabinet in the master suite. On the second shelf, she located three prescriptions. Searching for escitalopram, she picked up the bottles, reading the labels one by one: lorazepam, dextroamphetamine, escitalopram. She tucked the escitalopram in her pocket, shut the medicine cabinet, and then drew in a quick breath.

Dextroamphetamine. Why was Alma taking the same medicine a couple of the five-year-olds took for attention disorders? Maybe that explained her agitation yesterday. She hated to think a doctor would give her antidepressants and tranquilizers, only to counteract them with a stimulant like dextroamphetamine. Maybe it was an old prescription. She opened the cabinet again and took a good look at the dextroamphetamine label. It had been prescribed earlier in the month… to Baxter. She put it back on the shelf and made a mental note to discuss the matter with Alma. Mia would bet her chicken salad sandwich that Alma had been sneaking Baxter's dextroamphetamine. Why he was taking that was none of her business—but Alma's health was.

Back at the kitchen table, she took a small bite of her sandwich and smiled at Alma, whose plate held nothing but crumbs. "I was only gone a minute. You must've been hungry."

"Turns out I was." Alma shrugged. "I don't remember if I ate yesterday or not. Angelica says I didn't, but I really couldn't tell you. It's all these damn pills." Then she frowned and pointed at the prescription bottle Mia held. "I know you want me to take that, but I'd rather not."

Mia lowered her voice. She didn't want to patronize Alma, but she needed to have a frank discussion with her. "I've brought your escitalopram—Angelica said that's an antidepressant, and I think you should follow doctor's orders and take it. Yesterday, you said you didn't want tranquilizers, but I don't think it's wise to suddenly stop taking any of your meds. Lorazepam is for anxiety—I know because I used to take it. What if we call the doctor and ask her for a schedule to wean you off the tranquilizer—the lorazepam. Does that seem reasonable?"

"Perfectly." Alma leaned back. "I'm not trying to be difficult. I trust you, so if you want to call Dr. Zester, I'll give her permission to discuss my care with you."

The old Alma was back, and so was Mia's appetite. Alma *trusted* her. "Okay, we'll send over consent, and I'll speak with the doctor while you're napping."

"We've got too much correspondence for me to take a nap."

"Yes, but I can hardly keep up with you as it is. It'll give me a chance to catch up with stamping and addressing and to make a post office run."

Alma looked like she might be wavering.

All she needed was a tiny shove over the edge. "You have to stay strong for Celeste. And that means taking good care of yourself and getting proper rest."

"You're very wise, Mia. Your mother would be proud."

Mia hoped so. She wanted to make her mother proud—she always had. Dr. Baquero didn't approve, though. Once, she said that Mia, like a lot of children of alcoholic parents, had an excessive need for approval, and that Mia was in denial about her mother, putting her on a pedestal, burying her resentment. It crossed Mia's mind she might be putting Alma on a pedestal, too, but where was the harm? "That's kind of you, Alma. Thank you." She reached out and rested her hand close to her friend's. "May I ask you something personal?"

"Yes."

"Did you take dextroamphetamine yesterday—I noticed it in the medicine cabinet."

Alma waved her hand as if it were unimportant. "A few. I had to. I didn't have anyone helping me then, and I needed to get these letters done. There'll be a whole new batch tomorrow, you know."

"But the dextroamphetamine is prescribed for Baxter."

"If it helps him get his work done, it can help me with mine. He has adult attention deficit—that's what the doctor says."

Was there an unspoken *but* at the end of that sentence? "And what do you say?"

"I say he has too many businesses to run and not enough help. But not to worry, now that I've got you, I promise I won't take any more of his *get-er-done* pills. I won't need them."

"Won't need what?" Baxter said as he burst into the kitchen, a large brown bag in his arms.

"Your attention pills."

Baxter dropped the bag, with a thud onto the table. "Alma, stay out of my medicine. You shouldn't be mixing stimulants and tranquilizers or taking anything that's not prescribed for you."

"And you shouldn't work so hard."

"I'm not going to let you bait me into an argument. I brought you young ladies a surprise." He sent her a smile, then pulled out a carton of ice cream from the brown bag, and then another, and then another, and then another.

"Baxter, you shouldn't spoil me like this," Alma said. "I don't think all of that's going to fit in the freezer."

Ignoring Alma's complaint, he turned to Mia. "My darling wife has one weakness—she can't resist ice cream. I wasn't sure what kind you liked, though, so I brought a few to choose from. We've got Alma's favorite—banana nut—then there's strawberry, vanilla, and last but not least, chocolate. Choose your poison."

"I haven't had ice cream in a long time." In truth, she rarely partook. It reminded her of her mother's broken promises, of childhood dreams unfulfilled. It took a moment for Mia to find her voice, but, at last, she managed, "I'd like to try my mother's favorite. May I please have a scoop of chocolate?"

CHAPTER 33

Monday

Keisha's deadline had arrived. It worked out well for Mia that Alma and Angelica had plans this afternoon, giving Mia time off to move her mother's hope chest and take care of *personal business*.

This morning, Mia called Keisha at the Piano Man, and the two agreed to meet at Mission Beach. The trip from the Coopers' residence, via public transportation, took about an hour, and Mia thought she'd have time on the way to figure out what to say. Only she hadn't been able to come up with a single sentence, much less a compelling argument that would make Keisha see sense. It was impossible to concentrate when, from the moment Mia boarded her trolley, she'd had the feeling someone was following her—despite the fact she'd changed lines before deboarding at Mission Boulevard and San Rafael.

Now, she squatted, tied her shoelace, and glanced up and down Mission, promising herself this was the last time she'd check to see if Paul Hudson was among the foot traffic.

He wasn't.

Relax.

Mia turned up Toulon Court in the direction of the ocean and breathed in the signature smells of Mission Beach: sand, salt and hot grease wafting from the burger joints surrounding the boardwalk. Climbing the narrow, bungalow-lined street, she took comfort in a familiar symphony: gulls cawing, skateboards screeching, and laughter floating on the breeze. The full-body tension that had been with her for hours, at last, loosened its grip.

She could handle this. It didn't get more public than Mission Beach.

There's nothing to be afraid of.

Nothing except being called out as a liar—nothing except squandering the friendship of the Coopers, devastating Alma with her betrayal, and becoming a suspect in a missing person investigation.

Mia's past behavior had been beyond foolish, but it was a bell she couldn't unring.

The only thing left for her to do about it was to change. She needed to make better decisions, starting with the one in front of her. "Keisha! Over here!" Mia waved at her approaching, would-be blackmailer, smiling her best, biggest smile, to let her know she wasn't her enemy.

In return, Keisha smiled back.

Off to a good start.

"Love your earrings." Mia got the ball rolling with an honest compliment. Keisha looked pretty in a flowing rainbow-colored kaftan. Oversized silver hoops adorned her ears. Her coral lipstick matched her sandals, and her sun-kissed hair hung in natural waves to complete the perfect day-at-the-beach look.

"How'd you get here?" Keisha hooked an arm through hers.

"Trolley."

"You didn't drive? You weren't followed, were you?" Keisha whispered the question.

Mia pulled her arm free and stepped back, leaned against a retaining wall. "Why would I be followed? And why does it matter if I drove or took the trolley?"

"You can't be too careful, is all." Keisha lowered her voice once more, and looked over her shoulder and back. "I've got a feeling I'm being watched."

The first thing that came to Mia's mind was… "Do you know Paul Hudson?"

"No idea who that is, or why someone would be following me. It's just a creepy feeling. Don't make a big deal." Keisha threw her hands up, protesting a bit too loudly.

"I'm not the one making a big deal. Maybe that feeling is guilt."

"Excuse me?"

"Never mind. Look, a friend is picking me up later. He's bringing a truck to help me move some things, so I took the trolley because we don't want two cars. No one followed me. I've been very careful."

"You told him you were meeting me?"

"No." She was so jumpy, you'd think Keisha was the one being blackmailed instead of the other way around. "I said I was meeting a friend—I didn't mention your name—for a beer at the beach."

"Let's do that, then." Keisha stuffed her hands in her pockets and walked ahead.

Mia followed her to a liquor stand located less than a foot behind a "No alcoholic beverages beyond this point" sign. Keisha ordered two draft IPAs, and they took their foaming cups to the nearby "dining area", which consisted of rickety plastic tables shaded by even ricketier red umbrellas.

Keisha slurped her beer, then dabbed a foam mustache from her lips. "Hot today."

"Eighty-seven and muggy." Mia lifted her hair off the back of her neck. "Feels like two hundred to me."

"Same." Keisha studied her acrylic nails. "Thanks for calling. I, uh, really appreciate you helping me out with my repair. Did you, uh, bring the cash?"

"No."

Keisha shifted in her seat. Mopped her mouth with her napkin. "You need more time? I can, uh, give you a few more days if that's the problem. The shop says my car won't be ready today after all. I think maybe Wednesday. Can you get the money by then?"

"I'm not going to pay for your transmission, Keisha."

"Then what the hell are we doing here?"

"We need to talk."

Keisha rose and tossed her empty cup in the trash, the sun glinting off the rhinestones in her manicure. "It's a shame, that's all, what you did to poor Celeste. I feel terrible. You seem like a good person, but I'm sure you understand I can't keep information like that from the cops."

Mia jumped up to follow Keisha who'd turned her back and was heading for the ocean.

"I'm going for a walk on the beach if you want to come," Keisha called back to Mia. "Too many people around on the boardwalk for good conversation." Keisha slipped her sandals off and placed them on the wall.

Mia jerked her tennis shoes off without untying them and set them, with her ankle socks crammed inside, next to Keisha's pretty sandals.

She hopped on alternating feet across the scalding sand to reach Keisha, and they raced the rest of the way to the shoreline where the tide provided a cool path for walking. As they paced the beach, waves rushed out and back teasing their ankles. Overhead, gulls glided, occasionally dive-bombing for food. Surfers caught, and failed to catch, a ride, their brightly colored boards rising and falling on white-capped turquoise swells. To onlookers they must seem a pair of friends enjoying a stroll—but onlookers couldn't feel the pounding of Mia's heart, or the apprehension charging the air between them.

"Blackmail at the beach," Mia finally broke the silence. "Such a beautiful backdrop for extortion."

"Let's get this straight, I'm not a blackmailer."

"Not yet," Mia said. "And let's hope it stays that way, but no matter what, I'm not buying your silence."

"I'm asking you to pay for my transmission, not my silence."

"But if I don't, you'll tell anyone who'll listen that I took Celeste's keys. I don't know what you call that, but I call it blackmail—or extortion, I'm not sure of the difference."

"I need the money."

They were yards away from the nearest person, and the crashing waves drowned out their voices so they could barely hear one another even though they stood less than a foot apart.

Mia met Keisha's eyes. "I'm sorry about your expenses. But I can't help you. I don't want you to tell anyone I took Celeste's keys. It would hurt me, and maybe hurt Celeste, too, if the police waste time on something that has nothing to do with her disappearance. I know it was a rotten thing to do. And I really, really regret it. Which is another thing I wanted to talk to you about. When I picked up those keys, I didn't think it through. I acted impulsively, without considering the consequences. Now, I'd do anything to have the chance to undo it. It's too late for me, but you—you still have the opportunity to stop and think. Don't do something you're sure to regret later."

Keisha scoffed. "Nice speech. But why would I regret making a small profit off of inside information? You deserve to pay for what you did to Celeste."

"Believe me, I am paying a price. And I'm trying to stop you from having to do the same. If you really thought I had anything to do with Celeste's disappearance, I bet you'd have gone to the police right away. If you do this, it's going to weigh on your conscience." She shrugged. "Besides, the police will wonder why you waited to tell them."

"I'll come up with some excuse."

Enough was enough. Mia was going to make her stand right here and now. "I won't let you blackmail me. It's your word against mine. No one will ever find those keys, and the footage is gone—because you erased it. *You* destroyed evidence. You're the one who committed a crime."

"I didn't know it was evidence, so it can't be a crime. And who's to say I didn't make a backup?"

CHAPTER 34

A hand clasped Mia's shoulder, making her jump.

Isaiah.

How much had he overheard?

"You scared me." Mia tried to make her voice seem casual, teasing, but while she might fool Isaiah, she couldn't fool herself. If Keisha did have a backup tape, there really was something to be scared of.

Isaiah stuck his hand out to Keisha whose arms stayed at her side while she inclined her head, surveying him. "You came out of nowhere."

"I'm Isaiah, nice to meet you."

"This is Keisha," Mia offered. "I thought I was going to call you when I was done."

"That's what we said, but since it turned into such a beautiful day I thought I'd tool around and enjoy the beach." He checked his watch. "I can get lost until you're done with your friend, though. When do you think that'll be?"

"Right this minute," Keisha said. "Mia and I are finished. Aren't we?"

"I guess." Mia's only hope now was that Keisha had been bluffing about a backup tape. Even if she came up with the cash, there was no guarantee Keisha wouldn't go to the police, and if they learned Mia had agreed to a payoff she'd look even more guilty. From here on out, she needed to be extra careful. Keisha might even be wearing a wire. "We'll talk more later?"

"Whatever." With her back turned, Keisha waved a hand in the air and jogged off down the beach.

"She didn't seem too happy to meet me. I'm sorry I didn't wait for your call. I didn't mean to interrupt something important."

"You didn't. She's just socially awkward."

"Birds of a feather, then." His grin softened the blow of his words. "Joking. In case you haven't noticed, I'm a Mia fan. I appreciate a woman who doesn't pretend to be perfect."

Her face flushed, and the sun felt pleasant and warm on her skin. "A little backhanded, but thanks."

"I'm glad you're out with a girlfriend. I was beginning to think…"

"That I didn't have any?"

"Maybe I'm the socially awkward one. I'm trying to win you over, but I don't feel like I'm making much headway. I don't see why we shouldn't be friends—at the very least. I guess showing up early was my way of taking advantage of that fresh start we talked about."

His deep voice made her shiver. She wasn't used to male attention, and apparently she was rather susceptible. Angelica had warned her to be careful around him, but he had a way of looking at her that made her feel important—and that didn't happen often with either gender. "Thanks for coming. I know your dad volunteered you to help me move my mother's chest—"

"He said that? I volunteered myself. I'm happy to move whatever you want. Mom is already more relaxed just knowing you're going to be around. She really likes you—I do, too."

Today, his eyes reminded her of the ocean, probably because they were at the beach—in this light, they seemed bluer than usual.

"You want another beer before we go? I won't be partaking, of course, but I don't mind sitting with you while you do."

That pleasurable feeling, low in her belly, took an ominous turn. Had he been watching, perhaps listening, without being seen? "Who said I had a beer already?"

"You said you were meeting a friend at the beach for a beer, so I just assumed."

"No thanks. I'm good. Were you able to get a truck?"

"Parked on Mission. Anytime you're ready. But you're gonna need shoes. Let's hope they're still where you left them. If you ask me, you're too trusting by a mile."

*

"Wouldn't it make more sense to wait until your new apartment is ready and then come back for this?" Aunt Misty looked at Isaiah and Mia like they were planning to heist the crown jewels instead of moving an old chest full of moth-eaten garments no one had the heart to throw away.

"It might make more sense, but I don't want to wait. I want something of hers with me," Mia said. It would be different if she had pictures and family mementos—like normal people did, but she didn't. "Speaking of which, I've been meaning to ask you something. The other day, I was thinking about mother's bracelet—it was silver."

"With three charms—a star, a heart and a cross." Aunt Misty looked away and then back, pushed her hair off her forehead.

"That's what I remembered. She used to wear it all the time when Granddad was alive. But after that, I don't think she wore it anymore. Do you know what happened to it?"

"It was sterling silver so it was worth a little money. I'm sure she sold it—maybe for food or more likely beer. That bracelet was my mother's—your grandmother's. She left it to Emily because she was the oldest and because she had a daughter. It was meant to be passed on to *you*, someday."

The tone of Aunt Misty's voice, the slight tremor in her shoulders, told Mia this was a sore subject—one she shouldn't bring up again unless she wanted to cause her pain. "Okay. Don't worry about it. I just wondered."

Isaiah sat on the bed and put his hands behind his head. Aunt Misty raised her eyebrows.

He lay back, taunting her, stretching out, putting his shoes on the bedspread.

Aunt Misty glared at him. "I'll leave you to it, then."

If he was trying to get rid of her aunt, it worked. "We'll call you if we need anything," Mia said.

Once the door closed, Isaiah scrambled to his feet and crossed the room. Rattled the knob. "This thing lock?"

"Nope."

He came closer, and Mia backed up. He straightened his arms, caging her between his body and the wall. "So what do you do when you have a guy over?"

Heat radiated off his body, warming her. She felt an ache in her solar plexus. "I don't."

"Never?"

"I don't mean I've *never*. I'm saying if I have a friend, I don't bring him *here*."

"I understand."

"Do you?" She stared at his parted lips. She didn't have a lot of experience, but she had enough to know if she didn't stop him, he was going to kiss her. It took her a moment but she lifted her hand and gently shoved him back. "I don't think this chest will be too heavy for us to lift."

He stepped away and combed his fingers through his hair. "What's in it? If you don't mind my saying so, you and your aunt are both acting weird about this chest."

"These are my mother's things—it's really all I have left of her. Maybe your mother mentioned to you…"

He moved behind her, and his breath whispered over her scalp. "Yeah, she told me about your mother. And I want you to know I'm here if you need me to listen, or, for anything else."

She turned to face him.

He bent until his forehead touched hers. "And Mia," he whispered. "At our house, there's a lock on your bedroom door."

CHAPTER 35

Tuesday

Last night, in the Coopers' guest suite, with her mother's hope chest resting at the foot of her bed, Mia had slept fitfully. But this morning, she'd woken up knowing what she had to do. And that sureness brought with it a sense of peace.

In a way, Keisha had freed her.

Paying off Keisha today would not ensure her silence tomorrow. Of that, Mia was certain. And that left her with no other choice than to tell the truth—that acting on her worst impulse, she'd stolen Celeste's keys.

Not having to keep that terrible secret—even the anticipation of not having to keep it—made Mia eager for the day to begin. But it wasn't going to be easy to tell Alma and Detective Samuels. Somehow, Mia would have to convince the detective that she'd just made a mistake rather than his worst-case scenario—she'd have to make him see she had nothing to do with Celeste's disappearance. But if the evidence pointed to a serial killer, that shouldn't be impossible.

As for the Coopers, Mia had come to a realization:

True friendship can't be built on deception.

Secrets and lies are a lethal poison, and if Mia kept on drinking from that well, their friendship wouldn't survive. Alma, Baxter, Isaiah and Angelica all had the right to choose, based on the truth, whether they wanted Mia in their lives.

If they cast her out, so be it. She would keep them close in her heart and do all she could to find Celeste. She had to admit the truth. Alma should hear it directly from Mia—before anyone else, and first thing this morning.

Her hand trembled as she buttoned her blouse, and then pulled her hair back into a ponytail. Her face looked pale in the mirror, so she added an extra swipe of blush and a touch of pink lipstick.

Someone knocked at her bedroom door.

This is your moment.

Time to step up.

Mia opened the door to a smiling Alma and hurried to wrestle a tray out of her arms. "What's this?"

"We skipped breakfast before, and I want to be sure we don't make the same mistake today."

"Thank you." Mia rested the tray on the desk and peeked beneath the plate cover—bacon, scrambled eggs, and a cinnamon roll. The smell made her mouth water. "But you're not my hostess. I work for you, remember?"

"Nonsense. You're my guest, assistant, friend, and more. We should dispense with the labels. I've eaten already, but you've been looking after me so well, I want to return the favor. And I've been going through some photos of Celeste." She paused and took a long breath. "I thought it would be nice to have company on my stroll down memory lane. Is that too sentimental? Do you mind if I hang out?"

"Of course not. You want us to look at photos together?"

Nodding, Alma pulled a wallet-sized album from the pocket of her skirt. "Last night I dreamed of the old days, when it was just Celeste and me. This was before I met Baxter, of course."

"You were a single mom? I had no idea." She'd never have guessed Baxter wasn't Celeste's biological father, and it made his grief, his obvious love for her, all the more touching.

"Oh boy, was I. I got pregnant with Celeste at seventeen. Her father was nineteen and when he found out he threw me against a wall. After that, I was terrified of him, but thank goodness he wanted no part of his child's life or mine. I lost my parents in a car accident when I was twelve, but luckily, like you, I had an aunt who took me in when they died. After Celeste was born, my aunt's place was just too small, so we moved out. Not long after, my aunt met a wonderful woman and they fell in love and moved to Alaska together. I love her dearly and we've always kept in touch, but Alaska's far, and at the time, it seemed like all Celeste and I had was each other."

How long should she wait? She had to tell Alma the truth about the keys, but now wasn't the right moment. Not when Alma had that faraway look in her eyes. Not when she was lost in her memories of Celeste.

"These pictures got me thinking about you and your mother. Don't laugh, but I feel like you and I have parallels in our lives that connect us. I suspect you and your mother had to rely on each other like Celeste and I did. Sometimes, when you're lonely, it's hard to be a good parent. I think I leaned on my little girl too much. Anyway, and forgive me if this is too personal, but I wondered if your mother relied on you too much as well. Maybe you felt like you had to take care of her. Maybe that's why you're such a nurturer."

Mia backed up to the bed and sat down.

Don't cry. Don't ruin the moment. This may be the last time you have a heart-to-heart with Alma.

"I don't mean to pry." Alma looked concerned.

"No. It's fine. Come sit with me and let's look at that album."

"Don't you want to eat first?"

"In a minute." Mia patted the space beside her.

Alma sat down and began turning the pages. The album was just the size to hold snapshots. The cover was worn with plastic peeling off the corners. A lot of the photos were smudged and grainy—reminding Mia of the Polaroid she'd found in her mother's hope chest. She had a nearly irresistible urge to dig it out and compare memories with Alma, but realized she shouldn't.

Not now.

The only thing she should be thinking about in this moment was how to tell Alma about Celeste's keys. She couldn't keep putting it off. She didn't deserve Alma's confidence. Not until she told her the truth.

"See here—this is Celeste at four. She loved it when I braided her hair. It was kind of our thing."

"My mother used to brush my hair a hundred strokes before bed. She said it kept it shiny and healthy."

Alma tipped her head to the side, nearly touching Mia's. "Here we are at the diner where I worked before I met Baxter. That's Celeste sitting on the stool gobbling a hot-fudge sundae, hamming it up for the camera."

"How old was Celeste when you and Baxter married?"

"Six—just turned. He never batted an eye at taking on a ready-made family. In fact, I was the one dragging my feet; before I brought someone into our lives, I had to be sure that he would be good for both of us. Baxter was patient, unwavering, and one day I woke up and I just knew he was the one. He married us both—that's the way he puts it. A year later, he adopted Celeste. I know he's not perfect. He has his flaws, but unlike Celeste's biological father, Baxter has been good to us." Alma closed the album, and then stared down at the wedding ring on her hand. "We're very lucky. Or at least we have been until now."

"Maybe luck was part of it, but give yourself credit for taking your time. For making good choices."

"Mm. I suppose you're right."

Now's not the time.

When will be?

"Alma, I need to tell you something."

Alma looked at her, that faraway gaze changing to one of intense focus. She picked up Mia's hand. "Whatever it is, it will be okay."

How could she possibly know how terrified Mia was? Alma must have some kind of sixth sense. Her heart squeezed in her chest. She was probably going to lose Alma, and she didn't know how she would bear it.

Unable to turn away, yet unable to look Alma in the eyes, Mia closed hers. The sound of Alma's breathing, synchronized with hers, filling the room.

Time passed.

Mia didn't know or care how much.

And then Alma squeezed her hand. "I'll make this easier for you. I already know."

Mia opened her eyes. "You do?"

"I don't think we should make a big deal out of it," Alma said.

"I'm so, so sorry. I know that doesn't make up for anything, but I am."

"I appreciate your apology, and I promise I'm not mad. Only, if you don't mind, in the future if you need something, just ask. I prefer you not go into Celeste's old room again."

Mia drew in a sharp breath, realizing they'd been talking circles around each other.

Alma got up and walked to the closet, rummaged around and pulled out Celeste's favorite red cardigan. "If I'd known you needed a sweater, I would've loaned you one of mine, or bought you one of your own."

Mia's mind was racing. How did that cardigan get in her closet? Roseanne, the housekeeper, had been here yesterday morning. Maybe she'd put it there by mistake. Mia opened her mouth to protest, and then thought better of it. What if she really had taken the sweater and didn't remember?

Alma climbed to her feet. "Let's not speak of it again. Don't let your breakfast get cold. I've got some things to do to get ready for Detective Samuels. I'm fed up with him keeping us in the dark, so I insisted he come by later and give the entire family an update on the investigation. We're long overdue for an accounting from him. You'll be here, in case he has any more questions for you?"

"Of course." Her mind continued to spin. "What can I do to help?"

"Nothing at the moment. Take the morning off." Alma raised an eyebrow. "Maybe go buy yourself a sweater."

"I'll keep my phone on. You'll let me know when to expect Detective Samuels."

Alma nodded. "And don't worry. I found the sweater in your closet yesterday, but I was waiting for you to tell me you borrowed it. I knew you wouldn't let me down."

After Alma left the room, Mia went to her mother's hope chest and sank to her knees. Drained from her conversation with Alma, and longing to feel a connection to her own mother, she opened the lid.

Alma's trip down memory lane had made Mia intensely aware of the gaping hole in her life.

Aunt Misty had pictures of her mother, of course, and of Mia as a newborn. But the two sisters had become estranged after Granddad died, and Mia had no photos of herself or her mother from that time in the woods. Nothing from that period in her childhood had been memorialized so it was hardly surprising she couldn't remember much. There was only the one Polaroid she'd found in the chest. It might have been from a special day. A day she might remember if she studied the photo.

She moved the clothes from one side of the chest to another, picked them up, shook them out, one piece at a time, and placed them on the floor, until the chest was empty.

"Where *are* you?" she muttered aloud in frustration.

Inch by inch, she ran her hand around the inside edges of the chest.

Then she rocked back on her heels and let it sink in.

The old photograph was gone.

Celeste's cardigan had appeared in her closet out of nowhere.

And she had no idea how either of those things happened… unless… she'd been walking in her sleep again.

She did have the morning free—maybe Dr. Baquero would fit her in.

CHAPTER 36

Mia settled back against the couch. "I'm ready, but I need to leave my phone on. I'll keep it set to vibrate."

"Under the circumstances, I think we can break the no phone rule, but you need to take a deep breath. You seem agitated," Dr. Baquero said.

Mia didn't have a minute. Alma could call at any time and summon her back to the house for the meeting with Samuels, and she didn't relish facing either of them until she got some answers. "Can hypnosis help me remember something from a dream?"

"Possibly. There's evidence that if you give yourself a pre-sleep hypnotic suggestion it can help you recall your dreams vividly the next day. Is that something you'd like to try?"

That wasn't exactly what she had in mind. "What about after? I mean if you don't remember something that happened while you were sleeping, can you get that information from hypnosis later on?"

"I wouldn't go so far as to say it's impossible, but if you weren't awake at the time of the event, without any pre-sleep suggestion it would be very difficult." Dr. Baquero leveled her gaze. "What are we talking about, Mia? Have you been walking in your sleep again?"

Mia took that deep breath. "A couple of weeks ago, I woke up dressed, and then I found my old sleeping pills spilled open in a drawer. Later, I threw the pills away, like I should have done three years ago. I thought that would solve the problem." She wanted to reveal more, to trust her therapist with the whole truth—that she had found a receipt from a doughnut shop that was near Celeste's house, and it was dated the same night she went missing. Mia's jaw tensed. In her heart she didn't believe she would ever hurt Celeste… but what if she was wrong? "I haven't taken any medication since then, but I think I might have walked in my sleep at least one more time."

"You woke up dressed again?"

She shook her head. "No. But I found a sweater in my room that I don't remember putting there, and also something is missing—a photograph."

"I see."

"So I'd like to try to remember with hypnosis."

"Have you thought about asking your aunt? That seems like the most straightforward way to get to the bottom of things. She would know, wouldn't she, if this has been a frequent thing—before you moved out at least?"

"I'm not sure I can trust her."

The look on Dr. Baquero's face confirmed what Mia felt in her heart.

"She's raised you since you were a little girl, Mia. I don't know everything that's happened between you, but I have a hard time believing she'd lie to you about anything of consequence. I could be wrong, of course."

But she wasn't. Mia should have doubted herself before she doubted her aunt.

"I will ask her. I promise. But can we at least try? I really want to remember, not just about sleepwalking, but about my mother. Detective Samuels won't reopen her case unless I have something new for him." She looked around the room at the purple walls. How many times had she sat on this couch, pouring out her heart to Dr. Baquero? "I'm going to *insist* he look into what happened to my mother—just like Alma is insisting on an update for her family."

"I have to say, I think I approve of this new, more assertive, you. This is your session, your time, so if you want to plunge right into a trance it's your prerogative to try—but I'm not sure how well that will work. My advice is that you let yourself go wherever your mind leads, whether it's sleepwalking or back to your childhood. Don't try to force yourself in one direction or you may not get anywhere at all. Trust your mind to give you the information you really need." Dr. Baquero reached for the remote and lowered the shade until only a strip of light entered the room.

Mia's hands were already tingling. She looked at the coffee cup.

"When you're ready, your eyes may want to close." Dr. Baquero's voice was far away.

And just like that, Mia's arm floated, her eyelids slipped lower.

"See how good you are at this. I'm here if you need me. When you want to come out of your trance all you have to do is count…"

Mia's chest rose and fell. The rhythm soothed her. Her arms and legs went limp. It was dark now—so very dark.

She shuddered.

You're safe, now, Mia.

I'm with you.

Find the memories you need.

That's Mommy's voice!

She has me by the hand.

She's dragging me.

Mommy, no! Please, I don't want to go to the shed!

Mommy tugs harder. I try to pull my hand free, but I can't and my feet slide slowly across the room. We're almost to the front door, and I hear the sound of a car's wheels grinding up the road growing louder and louder… and then softer, more distant.

Mommy sinks to her knees.

I fling myself against her, and she grips my shoulders and holds me at arm's length. Her eyes are big, and she tells me, breathlessly, it was only a false alarm.

Thank goodness it wasn't him, she says. He almost caught you in here, but he didn't. We still have time. We can cuddle some more before I have to take you to the shed.

Outside, it's raining hard.

I'm shivering.

I want to climb under the covers with Mommy and read Goodnight Moon *and* The Little Prince *and* Cinderella.

I ask her why I have to sleep in the shed, why I can't stay with her.

Because Arnie's coming, she says.

Arnie! You love him more than me.

No, Mia! Don't say that. Her fingers dig into my shoulders, and she tells me she loves us both the same.

But I don't believe her, and I say so.

Mommy gathers me up and carries me back to bed. She climbs in and pulls me close to her.

I smell flowers and rain.

I love you, Mommy—I whisper it in her ear.

Close your eyes, baby, and go to sleep. Sweet dreams, she says, as she kisses my cheek.

I close my eyes.

She hums, and I feel warm and safe, but then I jolt awake. Was that a car? Is it time to go to the shed?

I start to cry.

Shh. Don't cry.

Now she's holding me, rocking me against her body. I know you don't understand, she says. But this isn't just for me. It's for both of us. It's because I love you so much. I have to prepare Arnie before I tell him about you. If he finds out about you and he runs away, I don't know what we'll do.

Her face is wet, and it makes me want to comfort her. I reach up and pat her arm. Please don't be sad, Mommy. I promise I'll be a good girl. We don't need Arnie. I can take care of us.

She laughs, but it's not a happy laugh. She asks if I remember the woman who came to the apartment after Granddad died.

The pretty one? I ask.

Pretty enough, yes. Well, she's from the state. And if she finds out we don't have a place to live…

We have the cabin, I say.

We don't have a place that's legal, honey. And I'm trying real hard not to drink too much. I'm trying to get another job. You know I want to take care of you all by myself, but Arnie can help us, and I love him.

Tell me about Arnie, I say. I don't want to hear the story again, but I know she likes to pretend everything will turn out happily ever after like in the storybooks.

I lean my head against her chest, and I feel her heart beating against my ear.

Arnie is tall and strong and he has black wavy hair, and a scar on his cheek he got fighting bad guys when he was in the Navy, she begins.

What's a scar, I ask?

A mark on his cheek where he got cut. It might look scary to a little girl, but you don't need to be afraid. Arnie is going to love you just as much as I do. And you're going to love him. I promise.

I try to picture him in my mind, but I can't. Is he coming tonight? Yes.

Then why can't I stay? Why can't I meet him right now?

Because, I have to get him in a good mood first. I'll pour his whiskey and make him real happy and then I'll tell him all about you, Mia. This time, I really mean it.

She won't tell him—I know she won't.

Look at me, she says. Tonight's the night! I'll tell him all about my brave little soldier. And then he'll take us to live in a real house, and we'll have dinner every night! Just think of it, Mia!

My tummy rumbles. Is Arnie rich?

She strokes my hair. Not rich, but he works hard, and he has big dreams.

Then Mommy says we have to dream big, too. Dreams are the future, and she knows how to make them happen for real.

You'll tell him tonight?

I promise, she says and crosses her heart.

She's crying hard. I won't let you down, my precious Mia. Not this time. We're going to live with Arnie, and I'm never going to have to worry again that the lady from the state will try to take you away from me.

Don't let her take me away! I'm sobbing, too.

In the distance, I hear the faintest sound of tires grinding.

Twenty. Nineteen. Eighteen.

It's time to go to the shed.

Seventeen. Sixteen.

My pocket vibrates.

Mia opened her eyes, took out her phone and looked down at the text from an unknown number: *I KNOW WHAT YOU DID.*

CHAPTER 37

By the time Mia arrived back at the Coopers', Detective Samuels had assembled the entire family, minus Angelica, in the study.

Mia crossed the study's threshold, feeling as empty as a bottomless well, unable to plumb the depths of her own darkness.

I KNOW WHAT YOU DID.

That had to be Keisha harassing her about the keys, didn't it? It couldn't mean anything else.

But what if it wasn't Keisha? What if someone had *seen* her that night on Celeste's street?

Doing what?

Mia didn't own a gun, and she doubted she could overpower Celeste in hand-to-hand combat—the very idea was ludicrous. But suppose she *had* somehow managed to knock her friend out. Then what? Would she have carried the body back to her car—which showed no trace of dirt or blood—driven to some unknown location, dug a grave with her bare hands, and then awakened back in her bedroom with only a pair of damp tennis shoes and a single twig in her hair to show for it?

She gritted her teeth.

Whoever sent that text might have succeeded in making her hands shake and her knees weaken, but if the plan was to scare her off, to paralyze her with fear, or to get her to believe she'd done something she hadn't, it wasn't going to work.

Stiffening her back, she nodded to Detective Samuels. "Sorry I'm late."

He motioned for Mia to take a seat next to Alma on the sofa, while two men, whom Mia recognized as detectives, rolled an oversized whiteboard into the room.

What looked to be a recorder stood upended on Baxter's desk.

Not brave enough to make eye contact with anyone, she stared straight ahead, waiting for Samuels to begin. The crackle of paper being smoothed and the cawing of crows outside the window provided a foreboding soundtrack as the two detectives attached a giant map to the whiteboard. Then they took up a position on either side of the door, their jackets open just enough to provide a peek at their service weapons.

Were they anticipating that someone—like her—might try to make a run for it?

With one hand, Samuels pushed his jacket back, and, his pistol in full view, moved to the whiteboard. "All right, we ready?"

No reply from the cheap seats.

"I'll take that as a yes. First off, I want to address, for the record, the purpose of this assembly. When Alma called me this morning, she made it known the family feels we, the police, either haven't been doing our utmost to find Celeste, or that we've been derelict in our duty to keep the family informed. I'm here, this afternoon, to assure you we are leaving no stone unturned, and to provide an update—to the extent I can do so without jeopardizing an ongoing investigation. I've brought all of you together for the sake of efficiency, and to see if sharing information as a group might lead to some new insights. I'll make a brief presentation, and then anyone with questions or information should speak up."

Mia nodded along with the others.

"These—" with two fingers, Samuels thumped about a dozen spots on the map that had been encircled with black sharpie "—represent areas where we've conducted searches—in some cases multiple times. As you can see, we've covered large portions, both urban and rural, of San Diego County."

"How did you determine which areas to search?" Baxter interrupted.

"Not randomly, if that's what you're implying."

"I'm not implying a damn thing," Baxter ground out. "I'm asking a reasonable question."

"Baxter, please." Alma sent him an admonishing look.

His face reddened. "Well?"

"The answer is that the determination is multifactorial." Samuels held his hand up to indicate he'd like to finish before taking more questions. "This isn't just us out there, folks. Our tip line is active, and we've been working Celeste's case in conjunction with a number of other agencies: the FBI, the San Diego County Sheriff's department, and the BI—California's statewide bureau of criminal investigation."

"But the case is under your primary direction," Baxter said. "It's your job to find my daughter."

"Understood. I'm not trying to avoid accountability here. I simply want to reassure you we're utilizing all our tools, calling on all our resources."

"And getting nowhere." Baxter folded his arms and sat back.

"Not as far as we'd like. We're working our usual avenues—for instance, we're checking on all the known sex offenders in the area—and we're not done with that monumental undertaking yet. I'm also sorry to say we're handicapped by a few things: the lack of a witness to a crime; the fact her car hadn't been moved from the lot near the Piano Man, and there were no unexpected prints or other evidence in it; and finally the fact we haven't located her cell phone—which nowadays is one of our most important sources of evidence. It last pinged off a tower near the alley where we found her empty purse. We believe the battery was removed shortly before midnight on Friday. We've canvassed her social media and subpoenaed her text messages, and those roads did generate leads."

"What leads? Be specific," Baxter said.

"I'm not at liberty to give names or full details, but suffice it to say Celeste was in communication with several young men via dating apps and social media. We interviewed them, and two were in or around the Gaslamp Quarter when Celeste went missing. One failed to provide a corroborated alibi. We got warrants for his phone records—and frankly, we don't like him for it. On the night she disappeared, he claims he binged alcohol and then went home and slept it off. Records seem to support that. However, we did use the location of his phone in the days *after* Celeste's disappearance to help us pinpoint new search areas—which, unfortunately, have not yielded anything of significance."

"So that's it?" Isaiah was on his feet. "You got one asshole's phone records and did some ground searches and that's a wrap?"

"It's not a wrap. We're not letting up. The searches are ongoing, and, thus far, we've logged about seven hundred hours of interviews with anyone who might be of interest in your sister's case. As you well know, we've had *you* in for questioning on four occasions."

Isaiah crumpled into his chair, and Alma threw back her shoulders. "And he's cooperated fully. You're wasting your time on my son."

"He has motive—Celeste urged your husband to cut him out of the will."

"Which I never did!" Baxter slapped his hand against his thigh.

"But you threatened to if you caught him drinking again."

"Excuse me—" Mia's throat was tight, her heart pounding "—did you get a warrant for Paul Hudson's phone records? Did you search any areas where his phone placed *him* in the days after Celeste went missing? Like you did for that other man—the one who claimed to be sleeping it off."

Alma shot her a grateful look. Isaiah kept his eyes to the floor. "No," Samuels said.

"Why not? Because Hudson is influential in the community?"

"Because Hudson has a corroborated alibi."

"From his *wife*. What about the rumors going around?" Mia wasn't giving up on the idea it could be Paul. He'd followed her; his wife had lied about her. Jane was sure he'd been bothering Celeste.

"We don't like Paul Hudson for this. His wife confirmed they were together all night. Your own story—that you were supposed to have dinner with Ruth, and that Ruth cancelled at the last minute, is consistent with the Hudsons' claims they reconciled that evening. We found no texts or calls between him and Celeste in her phone records. We're keeping an open mind, but at this point, we've moved on."

"To where?" Mia asked, unconvinced.

Samuels dusted his hands together and moved to perch atop the desk. "Look, I have some news that may be relevant. It hasn't hit the airwaves yet, but I'm sure it's only a matter of hours if not minutes until it does."

A hushed silence filled the room.

"We have a report of another missing woman. It's very early, but her co-workers are already canvassing, so I want you to hear it from me first. A hostess from the Piano Man didn't show up for work this morning."

Outside, the crows' caws amped up—as if they were about to crash through the window.

"We sent an officer around to her home, but there was no answer. Her car wasn't in the drive. We've tried her cell phone, and she's not answering. Like I said, she's only been gone a short time, but she's around the same age as Celeste, and obviously we're looking at a close geographic proximity. Yesterday, Keisha told her mother she was going to meet a friend at Mission Beach and would stop by later. But she never showed."

"Wait—Mission Beach?" Isaiah asked. "Keisha? Mia, does your Keisha work at the Piano Man?"

"Keisha Sims?" Samuels climbed to his feet.

Mia's heart was in her throat. "She's missing? But I just talked to her yesterday. Isaiah was with me."

"Not really," Isaiah objected. "We barely spoke. I got there just as Keisha was leaving."

"Where was she headed?" Samuels had the recorder in his hand.

"I don't know. Ask Mia."

She shook her head. She could barely breathe, much less speak.

"Okay, then. Where did you two go after the beach?" Samuels turned back to Isaiah.

"We moved a chest from Mia's aunt's place up to her room, here."

"And after that?"

"Mia and I answered correspondence until around ten o'clock, and then we both went to bed." Alma was on her feet. *Everyone* was on their feet.

"Good to know you can corroborate Mia's whereabouts. What about you, Isaiah? Were you home all evening?"

"No. I went back out—to church. I lit a candle for Celeste and stayed to pray for around an hour before heading home."

"You spend a lot of time in church, do you?" Samuels asked.

"As a rule? As little as possible. But that's where I went yesterday."

"I don't suppose anyone saw you there?"

Baxter rose, then strode to his son's side and rested a hand on his shoulder. "What are you driving at? If this young woman is missing, and it sounds like she is, I'd think you'd be blasting it all over the media. I'd think you'd be out there looking for her right this minute instead of haranguing my son."

"We've only been trying to reach her a few hours. I'd say calling her a missing person at this point is premature. Maybe she's off with her boyfriend somewhere."

Mia's entire body began to shake. "Or *maybe* there's someone out there snatching young women off the streets."

A vein bulged in Baxter's neck. "While the police do *nothing* about it."

"I've explained the steps we're taking to find your daughter. As for Keisha, we're still trying to determine whether she's missing, or just taking a ditch day from work. And I should point out, as of now, your son and Mia are the last people known to have been in contact with her." Samuels suddenly shifted then pulled his phone from his pocket and tapped the screen. He motioned to the detectives, grabbed the recorder and said, "We'll be back to collect the whiteboard later."

"Where are you going?" Alma asked.

"Mission Beach," Samuels called back over his shoulder. "They found Keisha's car in a parking lot."

They all stood silent, still staring after Samuels, when Angelica appeared at the arched entryway, something concealed in her hand. "Are the detectives still here?"

"He left. What have you got?" Isaiah asked.

Angelica opened her palm, letting a white pom-pom keychain dangle from her fingers, and Mia's heart somersaulted in her chest. Disbelief washed over her, and she struggled to contain a gasp.

Alma was looking at it too, her face ashen. "Is that... Celeste's?"

It couldn't be.

"Where did you get that?" Alma shoved past Mia and grabbed the keyring, turning it over in her hand.

"I found it—in *her* room." Angelica glared at Mia.

"What the hell are you doing with my daughter's keys?"

All eyes turned on her.

Her head went light, and her fingers numb. She forced out a breath. There was no way. It simply wasn't possible... "Alma, no. It's not what you think."

Of course, Mia *had* had Celeste's keys in her possession, but those were buried way up in the Torrey Pines State Reserve. This set had to be another look-a-like. Unless... had someone seen her?

Tears began to stream down Alma's cheeks. "Why are you torturing me? This is her keyring. It looks exactly the same."

"It isn't," Mia said softly. But she, too, would like to know why someone was doing this—and who. Keisha was the obvious choice since she was the one who'd seen her take the keys, but how had she gotten them and gained entry into the house? Angelica was the one claiming to have found them in Mia's room. Besides, it was beginning to seem like Angelica wanted Mia to steer clear of her family.

"There's an easy way to find out if these are really hers. Celeste has a house key." Baxter approached Alma and took the keychain from her, then went to the door. "This looks like it might be the right one."

The front doorknob made a scraping sound as it turned.

Alma's knees buckled, and Mia rushed toward her, but Angelica got there first and pulled her mother into her arms. "Get out of this house!"

Isaiah held up his hand. "Hang on. We should give Mia a chance to explain."

Mia would gladly have run, but Baxter physically blocked the door. "Damn right she'll explain. She's not going anywhere until she tells us what's going on—*then* she can get the hell out."

Mia backed against the wall, and slid slowly down, until her bottom hit the cold marble floor. "Celeste's keyring fell out of her purse on Friday night at the Piano Man. I picked it up. I should've returned it, but I didn't because I was mad about not being invited along with the others. Then, after Celeste went missing, I was too afraid to admit what I'd done. But I don't know how Angelica got them. I…" she trailed off. How would it look if she said she'd *buried* them? "I didn't bring them into this house. I swear."

"Like you didn't hang Celeste's cardigan in your closet," Alma's tears still flowed as she choked out the words. "You understand what's happened here? My baby walked home because she didn't have her keys, and now a serial killer has taken *my* child because *you* don't fit in."

Mia's chin came up. What she'd done was wrong. She knew that, but deep down she also knew that what happened to Celeste wasn't her fault. Celeste made her own decision to walk home. Jane offered her a ride. She could've taken a cab. And neither Mia nor Celeste had any way to know a serial killer would be lurking in an alley, waiting to strike.

If a serial killer had been lurking in an alley waiting to strike. Samuels was obviously still looking at people close to Celeste. In any case, Mia needed to start telling the whole truth.

"I think we should all go back in the study and sit down. There's more I need to explain." If Keisha had really made a backup tape from that night at the restaurant, the killer could be seen on it. It wasn't enough for Mia to confess about the keys, she had to tell them about the blackmail too.

CHAPTER 38

A knock sounded at the door.

As Mia watched from the window of her room, Baxter's Range Rover and Angelica's Mercedes rolled out of the driveway. After Mia had finished with her story, Baxter had headed out to tend to an urgent business matter, and Angelica had declared she would take Alma over to her place until Mia could gather her things and vacate the house—they'd given her two hours, and left her alone with Isaiah, presumably to stand guard and prevent any further perfidy on her part.

The knock sounded again, this time louder and more insistent.

Mia let the drapes fall back into place and crossed the room.

Isaiah entered without invitation and flopped down onto her carefully made bed. "Took you long enough."

"I needed a minute."

"Yeah, that was rough in there." He raked a hand through his hair. "In my opinion, though, screwing up once in a while makes you human. And at least, in the end, you told the truth."

"Thanks. I think." Isaiah's demeanor often changed from one minute to the next, and she never knew if he was being sincere or not. But right now she wasn't in the mood for company. She had to pack, and over the course of the last few days, something had changed inside her. Yes, she was scared, but more than that, she was sick to death of being toyed with.

And she was worried about Keisha. "I know it's only been a short time, but Keisha not returning calls, the police finding her car—that doesn't seem good to me."

"They found it in a parking lot—where people park cars. She's probably just ditching work for the beach. Come sit with me."

She moved to the bed and sat down, leaving a safe space between them.

He turned his body toward her, half sitting, half reclining. "What Keisha did to you, to all of us, using that footage for her own personal gain, is wrong. I, for one, am not wasting any sympathy on her."

"What happened to screwing up making you human and all that jazz?" Keisha might well have suffered the same fate as Celeste, making that statement about as cold as anything she'd heard from Isaiah since the day she'd first met him. And the fact that he was sober this time around only made it more unnerving.

"Blackmailing someone and screwing up are two entirely different things."

"I understand that, but I have a feeling Keisha just fell into it. She needed money—"

"You're so naïve. Surely you don't believe the BS about her transmission."

"Clearly you don't." She sighed. "So, then, is it naïve of me to believe your story about going to church to pray for Celeste? Where did you really go after you helped me move the chest?"

He clapped a hand over his heart. "You're killing me. I *really* went to church to pray for Celeste. I do love her, you know."

"I'm sorry. If you say you went to light a candle for Celeste, then I believe you." Though she wasn't quite sure she did. She inched farther away. "Do you think your mother will ever forgive me?"

Isaiah grabbed her wrists. "I think she just needs a little time to come around. In fact…" he tightened his grip "… I don't want you to go."

Be careful around my brother—I'd feel awful if anything happened to you.

"Your mother doesn't want me in her home—and frankly, I don't want to be here any longer." Mia's wrists hurt from the tight hold he had on them. "Please let go of me."

He dropped his hold, and she eyed the door, wishing he'd left it open in case she needed to run.

He leaned in and, reflexively, she drew back.

Red climbed from his neck to his cheeks. "Are you afraid of me, Mia?"

She kept eye contact and made her voice firm. "To be totally honest, you're making me uncomfortable, and I'd like you to leave."

His nostrils flared, and the bed trembled under his bouncing knee.

He lifted one hand, and she held her breath.

He bolted to his feet. "Your wish is my command. Now I'm the one who needs a minute. I'm sure you won't mind having the house all to yourself. I'm leaving until the rest of the clan gets back. I don't want to put myself in a position to be falsely accused of anything."

Part of her wanted to call after him. She *wanted* to believe him.

But his stories, his actions, they just didn't add up.

He'd dragged her into the back room of a strip club, claiming he'd mistaken her for Celeste. The first night she'd dined with the Coopers, he'd said, at the table, that their priest would be shocked if he darkened the door of a church—and now he claimed he'd been lighting a candle when Keisha went missing.

He'd been the one to find that menacing note on her car. So how could she be certain he hadn't pulled it out of his pocket? It was true, Samuels' handwriting expert had ruled Isaiah out as the author, but what were that expert's qualifications? He'd taken a class. He'd been awarded a certificate. The same expert who wouldn't rule out Mia herself was the one who claimed Isaiah was in the clear. Had she been a fool for believing the so-called expert?

And what about that day at Torrey Pines? Isaiah had shown up out of nowhere. True, it was Celeste's favorite hike… but she'd been so worried he'd seen her burning those articles or burying the keys…

Of course, he'd been right there!

Isaiah was the only one who could have seen her bury those keys. The only one who could've dug them up and then planted them in her room for Angelica to find.

The whole time he pretended to be on her side, he'd been lying, manipulating her, playing her for a fool—just like he was doing now.

"Please go," she repeated firmly.

He glared at her, then stalked from the room, and she raced to lock the door behind him.

Minutes later the screech of tires in the drive told her he'd made good on his promise.

She was alone in the house.

So why did she still feel unsafe?

Propping herself up against the headboard on the luxuriously soft bed, glancing about the perfectly appointed room, she rubbed her arms, willing herself to stop shivering.

Then she picked up her phone. "Aunt Misty?"

"Mia! I'm so relieved you called."

She put the phone on speaker and laid it on the bedspread beside her. Just the sound of her aunt's voice was a tonic. Mia's tight muscles relaxed like someone had wrapped her in a warm blanket. "I'm sorry I didn't get in touch sooner. How are you?"

"Mia, I'm worried sick. I just heard on the news that another young woman is missing. And she worked at that restaurant—the same one where Celeste had dinner the night she disappeared."

So the story was already out. "I heard. I'm hoping for the best, but it seems too much of a coincidence."

Eventually, she'd tell her aunt everything about Keisha, but now wasn't the moment.

"Are you being careful? I hate to think of you being away at a time like this."

"Totally. And don't worry. I'm packing up as we speak. I was wondering if I could come home for a couple of weeks, just until my apartment is ready."

"You don't need to ask me that. You know how much I love you and miss you. But what changed? Has something happened? Is it your sleepwalking?"

She sucked in a breath. "No, but why do you ask? Have you seen me sleepwalking lately?"

"Only the one time—a couple of weeks ago. The night Celeste disappeared. Don't you remember?"

"Not really. I woke up dressed but that's all I know."

"I'm sorry, sweetie. I thought you were awake at the end, but I guess not. You came out of your room and started walking in circles. I hugged you and steered you back to your room. I asked if you were okay. You nodded and kissed me goodnight, so I thought you'd remember."

"What time was that?"

"My talk show was just ending, so around eleven p.m., I think."

"You didn't see me leave the house later?"

"No. I was worried though, and I stayed in the living room and binged watched that British cooking show until two a.m. to make sure you didn't get up again. You were still sleeping soundly when I finally went to bed."

So Mia couldn't have left her house until after 2 a.m.—but according to Samuels the battery had been removed from Celeste's phone shortly before midnight.

Her hand flew to her heart, and a tear of relief slid down her cheek.

She didn't do it.

She'd taken a pill that had triggered disordered sleep and she'd made a late-night doughnut run—that was all. Nothing to be proud of, but she hadn't hurt anyone. She wished she'd confided in her aunt before. She wished she'd talked over a lot of other things with her, too.

"Are you still there?"

"Yes. And there is something I want to tell you—about my mother." When it came to the subject of Mia's mother, her aunt didn't always take things as well as Mia would like. "I've been undergoing hypnosis with Dr. Baquero, and I've recovered a memory from my childhood."

Audible on the other end of the line, a chair scratched across the floor.

Good.

Better her aunt was sitting for this.

"Did my mother ever mention a man named Arnie to you? Someone with a scar on his face? A Navy man with dark, wavy hair?"

"No. But we never talked about her boyfriends. It was a sore subject because I didn't think she should bring men around with you there."

Mia's mother used to hide her in a shed whenever men came around. And as wrong as that seemed, as terrible as it truly was, in the end, that had probably been Mia's salvation. Knowingly or unknowingly, her mother had most likely protected her from an evil predator.

"I don't think Mother ran away. I *know* she wouldn't have left me," Mia said, then waited for her aunt to try to argue her out of it.

"Honestly, I don't think so either. She was terrified of losing you, scared to death social services would take you away from her." Aunt Misty's took a ragged breath. "And the truth is, I'm the one who called them on her. I'm the reason she took you and ran and hid out in the woods."

"What happened to my mother, what happened to me, isn't your fault. If I were in your shoes, I would have called protective services, too. It was the right thing to do." Mia's face was wet, and she reached for her purse from the bedside table. She stuck her hand deep inside, rummaging for tissue, and found none.

"Are-are you still there?" Her aunt was sobbing now—great gusting sobs.

"Hang on a second." Mia, too, was crying in earnest now, along with her aunt. Mia turned her bag upside down and dumped everything out.

Really? In this entire bag of junk, not one tissue?

She jerked her arm, and the empty purse flew up and banged her in the eye.

Her bag was soft, but something in it was really hard. She squeezed the fabric between her fingers and found the offending object, a tiny rectangle, buried deep in one of the many zipper compartments.

A flash drive maybe?

"Mia?"

With some difficulty she managed to get the zipper unstuck and slide open the pocket, grasp the object between her fingers and yank it out.

"Oh God," she said, her throat so tight she could barely speak. After Samuels found that tracker on her car, she'd done a search of spy shops to check out the latest surveillance gadgets. This innocent-looking thing she held between her fingers wasn't a flash drive—it was a recording device.

CHAPTER 39

Mia had been bugged.

For how long and by whom was the question—and her suspected answer made her want to rip everything in sight to shreds.

Keep calm.

She dropped the recorder, put her head between her knees and forced herself to breathe.

"Mia, what's going on?"

Aunt Misty was still on the phone.

"I have to go. I'll call you later," she managed.

She grabbed a pillow and threw it against the wall, then locked her hands around a paperweight, sighted her target—a vase of fragrant red roses on the writing desk—and paused with her arm in mid-air.

Tearing up the Coopers' guest room would only make her look crazy to Samuels.

But searching it, carefully, might provide the evidence she needed to prove it was Isaiah who'd put the note on her car, Isaiah who'd been tracking her and listening in on her private conversations.

He was the only one who could've seen her bury those keys.

And if he'd put a tracker on her car and a bug in her purse, he wouldn't have stopped there. In her online search of spy shops, she'd learned about all kinds of dirty tricks people play on one another, and unless she was dead wrong about Isaiah… unless she was completely off base… then somewhere in this room she'd find a secret camera. One that would almost certainly be overlooked by an unsuspecting guest, but might be easily spotted by someone with her guard up, someone who had spent several hours educating herself online about covert surveillance, someone like her.

And it wouldn't require turning over tables or ripping out drawers. There were favorite places to hide miniature cameras.

So start looking.

There was no clock in the room, but there were several framed photos of San Diego on the walls.

That seemed the most likely place to her.

Mia closed the drapes in hopes of making it easier to spot a glowing lens. Then, taking her time, she carefully inspected each picture frame.

No luck.

Maybe embedded in a doorknob.

Mia got down on her knees, first peering into the knobs on either side of the bathroom door, and then the door that opened from the hall into the bedroom.

Where else?

The overhead light was a possibility, but surely she'd have noticed it flashing in the darkness during her stay. Still, it might be worth climbing up on the dresser to check it out.

Considering, she looked up, and then, closed her fists tight.

Two smoke detectors?

One of them had to be a dummy—and that flashing light a camera—not a battery indicator.

She clenched her jaw.

Isaiah had been *watching* her.

In her bedroom at night.

That sick bastard.

But would this be enough for Samuels? He'd seen the tracker on her car with his own eyes, taken custody of the menacing note, and still, he hadn't believed her. He'd taken the easy way out, accusing her aunt.

Accusing *Mia*.

Should she get out of here, now, or take the time to search Isaiah's room? Even if Samuels took her at her word, unlike Mia, he'd need a warrant to search Isaiah's belongings—and that would give Isaiah an opportunity to get rid of evidence. But if she found something in his room, something that closed the loop between him and the camera hidden in that dummy smoke alarm, it would be the nail that hammered her case shut.

Her heart banged against her rib cage—she knew what she had to do.

With her hand over her mouth, she crept out her door and down the hall until she reached the back stairway—the one leading to the third floor and Isaiah's quarters.

Maybe his door would be locked.

Maybe the Coopers, or Isaiah himself, would come back early and catch her sneaking into his room.

She put a hand on each rail, and then steadily, stealthily climbed the steps.

At the top, just past the landing, a door stood slightly ajar, light pouring from the room beyond it.

Holding her breath, she pushed open the door.

Waited.

No one came thundering around a corner or flying out of the room so she stepped inside. Isaiah's bed was unmade, but otherwise the room was tidy. A shelf against the far wall held books arranged in an orderly fashion by size and type—hardbacks on the top shelves, paperbacks filling the lower half. An open laptop, facing away from her sat on a desk similar to the one in her room.

A guitar hung by its strap from a hook on a closet door.

The closet held promise, but the laptop was pure gold. She'd grab it, and then get the hell out before the others came home.

Let the Coopers accuse her of theft.

She didn't give a single damn.

A few steps forward... and then a door slammed shut behind her.

She whirled to find Isaiah glowering at her.

"What are you doing in my room, Mia?"

Her knees threatened to give way, but she could still salvage this if she kept her cool.

He didn't know she'd found the camera.

Unless he'd been laying a trap, unless he'd been watching her search!

"I was looking for you." Mustering all her courage, she squared her gaze with his.

"I told you I was leaving the house."

"You weren't gone long. I heard your car, so I thought I'd come up to finish our conversation. I didn't like the way we left it between us." How had she missed the sound of his car returning up the drive?

"You should knock before barging into someone's room."

"I did knock. Where the heck did you come from anyway—a secret passageway or something?" She laughed, amazed at how easily the lies came, the way her knees had stiffened up and her survival instincts had kicked in.

His smile tightened. "It's odd you heard my car return, since I never left the house. I just pulled into the garage so you'd think I'd gone. I wanted you to feel comfortable. Then I came up here to my lair." He paused. "I've been hanging out in the study since then."

"I guess I was wrong, and yet here you are. You have a study up here?"

"In case you haven't noticed, my parents are rich. It's like a second house."

He lounged against the door. The only way out would be to knock him down, which didn't seem feasible—or else she could lure him away from the door, and then make a run for it.

"I didn't know you played guitar," she said.

He jerked his head back, bumping it against the door. "What do you want, Mia? I know you didn't come up here to ask me to play you a tune. Be honest for once."

"Okay." She moved to the bed and balanced on the edge. "I have questions I'd like you to answer."

He moved in closer, still blocking her escape, but at least there was space for her to get around him, now.

"Ask away," he said.

"At the strip club, when the bouncer found us in the back room, before he kicked us out, he told you never to come back. He said it wasn't your first offense."

"It wasn't."

She bit her knuckle.

"I'm making you uncomfortable again. But you came to my room, so you can hardly blame me for that."

"You want honesty? Then yes. I'm nervous. But I'm here to listen. To give you the benefit—"

"That's big of you. How about I give *you* the benefit of the doubt that you came up to talk, not to snoop?"

"There may have been a little snooping intent, too. But what was the bouncer talking about?"

"Another time, he'd caught me in the back room arguing with a woman. With Celeste—though apparently he doesn't realize it was her."

"When was this?"

"About a week before she went missing. She found matches from the club in my pants pocket and, naturally, she assumed the worst." He took another step closer.

From where she stood, she could reach the laptop, but she didn't dare turn it toward her. "She thought you were drinking again."

"I wasn't. Not then. But she didn't believe me. No one ever believes me because most of the time I'm lying—when it comes to my drinking. Celeste followed me to the club, and we got into a bad argument."

Mia edged toward the desk. "So you went to enjoy the show, but you weren't drinking. Have I got that right?"

He leaned in. "Even if I tell you the truth, you won't believe me."

But he wasn't telling the truth. If she hadn't found that dummy smoke alarm with a hidden camera blinking down at her, she might buy his story—but she *had* found it, and the bug in her purse, too. And the keys—she mustn't forget the real keys turning up in her room. "Try me."

"I wasn't drinking, and I wasn't there for the show either. I was looking for Dad. I found several receipts from Lacy's in his coat pocket—while I was digging for cash. I didn't want to believe Dad was at a strip club, maybe even cheating on Mom. I thought there might be some relatively innocent explanation. Maybe he was going with work colleagues or something. I had to find out for myself if he'd go there again. So I went to the club a few times."

"Lying in wait for your father?" Hopefully the incredulity she felt didn't come through in her voice.

"Celeste didn't believe me either. She said she was going to tell Dad I'd been out carousing and that then I tried to put the blame on him, and that this time he'd cut me out of his will for real."

Mia had actually believed that story Isaiah told her up at Torrey Pines, about how Celeste had been the one to get him into rehab. He'd acted like he was *grateful* she'd tried to come between him and his inheritance. Mia had been so easily taken in by him. Isaiah knew how to get under her skin—playing up his vulnerable side, taking an interest in her, pretending to *like* her, all the while knowing she had no real friends. She shouldn't have fallen for his act, not when he'd showed her his real self that day at Pocket Park, and again at the strip club. But she'd been drawn to him, and she hadn't wanted to believe he was capable of evil. And now, here he was, laying out a motive for murder as old as time—*money*.

If only she'd brought the recording device up with her. "If that's true, why didn't Celeste actually tell your father about any of this? I assume he still doesn't know about the argument you had with your sister." And the police didn't either, but Mia would be sure to tell them if she made it out of this room alive. She reached her arm across the desk and stretched her fingers until they touched the corner of the laptop. There was still one more thing she needed to confirm—that it was Isaiah who'd been watching her.

This would've been his last chance to spy on her in her room, so there was a good chance…

"Celeste said she'd give me one more opportunity. I had to swear to stay sober and start going to AA."

"And then she conveniently disappeared," Mia said.

He looked down and pinched the bridge of his nose.

Mia pivoted the laptop toward her and gasped.

It was what she'd been expecting, but still, seeing it was like a punch to the gut.

On the screen, she could see the live feed.

"What are you doing?" Isaiah lunged for her, grabbing her by one arm.

With the other hand, she picked up the laptop and swung it with all her might, cracking it against his skull.

Blood gushed from his scalp, and he fell, cursing, to his knees.

Mia didn't look back, just ran like hell for the door.

CHAPTER 40

Mia flew down the stairs, the balls of her bare feet slapping against the cold treads, her mind reeling, not registering the approaching ninety-degree bend until it was too late. She fell, face first, onto the landing, and her head smashed against unyielding marble, as she tumbled down the remaining steps. Then, fueled by adrenaline, she catapulted to her feet.

Pain seared through her, but she had no time to catalogue the source.

Blood poured from her nose and drained down her throat, making her retch.

She kept moving.

My keys?

When she'd dumped out her purse in her room, she hadn't seen them.

On the kitchen table?

For a millisecond, she hesitated.

Should she take the time to retrieve them for a surer escape, or simply keep running?

Footsteps overhead.

Isaiah had gotten to his feet, but he was still upstairs.

She raced down the hall for the kitchen and burst through the doors, but her keys weren't on the table.

Or the island.

Dammit.

She slammed her hand on the white countertop, and when she pulled it away, a bright-red handprint, like a child's finger painting, made her gag.

Get a grip.

Were her keys in the car?

Why had she wasted precious minutes?

Her cheek was throbbing and wet.

She kept going—raced out the front door for her car parked in the big, circular driveway.

Go. Go. Go.

She reached her Jetta; yanked the handle, but the door resisted.

She yanked again, and her elbow zinged like she'd stuck her hand in a jar of lightning. She remembered landing on her outstretched arm when she fell down the stairs. Was her elbow dislocated? And, *oh dear Lord*, there they were—her keys on the passenger seat—locked inside.

No! No! No!

She pounded a bloody fist against the driver's window, then whirled around in search of a rock.

Powerful arms closed around her.

She pummeled them with her fists. "Let me go! Let me go!"

"Mia, I've got you. It's okay." Baxter's voice echoed in her ears, his words soothing. "Shh."

He loosened his hold, and she buried her head against his chest, while pain, coming from everywhere, flooded her senses. "Help me. Please, help me."

"I'm here. You're okay." Keeping his hands reassuringly on her arms, he stepped back and surveyed her, then sucked in a sharp breath. "What the hell is going on? Who did this to you?"

She turned her head side to side, checking to see if Isaiah had followed her, then looked up. From a third-story window, he watched. She released her breath. "I-I'm not safe here. I need to leave, but I locked my keys in the car."

"I'll take you home to your aunt," Baxter said, the pitch of his voice rising. "But first we need to get you fixed up—you're hurt. Let's go inside."

"No!" she cried. "I need to go now. I'll explain in the car."

Nodding, he released her, followed her to his Range Rover and opened the front passenger door, then boosted her up to the seat.

From the window, Isaiah stood watch.

The Range Rover's engine roared to life, and Baxter drove around the circle, then down the road through the gates. Now, the one time when Mia would've been glad for their presence, reporters were nowhere to be found. With Keisha missing, the press had likely gone to harass the family of the latest victim.

They'd traveled no more than a mile or two when Baxter said, "Now that you've had a minute to catch your breath, it's time you tell me what's going on."

"Pull over, please."

"Mia—"

"Please. I'll explain it all, but you shouldn't be driving when I do."

He slowed the car and veered off the road, finally coming to a stop on the widest part of the shoulder. He switched his hazards on and turned to her, pulled a handkerchief from his vest pocket and offered it up.

"Thank you." She wiped her face and then looked down to see the handkerchief smeared with blood. She touched the bridge of her leaky nose. It felt swollen and bent. "It's Isaiah."

"You're saying my son did this to you? He beat you up?" A vein pulsed in Baxter's neck.

"I-I fell down the stairs."

"Did he push you? You just said *it's Isaiah*."

"No. I fell… because I was running from him."

"He was chasing you?"

"I thought he was, only he wasn't. But up in his room, he *grabbed* me. This is the second time he's done that. I hit him over the head with a laptop, and I got away."

"You hit my son over the head?" Baxter punctuated each word with a separate breath.

She met his gaze. "Just let me talk. Let me get this out."

He nodded, the vein in his neck now a fat blue bulge.

"I think Isaiah killed Celeste. Or else he's taken her somewhere. I'm not absolutely sure but I think it's him—"

Baxter set his jaw. "I know I agreed to let you tell your story, but I cannot sit here and listen to you accuse my son of *murder*. Isaiah would never harm a hair on his sister's head."

"But you were prepared to believe he'd hurt me."

"You're not his blood, Mia. I'm sorry to say so, but it's not the same thing."

"Celeste and Isaiah argued—heatedly."

"He told you that?"

"Yes. May I finish?" She paused, and when he didn't jump in, she continued, "I'm going to start from the day I first met him—at Pocket Park. Okay?"

"Okay." He stared ahead, his eyes glazed, detached, like he was watching a movie on a screen in front of them.

"That day, after he tore my blouse, I changed into one of Celeste's dresses, and I found a matchbook from a strip club in the pocket."

His eyes widened, but he let her keep going.

"I thought maybe she'd met someone at that club. Or that someone there might know something about her disappearance so I went to Lacy's—that's the place—to check it out. Isaiah was there. He grabbed me and pulled me into a back room. Later, he said he didn't realize it was me, and that it was all a big mistake. But now, he's confessed—"

"Confessed to what?" Baxter interrupted, his knuckles white from gripping the steering wheel.

"That he'd had an argument, at that very same club, with his sister. He said Celeste followed him there, and she confronted him about his drinking. She *threatened* him, told him she was going to talk to you, and this time, she was *certain* you would cut him out of your will. He believed she would get him disinherited. He admitted all of this to me, just now."

Baxter dragged a hand across his face. "Dear God."

As her heart rate slowed, she became more and more aware of the damage to her body from the fall. Her ankle was aching and swollen. Her brain threatened to explode out of her skull. She could barely breathe through her nose—and she couldn't lift or turn over her left arm.

But she was alive.

She was safe.

And she had to make Baxter understand how dangerous his son was. "I didn't want to believe it was Isaiah, either."

"It wasn't," Baxter said, his voice eerily calm. "I don't believe it."

"Someone put a tracker on my car and a bug in my purse. So I searched my room, and I found a dummy smoke alarm—the kind with a camera in it. Isaiah's computer, the one in his room, shows feed from *inside* the house. He's been watching me. I buried Celeste's keys in Torrey Pines, and Isaiah showed up on that very same trail. He has to be the one who planted them in my room. And you heard Samuels—no one has seen Keisha since we met her at the beach. Isaiah doesn't have an alibi. No one saw him at church praying for his sister. Celeste was going to persuade you to cut him out of your will—at least that's what he believes. I'm sorry, but from where I'm standing he looks guilty."

He looked at her, and her heartbeat counted down the seconds. Had she convinced him?

"I know my son didn't do it. But I'll take you wherever you want to go. To your aunt's or to the police—only we should get you checked at the hospital first. You've lost a lot of blood. You're white as a sheet."

"It's just a nosebleed."

He shook his head. "I'm afraid not. You've got a gash on your head, too. Let me take you to the hospital, and we'll call Detective Samuels from there. You can tell him your story. But I give you my word, you're wrong about Isaiah." His unbending tone set her fingers twitching. He simply could not, or would not, see what his own son was capable of. No matter the differences between him and Isaiah, Baxter was going to defend his son.

He shifted into drive and pulled back onto the road. "I'm taking you to the hospital."

"I want to go straight to the police. Whether you believe it or not, I have to talk to them."

"We're going to the hospital."

"You just said you'd take me wherever I want to go."

"I lied." He reached over and pressed a button, and the door locks clicked into place. "You're going to be a good girl and do what I say."

"I'm not a child. I don't want to go to the hospital." Her queasy stomach sounded a sudden warning. "Pull over! I'm going to be sick."

He kept his eyes on the road, not letting up on the accelerator.

She pressed the window control, but the window didn't slide down. "Pull over! Now!"

Baxter straightened his leg, and jammed the gas pedal to the floorboard.

CHAPTER 41

As her brain attempted a reboot, Mia looked up from the pool of blood-tinged vomit in her lap. She no longer felt pain—her tactile receptors had shut off, and yet, her other senses were zooming into overdrive.

The sour smell in the car, the relentless whirr of the tires, the sickening surge of forward velocity all, simultaneously, reached maximum intensity.

Maybe if she stayed perfectly still and closed her eyes this would all disappear.

Don't you dare be a good girl, little Mia's voice screamed in her head.

"Where are you taking me?" *Amazing.* She sounded like she was asking a reasonable person a normal question under ordinary circumstances.

"To the hospital." Baxter, too, seemed unperturbed.

Had his prior apparent distress been an act, or was he, like her, finally coming to grips with the problem before them?

The feeling returned to her fingertips, and her thoughts began to drop into first one slot and then another, trying to sort themselves into truth.

It's okay. You don't have to figure it all out right this minute.

She clasped her hands in front of her, resting them on her knees.

Focus on what you know: Baxter Cooper is not going to take your side over his blood. You're not safe with him.

"Which hospital?"

"Closest one is Samaritan."

You can survive—you've done it before.

So figure a way to get out of this car.

She had to get her head on straight, *now*. She would not shut down, fall apart, or back away from the truth. She would be just as calculating as him. She would play whatever part she needed to buy time, and then, she would do whatever it took to make it home to her family—to the imperfect, but always loving, woman who'd raised her.

Aunt Misty.

"I think we'd have better luck on a main road," she said.

"I'll do the thinking for both of us. You're hysterical."

"Do I sound hysterical?"

"Actions speak volumes. Just look at what you've done to yourself."

"What *I've* done?"

"You look like you've been spit out of a meat grinder. And you did it all to yourself, because you're paranoid."

Her pulse quickened, and she counteracted it with a slow, deep breath.

Dr. Baquero gave you all the tools you need to cope with anxiety— they should work for terror, too.

She straightened her spine.

"I'm not paranoid. Isaiah's been watching me."

"You're running away from people and things who aren't even chasing you. Isaiah was upstairs the whole time. He never went after you, did he?"

Thump, thump, thump.

Her heartbeat sounded steady and strong.

She glanced at the dash.

They were doing eighty.

That meant lunging for the wheel was out, and Baxter had control of the door locks.

"I told you, Isaiah grabbed me."

"Because you were in his room, nosing around. You hit him over the head with his laptop. You attacked him. Not the other way around."

"He was watching CCTV footage from *inside* the house." There was probably a screwdriver or something in the glove compartment she could use to defend herself. She reached for the latch.

Locked.

"Looking for something?" Baxter asked, his tone lilting like one kid taunting another.

"A rag. Anything to clean myself up with. You refused to stop, and I threw up in my lap in case you didn't notice."

"Key's in the center console. Knock yourself out."

She dug around inside the console until she encountered a small metal object and pulled out a key. Too tiny to be of use except for opening the glove box. She could do more damage to his eye with a finger.

With unsteady hands, she fit the key in the lock and popped open the glove box, then started tossing papers everywhere—as if he would allow her to find a knife or a letter opener.

A cell phone!

She took it out and powered it up.

"I see you found my other cell." The smile he sent her froze her blood.

No service.

Dammit.

"Think hard, Mia. When you were in Isaiah's room, and you saw the CCTV on his laptop, did you see footage from your bedroom?"

"What?"

"You heard me."

She hadn't been able to get a long look. She'd glimpsed video grids, just like when Keisha had turned the computer toward her at the Piano Man. She'd seen footage of the hallway outside her door, but then Isaiah had grabbed her. Was Baxter trying to trick her into doubting her own eyes? "I know what I saw."

"We have security cameras outside the house. You know that. *And* we have them in the hallways, where they're hidden in picture frames so as not to disrupt the décor. They're aimed at the stairwells, in case of intruders. A common practice."

"It's not common practice to hide a camera in a dummy smoke detector in a *bedroom*. Isaiah was *watching* me. He's sick. You need to get him the help he needs."

"He wasn't watching you, Mia. He has his laptop set up to view our home security footage. That's all. Your bedroom is *not* part of that system."

Baxter was in denial, and there was no talking him out of it.

Or maybe not—maybe he knew the truth.

What if he'd known all along?

How far would he go to protect his son?

Again, she checked the phone in her hand.

Still no service.

"I tried to warn you," Baxter said.

It would be so easy to let him convince her she was crazy. Only trouble was, she knew she wasn't.

"I never wanted it to come to this. That's why I put a note on your car. You should've heeded my warning."

The cell felt cold and slick in her damp palm.

Silently, she repeated his words in her head.

"Cat got your tongue?" He chuckled. "Since you're so fascinated with that phone—the code is three-four-eight-five. Why not open the My Home app? The blue one."

Her scrambled thoughts rearranged themselves, attempting to accommodate this new information. *Baxter* had left the note on her car. And what had Detective Samuels said? Do the math and you'll realize the person who left the note and the person who put a tracking device on your car are one and the same—something like that.

She did a quick calculation.

"Did *you* follow me to the overlook at Torrey Pines?"

"I kept behind a bunch of hikers, close enough to seem like the straggler of the group. I knew exactly where to dig—I just didn't know what was in that paper sack you buried until I pulled it out of the ground."

And the camera inside the smoke detector? She punched in 3485, opened the My Home app and clicked "History".

A video began to play.

It was of Mia in her room at the Coopers'—kneeling in front of her mother's hope chest, searching frantically for the missing photograph.

She held back a gasp.

With her heart knocking against her ribs, she tapped the phone, then selected "Messages" and opened the top message:

I KNOW WHAT YOU DID.

The phone slid from her hand and thunked off the dashboard.

Take it easy. Don't let him see your fear.

"And the red sweater?" Baxter had been the one to retrieve it from the school. "Was that you, too?"

"Who else?" He winked, obviously pleased with himself.

This whole time it had been *him*.

Deep breath.

She placed her hand on her stomach, felt it rise and fall. Willing herself to remain calm—at least outwardly—she asked, "Why?"

"Oh, come on. I'm not going to make this easy for you. You're the amateur sleuth—much to your own detriment."

She eyed the open glove box. He wouldn't let her dig in it if he thought she'd find a weapon. But sometimes people forget what they leave in these things. And sometimes objects can be put to use in unintended ways.

Like empty cans for digging.

She reached in the glove box again, using her one good hand—searching. There had to be something she could use—a pen, a paperclip…

She pulled out an old Polaroid.

Her mouth fell open.

"Oh, darn. You found the picture. You're onto me now."

"This is the photograph from my mother's hope chest? *You* stole it?"

"Reclaimed—it's always belonged to me. It was never yours to begin with."

She wiped her eyes, trying to bring the image into focus through her tears—a little girl in a too-big dress.

This time she recognized the little girl, and it wasn't *her*.

"This is a picture of Celeste. I don't understand."

"Try harder, Mia."

"This is the photograph I found in my mother's hope chest? The same one that disappeared?"

He showed her his teeth, more snarl than smile.

Stay rational. Don't let him distract you. "Why would a picture of Celeste be mixed in with my mother's things?"

His breathing came faster and louder.

The wipers whooshed furiously against the downpour.

The engine roared as the speedometer climbed to ninety.

"Slow down! We're going to skid off the road."

"You disappoint me, Mia. You're not even trying. If you want me to tell you the truth, you need to earn it. Let's play a game. I'll give you three guesses, and if you get it right, I'll slow down."

He let his foot off the accelerator, and for a fraction of a second, she thought he might come to his senses. The car slowed to seventy, fifty, and at forty, she reached for the wheel, but he knocked her away. Her head banged against the side window, then snapped forward.

No pain.

Good.

Stay in survival mode.

The car skidded into a turn, and then straightened, before accelerating again.

He'd slowed, just then, in order to turn onto a dirt road, and she'd missed her chance to take the wheel.

No problem—just wait for the next opportunity.

Trees rushed by.

Houses grew fewer and farther between, as they passed the time in silence.

The sun set, and the sky turned a deep, beautiful shade of purple.

The faintest glimmer of stars adorned the evening sky, and then, suddenly her mind rang like a bell.

She knew this area. She'd been here before. "Where are we?"

"Don't you know?"

If only she could reach the memory.

The photograph holds the answer. Ask him.

"How does your game go? What are the rules again?"

He grinned. "I knew you'd be too curious not to play along. You make a guess, and I'll tell you if you're hot or cold."

She held up the snapshot. "This photo is of Celeste when she was a little girl. But it was with my mother's things."

"We've established that. That's not a guess. Try again."

"Did Alma and my mother know each other?"

He clucked his tongue. "Cold."

It still made no sense. "Did *you* know my mother?"

"Hot."

She tried to breathe through it, but her body refused to exhale. An unbearable tension was building in her chest.

Look at Baxter.

Could it be?

She was breathing again—back in control.

Baxter's silver hair was thick and wavy.

In his youth, it might've been dark.

No scar on his face, though. His skin was smooth—perfect.

Too perfect for a man his age. Easy enough to laser off a scar these days—plenty of men get work done, especially ones who've been on TV.

He told you he'd traveled the world, and Alma was his compass.

"Were you ever in the Navy?" she asked.

"Hot," he said, making her heart jolt in her chest.

It'd been ages since they passed any houses, and the roads had long since turned rutted and bumpy. As she gazed out the window at the driving rain, the Range Rover, at long last, skidded to a stop.

Then he turned to her, his eyes gleaming with mirth. "You've had your three guesses, but I'll allow one more."

They were deep in the woods, far from any well-traveled roads, but it didn't matter. Mia wasn't planning to run—she was planning to fight.

"You're him," she whispered. "*Arnie.*"

CHAPTER 42

Mia thought her body might levitate. The weight of twenty years had just lifted off her chest, all the tears, the nightmares, the fears—banished in a single moment.

She'd found *him*.

Soon, she would learn her mother's fate.

Outside, the rain continued, gentler now, more of a slow plop, plop against the windshield. Arnie had stopped off-road in front of a clearing surrounded by tall pines. The sky was darkening, the stars shone brighter.

He shut down the engine. "We're here."

Her heart pounded against her ribs, adrenaline screamed in her veins, and she welcomed all of it. She would take no more deep breaths to counteract her body's reaction to this man. "You don't scare me, Arnie."

"We'll see how long that lasts." His lip curled. "And my name's not Arnie. That's just what I call myself around whores."

"I'll call you Arnie, too, then."

"You want to be my whore?"

"Not your *whore*. But that's the name my mother called you, so I'll call you by it, too. How many women have you been with? Besides my mother and Alma."

"Don't mention Alma in the same breath, please, but since you asked, I haven't really kept track of the number of whores I've slept with—too many to count, you see. But your mother was special.

One of my favorites." He unhooked his seat belt. "A shame I had to… well, we'll talk more."

Her heart was kicking like it wanted to escape her body. If she died tonight, she'd make him pay for his crimes first. She'd gouge an eye out, smash his face with a rock—he wasn't going to get away clean.

Not this time.

Not from her.

"What did you do to my mother? How many women have you murdered?"

"Let's walk and talk." The door locks clicked open. "I love the rain—it's romantic."

Did he have a gun on him? Maybe in his jacket or tucked beneath the back of his shirt. If she could grab it, get a drop on him…

"Get out."

With her good arm she opened the door and climbed down from the SUV, careful to avoid landing with her weight on her swollen ankle.

"Let's hold hands." He came around, grabbed the wrist that hung limp at her side and twisted.

A moment of blinding pain—and then exquisite relief.

She looked down at her arm and smiled.

Little did he know he'd just popped her dislocated elbow back into place.

Now her arsenal included the use of two arms instead of one.

"You want to walk side by side? No gun in my back? Seems risky," she said.

"I'll take my chances." He smirked. "I don't think you're in any shape to put up much of a fight. And it's nice to have someone to talk to. You've got that therapist of yours, but I don't. Secrets are heavy, and I haven't slept well since Celeste. I'd like to unburden myself."

"I'm not a priest." She pulled up short and turned to meet his eyes. "And I wouldn't give you absolution if I were."

He resumed walking, still gripping her hand. "Maybe I'm just looking to be understood. For *Arnie* to be seen and heard. You have questions. Let's see which of them Arnie feels like answering."

She quickened her pace lest he pull her sore elbow out of its socket again. As they moved across the clearing, she kept her eyes peeled for stones and sticks, anything she could use against him. But it was getting darker by the minute. She could hardly see a foot in front of her, and the tall grass obscured the ground.

"How many women have you murdered?" she asked a second time, bracing for the answer.

He gave her hand a crushing squeeze, and then dropped it.

Thank God.

Rain harder.

May a downpour from heaven wash away the poison from the places he touched my skin.

"Again with the how many? I'm no serial killer—at least not the one the FBI is looking for. I didn't kill those women in Colorado and Arizona. Whoever that guy is, though, he's provided me with nice cover. But, no. I'm a good man—a family guy. You think I'm some kind of monster but you've got it all wrong. I only kill when necessary. And if you need proof, consider the fact that I could've gotten rid of you twenty years ago, but I didn't. I let you have a life, all this time, when I could've—should've—snuffed you out."

He was definitely going to kill her.

She didn't want to run—she wanted to fight—but life suddenly seemed sweet, too precious to give up the chance to go on living.

They were too far from the trees for her to make it to cover if she ran now. But when they got closer to the woods, up ahead, she might make a break for it.

He pulled his phone out and shone the flashlight on the ground.

"Why didn't you kill me twenty years ago, then?"

"Oh, I considered it. Your mother hid you so well I didn't even know you existed until I read about you in the papers. A six-year-old girl digging her way out of a shed." He whistled. "Impressive. Too bad your mother put me in a position where I had no choice except to get rid of her."

"Where is my mother? What have you done with her?" She wanted to know the truth. No matter how terrible.

"Be patient. We're talking about you, not her. Like I said, I read about you in the papers, and you presented quite a dilemma for me. I was worried you might've seen something. But you didn't, did you?"

"No."

"Good to know. I've never been sure. Anyway, I didn't want to kill a little girl. I'm not a monster—not at all."

"You expect me to believe you let me live because of your conscience? You don't have one. You killed your own daughter."

"Perhaps I don't then—though Celeste isn't my blood, so I'm not sure your point is valid. As for you, in the end, I made a practical decision. I already had one murder to cover up, one chance of being imprisoned for the rest of my life. If I'd killed you, too, then I'd have double the chances of being caught. So instead, I've been waiting and watching. Patiently observing, making sure you never came close to truth, that you never had a chance to screw up the life I've worked so hard to build for my precious angel."

Aunt Misty was right.

"You've been watching me for *twenty years.*"

"Some years more closely than others. There were times I almost let you fall off my radar, but then you started seeing that shrink, and I got worried you might dredge up old memories. I put a tracker on your car. I even went to the preschool where you worked on the pretense of checking it out for a friend—just to see if you recognized me. Of course you didn't, and it all might've ended there if Celeste hadn't been looking for a job."

A bolt of lightning seared the sky.

Mia scanned the clearing, estimating the distance to the trees ahead, where at least she'd have a shot at hiding.

Too soon.

Even with the adrenaline flooding her body, she'd never make it that far on this ankle. And Arnie could decide any minute to do his worst. What chance did she really have against him?

What chance did you have to get out of that shed?

Just make it to the trees.

Keep him talking.

"Celeste needed a job?"

"She wanted to teach at a private school, and she found the Harbor Youth Academy brochure in the back of my car—after I'd paid that visit there to see if you'd recognize me. I tried to talk her out of applying. I didn't want my family anywhere near you, but the more I argued with her, the more determined she got. Celeste had quite the stubborn streak. I suppose you both do. Anyway, I decided to let it go and hope for the best. I didn't think you'd be a problem since you didn't seem to know anything about me. But just look where we are now."

"Did Celeste find out about my mother? Is that why you killed her?"

He let out a heavy sigh. "We're almost there."

"Where?"

"You'll see. How's your ankle holding up? Do you want to lean on my shoulder?"

No!

"I'm fine." It was true. Her gait was slow and wobbly, but for all the pain she felt she might as well have had a double shot of morphine.

He still hadn't answered her question about Celeste. Maybe if she rephrased it… "What happened to Celeste?"

Silence.

"You said you haven't slept well. You said you want to unburden yourself so go ahead. I want the truth, and we both know I'm not leaving this place alive."

"So it's a win-win?" He pulled up short.

No. Keep walking!

He put his hands on her shoulders, and she instantly retched.

"Go ahead, get it out of your system."

She fell to her knees, spewing her stomach contents onto the grass.

He widened his stance, looking down at her with folded arms. "Celeste left me no choice. If it's any comfort to you, your taking her keys had nothing to do with her death."

"Why put the knockoff keyring on my desk?"

"I saw you take Celeste's keys. I left that other set on your desk at school so you'd *know* you'd been seen. It was an obvious signal to stay clear of things. Later, I tried to rattle you with the sweater and that warning text. I really did hope you'd leave on your own and go running back to your aunt. And I think I did a pretty good job making you seem unstable—now when you disappear it will seem like another one of your crazy antics, another cry for attention. Why did you ignore all my warnings, Mia? I gave you so many chances."

"You *saw* me take Celeste's keys? You were *there*—at the Piano Man that night?"

"I had a date with an escort. I thought if I were seen, I could explain away dinner with an attractive woman. I'd just say she was a business associate."

"Seems risky."

"Yeah, but I like taking risks. Luckily, I'm more *has-been* than celebrity, so I don't get recognized often. Besides, ever since the mess with your mother, I arrange all kinds of backup plans and excuses for any escapade I embark upon. But I didn't expect to bump into Celeste. And I didn't expect her to see me *kissing* that whore. Celeste didn't confront me at the restaurant—she doesn't like scenes. That was a mistake on her part. She walked home, and then she called me to come over to her house and discuss that and some other things. We had a terrible argument. She said she was going to tell Alma, and I simply couldn't allow that."

Mia stretched her arms in front of her, and doubled over, feigning another retch. She ran her hands through the tall, wet grass, searching. There had to be a rock somewhere.

"So you killed your own daughter to cover up an affair?"

"Again, she's not *my* daughter. Isaiah and Angelica are my blood. Alma was a single mother to Celeste when I met her. When I think of all the things I've done for a child who isn't even mine. I did it all for Alma's sake and Celeste was going to repay me how? By telling her mother about my affairs."

Mia raked her fingers deep in the mud.

Yes!

Her palm closed around something hard and sharp.

She craned her neck, looking up at him.

He stared off into the distance. "Of course I'm not heartless, and if it had been only that one thing—the escort at the Piano Man—I could've wormed my way out of it. I might've admitted to a lapse in judgment, confessed to a single kiss and begged Alma's forgiveness. For Alma's sake, I would have let Celeste live if there'd been any way. But, sadly, there was more to it. Celeste had nosed around my office looking for dirt; it seemed even before that night, she'd become suspicious. Someone told her I was cheating on her mother. After what happened today, I'm wondering if that someone was my own son—but that's a problem for tomorrow. I've got enough to deal with right here and now with you."

Now Isaiah was in danger, too. If she didn't stop this evil, right here, where would it all end? "Celeste found out about more women? Strippers?"

"Worse. It seems she'd broken into my lockbox in my study and found a newspaper clipping."

That must've been what was upsetting her at school Friday morning.

Mia got up on her knees, concealing the rock in her hand behind her back.

"One about your mother. A story about the disappearance of Emily Thornton and her poor little abandoned daughter, Mia." He looked down at her. "She left me no choice at all. I didn't want to kill Celeste, but she simply knew too much. There's no containing a situation like that. So I did what needed to be done, and the next day I dumped her purse in the alley for the police to find—to make it look like she never made it home. I'd heard about those other missing women but I never thought it would be so easy to mislead. It seems the police are always happy to add a crime onto a serial killer's list of accomplishments if you give them half a chance. Do you need some help up?" He extended his hand.

She took it, and he helped her to her feet, almost gently.

Do it. Do it.

The stone was heavy in her hand.

Do it. Do it.

She brought her arm up, and, with all her might, heaved the rock.

Smashed him in the face.

"You little bitch!"

Run! Run! Run! You can make it!

The grass rustled behind her.

Thunder clapped in the sky.

Just a few more yards.

Her head jerked back—he had her by the hair.

Her back slammed against the ground; she tasted dirt.

He kneeled over her, blood dripping from his mouth, and laughed.

CHAPTER 43

"Get up!"

No way. She wasn't going to make this easy for him. Plus, her legs had turned to water. Without a break, she couldn't hike the rest of the way to wherever the hell he planned to kill her, even if she wanted to.

Which she did not.

Lying on her back, like this, she could see the Big Dipper.

"Come on. Get up. Or should I drag you by your hair?"

"Go ahead."

At least it would tire him out.

The stench that had been making her sick for ages was gone. Her queasy stomach all better. She inhaled deeply, making the most of what would probably be the last time she smelled rain and gazed up at the stars.

He shoved his hands under her armpits.

Apparently, he'd thought twice about dragging her by the hair. Maybe he needed a more even distribution of weight. They started to move, her shirt riding up her chest.

The cold mud felt good against her stinging skin, and though the ground was rough, and stones scraped her back as he hauled her across the clearing, her body's natural morphine, or whatever miracle was keeping the pain at bay, was holding strong.

"God almighty." They stopped moving. He pulled his hands out from under her and huffed down to the ground beside her. "We're gonna rest a minute. And then you're gonna get up." He didn't sound like Baxter anymore. That low, refined voice of his, even his diction had changed.

"You still haven't told me what happened to my mother."

"I don't think you really want to know. Let's make a deal. You make it easy on me, and I'll make it easy on you. Get off your lazy ass and walk, and I won't rip your nails off one by one, and then beat you to a bloody pulp before I kill you."

Scanning the sky, she found Orion. How long had it been since she'd lain in the grass, studying the night sky with her grandfather pointing out the constellations? And yet, she still knew them.

"Thank you, Granddad," she whispered.

"Shit. Don't lose it. I need you to stand up." The voice came from far away.

His voice—Arnie's voice.

She lifted her head and turned to look at him. His face was scratched and dirty, his hair matted with blood.

She laughed.

She'd done that to him. "Where's my mother?"

"I'm taking you to her. Stand up and we'll get there faster."

"I don't think I can. Tell me what you did to her."

He put his face between his hands. "I don't know how many ways to say it to make you understand—Emily left me no choice. I love my wife. Alma's mine, and no one is allowed to take her away from me, but your damn whore of a mother sure tried her best."

"So women come in two kinds? What makes Alma the angel and my mother a whore? They were both poor. They both had a child outside marriage—"

"I told you, I didn't even know you existed. It was nothing to do with that. I picked Alma, that's all. I *chose* her, and that's what makes her special. But anyone can see what makes your mother a whore."

She wanted to go to sleep, now. She wanted Mommy.

Don't come to me yet, Mia. It's too soon.

"Help me sit up."

He hoisted her into a sitting position, facing him. "Will you walk?"

"In a minute. I want to know everything. Start at the beginning, and then I promise I'll go with you."

He nodded. "Emily came into my shop one morning, all done up like Saturday night on Hollywood Boulevard. She pawned a charm bracelet. That bracelet was worth something for the silver, and I gave your mother a fair price. I don't know how she came by jewelry that costs that much. Probably stole it."

"It was my grandmother's."

"Whatever. Emily's eyes were big and brown like yours. Full, sexy mouth. She was so skinny I suspected, rightly as it turned out, that she didn't eat regularly. But still, I liked the way she looked. I like all kinds of women."

"You like vulnerable women."

"Is that a crime?"

"When you murder them, yes."

"They left me no choice? Remember?"

Mia stared at the devil in front of her, watching his lips move, listening to his words, devouring every morsel of information.

He'll never hurt you again, Mommy.

"She pawned her bracelet and then what happened?"

"Emily wrote down her name on the pawn ticket. She didn't have an address, but she told me how to find that cabin of hers, and I promised to drop by. That night, I took her some groceries and beer, and we started up from there. I swear I didn't know she had a kid locked in a shed. If I had, I would've beaten the crap out of her."

The wind was like silk caressing her face. "I'm ready to go, now. I think I can make it."

He stood—his legs shaky. The journey had taken a toll on him, too, and it showed. He offered her his hand.

She got on her knees and then planted both hands in front of her, pushed off the ground and climbed to her feet on her own. Never again would she let him touch her—at least not of her own free will.

"That's my good girl."

Not even close.

"Where was I?"

The trees were just a few yards ahead, but Arnie was talking.

She was going to learn the whole truth, no matter the cost. "You started up with my mother."

"At first, Emily was mostly sober around me, tried to put her best foot forward and all. But she was a hopeless alcoholic and couldn't hide it forever. I hate a boozer, but there was a silver lining: when she got drunk enough, she'd go along with a little kink. Life was good. My business was taking off. I had my precious Alma. We'd just gotten engaged—I loved her so much I didn't mind her baggage."

You monster.

"Celeste was the baggage?"

"Yeah. But I still gave her everything the same as I did my blood. But we were talking about Emily. I guess she didn't see things the same way I did. She was suffering from the delusion I was her boyfriend, and that we were going to be together forever. White picket fence, the whole nine yards. But that last weekend, while I was sleeping, she went through my wallet and found a picture of Celeste and another of the three of us, Alma, Celeste and me—with Alma showing off her new diamond ring. Emily took the photos to use against me as proof I'd been with her. She said she was going to show them to Alma, tell her all about me, unless I came clean and left Alma on my own." He stopped and gaped at her. "You believe that? Me leave my fiancée for a drunken, beat-down whore like your mother? Anyway, I pried the one family picture out of her hands, but I never knew what happened to the other until you brought that old chest to my house."

They arrived at the trees.

"Careful, watch your step." He reached for her hand again. She recoiled.

"Fine, but keep up or its back to dragging. I'm gonna put my hands on you sooner or later, regardless—I don't do guns or knives anymore."

"Too much evidence?" He was so cold she'd need an ice pick to open his veins.

"Hands are much cleaner—more work, but worth it in the end. I used a steak knife on your mother, and you don't want to know the problems that caused me. I learned my lesson after that—strangle 'em—leave no trace. You want your mother? I'll show you where I buried her."

She stumbled forward, then halted in her tracks. To her right, the ground was grassless, smooth except for leaves, blowing across a long swath of newly turned earth.

A fresh grave.

Thank God her stomach was empty.

"Not there. That's Celeste and Keisha."

Her feet froze. "Keisha?"

"She was supposed to have my back. I've greased her palm enough times to get me a good table or arrange a special treat for a lady. And I paid her well to erase the security footage that showed me with an escort at the restaurant that night. Then she tells you she made a backup? I knew right then, she had to go."

"You heard that? When did you put the bug in my purse?"

"The first time you came to dinner. I've been getting an earful since then. The blackmail, the therapy, the conversations with your aunt." He sent her a mean smile. "Anyway, Keisha, Celeste, all you ladies brought this on yourselves. Your mother tried to ruin my marriage. Celeste spied on me—the father who adopted her and gave her everything. Keisha said she'd made backup footage, which could've created all kinds of problems for me if true—with Alma and with the cops. And you, Mia, you simply wouldn't heed my many, many warnings to stay away. When Alma showed you that photo album this morning, I knew then, it was over. She was getting so sentimental with you, I saw that a real bond was developing between you both, and I simply couldn't allow that to happen. It was far too risky. I either had to scare you off or else I had to make *her* want *you* gone for good. The only way to accomplish that was to show her what you did to Celeste."

"That's the reason you left the *real* keys out for Angelica to find. You knew she'd show the family and Alma would hate me for hurting Celeste."

"If I had let Alma get any more attached to you, sooner or later she was bound to slip up."

Her head felt fuzzy, and her ears were ringing. She must have heard him wrong. "Slip up how? Are you saying Alma knows about Celeste?"

"Alma would murder me in my sleep if she did. But she sure as shit knows about your mother—and she's made all our lives hell trying to atone for my sins with her charity work. I should never have told her about Emily, but she got the truth out of me when I came home bloodied up. No one can ever say I don't love that woman. And she loves me. Who do you think cleaned up all that blood?"

"I don't believe you. You sick, murdering bastard."

"I got no reason to lie now, do I? But playtime is over. Let's finish this." He gestured. "Your mother's this way. It's too crowded over here, so I'm putting you right beside Mommy."

He turned his back.

She pictured him lying on the ground in a pool of blood.

If only she had a pistol, or a knife, or another rock.

She put one foot in front of the other. The wind picked up, singing sweetly through the branches.

She kept walking until she saw it—a gaping hole, freshly dug—a shovel cast to the side.

Could she reach the shovel?

She broke into a run.

Panting sounded behind her, and then he had her by the collar. Elbow bent, his arm dropped across her neck.

She ducked her chin, and he squeezed, tighter and tighter. "I'm not a bad man. I'm only doing what has to be done."

Me too.

Above her, the stars blazed in the sky.

It takes a dark night to reveal heaven's beauty.

With both hands, she grabbed the arm he'd clasped around her neck and dropped her body weight, opening up just enough space for her to take a breath.

And then another.

"You're a hellcat, just like your mother. She fought like crazy. But you can't beat me. Take it easy, and it'll be over quicker."

He's panting, tired.

Fight!

She flailed one arm above her head, found his hand, and jammed her fingers between his.

Pull! Twist!

"Whore!"

"Not a whore! We're not your whores!" She kicked her leg back, connecting with his crotch.

Screaming, he loosened his hold on her.

She spun around, punched him in the chest.

He lunged back, and then his foot slipped out from under him.

He tumbled into the open grave, sending mud blasting up like shrapnel.

Run!

No! Stay!

She dropped to her knees, her body racked with sobs. Her mother was *here*, and she wasn't going to leave her alone in the woods.

Nor Celeste, nor Keisha.

Mia was going to stay put and make dead certain that Arnie never hurt anyone again.

Stretching out in the mud, she coaxed the shovel toward her. Then she crawled to the edge of the open grave and looked down.

Arnie lay at the bottom, prone, blood oozing from his skull.

She sat back on her haunches and raised the shovel overhead, ready to knock him down if he came to and tried to climb out of the hole where he belonged. She'd stay here all night, all day, however long it took.

Her hands cramped, but she didn't quit.

Her back ached, but she didn't relent.

Rain came and went.

Wind blew.

She was still at her post, shovel raised, when, at last, she heard the sirens.

EPILOGUE

Four months later

The echo of a heavy metal door slamming shut behind her reverberated in Mia's ears. In a show of bravado, she pushed up her chin. She might fool the casual observer, but she couldn't fool herself. Though unblemished on the outside, beneath her skin the dead had carved ciphers into her bones.

Striding beside her, Isaiah kept his eyes lowered, his hands pushed into his emptied pockets. Per the rules, his belongings, and Mia's, had been stowed in lockers outside the family visitation room. They'd followed the dress code, avoiding khakis and denim so as not to be confused with prisoners or guards.

"Don't be scared." Isaiah kept his voice low.

"I'm not."

She'd pictured prison differently. Stark walls. The stench of unwashed flesh.

But here, in the visitation room, the walls were a blue-gray, which, if not for their industrial sheen, might be considered soothing. The air smelled like shampoo and cookies, and children climbed the bolted down furniture, the chirp of their young voices bouncing off the walls.

Still, though uncuffed once they entered the room, the women were dressed in prison garb, and the weight of decimated lives hung oppressively in the air.

In a far corner of the room, Alma raised a thin arm, signaling them. She waited at a round metallic table, whose seats were attached to long tubes arcing from the body like spider legs.

Through a maze of tables and families, Mia and Isaiah picked their way over to her. The fluorescent light bouncing off her orange jumpsuit, gave her skin a jaundiced tone. Like trellised ivy, streaks of gray wound into her auburn hair. Her eyes seemed big and beautiful.

"Thank you for coming," Alma said.

"We're here like we agreed." Isaiah's voice sounded strained.

Mia said nothing as she sat down on one of the attached seats. She wasn't here to gratify Alma.

"I thought you might have questions, Mia." But Alma wasn't looking at her. She was watching Isaiah as she spoke. She and Mia hadn't talked since the day Baxter had abducted her.

Mia had no more illusions regarding this woman. She realized Alma orchestrated today's visit to win back her son. Isaiah had refused to visit again unless she gave an accounting to Mia. All Mia wanted from Alma was the truth, and she didn't care one whit about her motive for offering it up. "Tell me everything."

"I hope, dear, that someday you'll find a way to forgive me."

The *dear* made Mia cringe. "I just want to know what role you played in my mother's murder. That's the only reason I came."

Alma lowered her eyes. "What you've suffered is terrible. But you do know I've paid the *ultimate* price."

Alma had cooperated with the police and pleaded to accessory after the fact in the murder of Mia's mother. In exchange, she'd received a reduced sentence: a five thousand dollar fine and one year in prison.

Hardly justice.

"Tell me about my mother," Mia said.

"Samuels has filled you in on some of it, I know. Where should I start?"

"At the beginning. I want to hear it all from *you*." Mia reached for Isaiah and briefly touched his shoulder. "I'm sure Isaiah does too."

"That's right." His voice didn't break, but Mia could feel his body trembling beneath her hand. He'd lost a sister. His father was the cold-blooded monster who'd killed her. And then there was his mother, who'd helped Baxter cover up a different murder. Isaiah deserved the truth as much as Mia did.

Isaiah was the one who'd phoned 911. He said, later, that as he'd recounted the details of the incident with Celeste at the strip club to Mia, he'd begun to see Mia's point. It *was* suspicious for Celeste to disappear just days later. Only he knew *he* hadn't hurt her. But he *had* confided to Celeste that Baxter might be leading a secret life. Then, after watching Mia climb into Baxter's Range Rover and finding the trail of blood she'd left on the stairs, he'd gotten an awful feeling. When neither Baxter nor Mia picked up his calls, he'd tracked them on his computer using his family phone-finder app. Once Baxter's signal began traveling off the main roads, Isaiah knew he had to act. Whatever his father was up to, it wasn't getting Mia to the hospital where she clearly belonged. So he'd called the cops and guided them to the location of Baxter's phone. Eventually, the signal failed, but not before the cops got close enough to spot the Range Rover parked off-road. If the police hadn't arrived when they did, before Baxter regained consciousness, Mia might not be here today. Instead, she could well be the one incarcerated for giving in to her worst instincts and using that shovel to finish off Baxter, or else she might be lying in a secret grave beside her mother if Baxter had come to and attacked her. She owed Isaiah—but more importantly, she trusted him.

Alma clasped her hands together, resting them on the table, and Mia noticed marks where handcuffs had gouged her wrists. "First, I want to say, to Isaiah, that I love you with all my heart—such as it is. No matter what I've done, please don't doubt that."

"Just get on with it, Mother. You promised to tell Mia everything. She deserves that."

Alma lifted a bottle of water to her lips, then screwed the cap on and set it down. It wobbled on the uneven table before coming to rest. "I was twenty-three and Celeste was six. Baxter and I were engaged, and I'll be honest, I wasn't head over heels for him like he was for me, but that only seemed to make him want me more. My life was a struggle—every single day was hard. And Baxter promised to take care of Celeste and me. He promised we'd never go without again. When I was growing up, my mother moved us between shelters and relatives' couches. Once, we were on the street for weeks, and I slept in a toy wagon. I was determined my child, my lovely little Celeste, would never have to go through anything like that. When Baxter proposed, I wasn't too keen on him, but eventually I realized he could be my way out."

"That justifies nothing." Isaiah looked away.

"I'm not trying to justify. I'm explaining. I want you to understand my side of it."

"Just let her talk, Isaiah," Mia said. The *why* haunted her. She wanted to know what had been in Alma's mind.

He nodded.

Alma looked from one to the other and continued, "One night, shortly before our wedding date, Baxter came home past midnight and rushed right past me. He ran for the shower, and when I followed him, I found his clothes, bloody and torn, stuffed in the trash. I confronted him, and after a while, he confessed that he'd been seeing a woman named Emily. He said he tried to break it off with her, and she threatened to find me and tell me he'd been cheating. He said the thought of losing me made him go berserk. She ran outside. He chased her with a kitchen knife and finally caught her in the woods. After, he loaded her body up in the trunk of his car, drove further into the woods and buried her. I was horrified."

"But you married him." Isaiah covered his face.

"I didn't dream he'd ever hurt *me*—or Celeste. Emotionally, Baxter was the needy one. I'd been counting on that marriage, and I didn't think I should have to give up my ticket out of poverty just because he did something stupid. I was sick of working two jobs to keep a roof over Celeste's head." She gave Mia a pleading look. "Your poor mother was already in the ground when I found out. It wasn't as if I could bring her back, and Baxter was so remorseful. He sobbed for an hour, begged me not to leave him. He swore he'd never look at another woman again, and I was naïve enough to believe him."

"So by remorseful, you mean he regretted *cheating on you*," Mia said.

"That's right." Alma took another sip of water, seemingly unaware of the inhumanity of that statement. "So I helped him cover up. I burned his clothes and helped him clean up the car. I scrubbed bloodstains out of the trunk, and he vacuumed it. That night, it poured rain so we didn't worry about them finding blood or footprints in the wilderness. Then, the next day, we went down to the courthouse and got married. Baxter said no one could force spouses to testify against each other, so I would never have to lie to the police. I thought I'd never have a problem with him. And for a long time, I didn't. He did everything I asked of him. Worked his tail off at the store, and even let me sign him up for a reality show for the publicity. He never wanted more than that one pawn shop, but he knew I hated being poor. If you think my wanting to be rich makes me shallow, so be it. I craved the things I saw in the movies and read about in books, and Baxter got them for me."

"Oh my God." Isaiah shook his head. "All the time you were playing the concerned wife, pretending to be worried about how hard he was driving himself…"

"I admit I pushed him to succeed. I was the one who subtly nudged him into asking the doctor for amphetamines. And it worked, too. Look where it landed us."

"In a miserable family where everyone escaped from each other in their own way. Me with booze, you with tranquilizers, and Dad with uppers—even Angelica binge drinks."

"I was miserable. Think of what I went through. I had to stay married to a *murderer*, pretending to love him all those years for the sake of you and Celeste and Angelica. I made that sacrifice for *you*."

"Don't put that on us. You were the one who wanted the big house and the expensive things. I never cared."

"Well, you sure weren't happy when your father said he'd cut you out of his will."

Mia slapped her hand on the table. "Can we get back to what happened? Did you know who I was, Alma? And if you did, why on earth bring me into your house and show me those pictures of you and Celeste? Didn't you realize you were risking exposure for Baxter?"

"Of course. I knew you right away. Not like I'd forget the child of the woman my husband murdered. I'd read all about you in the papers. And when you showed up with Angelica at Celeste's place that day, I did see an opportunity."

"I was an *opportunity*?"

"After twenty years, Baxter didn't worry as much about being found out. I'd been gradually losing control over him. He still adored me, of course, but he'd been indulging his—shall we say indelicate proclivities—on the side, and worse, arguing with the children—particularly Isaiah. I hoped having you around, Mia, would bring Baxter back into line. I wanted to protect Isaiah's inheritance." She reached for his hand.

He pulled it off the table as if she were a coiling viper.

"I felt sorry for you, Mia. And I thought you'd be a good reminder to Baxter that he might still be caught. I was furious over the way he treated Isaiah, so I used you to rattle him."

"Ease up on Isaiah? Toe the line or else," Mia said.

Alma paused, her throat working in a long swallow. "I wasn't so obvious as that, but he got the message. And then, toward the end, I started to wonder. How could I trust a man who'd murdered someone and never looked back? And one morning it hit me that if he could kill Emily—" her breath hitched "—what if Celeste found out about him and he'd done something to *her*? I suspected the whole serial killer grabbing her up in an alley scenario was a little too convenient. I wasn't sure—not at all. If I had been, I'd have killed him. I didn't want to believe Baxter could've hurt Celeste, but whether he had or not, I wanted him out of my house."

"You could've divorced him," Mia said.

"I didn't want a divorce. I wanted *everything*. And if Baxter was arrested for Emily's murder, that's exactly what I'd get. But I couldn't go to the police with what I knew. I'd cleaned up the blood and burned evidence, and besides, I didn't want to enrage a murderer."

"None of what you did seems like a foolproof plan to me."

"No, there were no guarantees, but it was more of a game than a plan—I saw a chance and I took advantage. Having you in the house made him crazy, and I hoped he'd do something foolish, which he did. He stole that photograph from your mother's hope chest the very same day you brought it over, and then he made the mistake of showing it to me. He was so relieved to find it, but it reminded me of the story he'd told me all those years ago about your mother hiding it from him. I'd almost forgotten, and that gave me the idea of feeding you clues with our old photo albums. I was tired of protecting Baxter, and our perfect life was far from it. I not only didn't care if he got caught for Emily's murder—I prayed he would. I might not have my precious Celeste, but at least I'd have money, and justice would be served."

"You have a very warped sense of justice." She could hardly believe this petite, soft-spoken woman in front of her, the woman she'd idolized, was a sociopath, a master manipulator—and she'd relayed her story without a hint of remorse. It was almost as if she wanted them to see how clever she'd been. "If you hadn't covered up for Baxter twenty years ago, your daughter and Keisha would be alive today."

"Like I said, I paid the ultimate price."

"No, Mother—" a tear slid down Isaiah's cheek "—*Celeste* is the one who paid."

*

Back at the car, Isaiah opened Mia's door for her and went around to the driver's side. She clicked her seat belt into place and turned to him. "I don't blame you for what your parents did. Please know that."

"I'd understand if you hated me, but I don't know if I could handle it. Right now, you're the only friend I have."

"You've got Angelica," Mia said softly.

"Not at the moment. She's furious with me for not 'standing up' for Dad. According to Angelica, Samuels violated his rights, coercing him into a plea deal because he was afraid of the death penalty."

Mia now knew more than she'd ever hoped to about the California capital punishment statutes. Despite the governor's suspension of all executions, the death penalty was still legal in California, and plenty of criminals were being sentenced and sent to death row. If the moratorium on executions was ever lifted, they could be executed. So Baxter had provided a full confession to the murders and spared the families a trial in exchange for taking the death penalty off the table.

"He kidnapped me and took me to the grave sites."

"There's no logic on Angelica's part, just blind loyalty to Dad. Sooner or later, I'm sure she'll come around, but meanwhile, she wants nothing to do with me."

"I'm sorry."

He cleared his throat. "Change of subject?"

"Sure."

"I know it's been a rough day, and I hope this won't make it harder on you, but I don't think there's ever going to be a good time." He pulled a long slender box, wrapped in gold foil from the car's glove compartment. "This belongs to you. I hope it's not too sad a reminder."

Mia unwrapped a jewelry box.

She snapped the lid up, and her hand flew to her throat.

It couldn't be the same one.

She closed her eyes, picturing her mother turning the pages of a storybook, in her mind she heard tinkling bells. She could see the silver rungs of a bracelet, the beautiful charms: a cross, a heart, and a star. She opened her eyes. "Is this… is this my mother's? How can that be?"

"Dad's original pawn shop has been closed for years, but he kept boxes and boxes of unsold inventory. He also kept meticulous records. So when I heard your mother used to come into the shop, I promised myself that if anything of hers was in storage, I'd find it."

He brushed his hand across his eyes. "I've been wanting to give this to you since the moment I found it. But knowing that it led your mother to my father… I-I worried it would be too painful for you to see it or touch it. But in the end, I realized I had no right to make that decision for you."

Mia nodded, her throat too clogged to speak.

She held up her wrist, and he helped her with the clasp.

"Thank you." She lifted her eyes to his. "I admit this is a bitter-sweet memento—some people might even think it's morbid to wear it. But my mother loved this bracelet, and in spite of everything, I loved her. I don't want to push away my past anymore. I didn't choose it, but it's part of who I am."

"What about the future?" he asked.

"I have no idea," she said. "But getting the hell out of this prison parking lot would be a good start."

A LETTER FROM CAREY

Dear Reader,

Thank you for taking time out of your busy life to read *Her First Mistake*. I loved creating these characters, and I hope you enjoyed getting to know them and taking their journey as much as I enjoyed sharing them with you.

If you'd like to be the first to know about my next book, please sign up via the following link. Your email address will never be shared and you can unsubscribe at any time.

www.bookouture.com/carey-baldwin

Building a relationship with readers is one of the best things about being a writer. I love hearing from you, so please stay in touch by connecting with me on Facebook, Twitter, and my website, and following me on BookBub. I've posted the information below for your convenience. Meanwhile, if you enjoyed this story, I would be grateful if you could leave a short review. Reviews are one of the best ways to help other readers discover my books. You can make a big difference simply by leaving a line or two.

Thank you very much for reading and don't forget to stay in touch!

Love, Carey

Carey.Baldwin.10

CareyBaldwin

CareyBaldwin.com and CareyBaldwin.net

Bookbub.com/authors/carey-baldwin

ACKNOWLEDGMENTS

Thank you so much to my wonderful agent, Liza Dawson, who is unendingly supportive and always wise. I'm so grateful to everyone at Bookouture for taking me on and working so hard to make this book a success. In particular, I want to thank my fantastic editor, Lucy Dauman. Where there was an opportunity to make the story better, she spotted it, and brilliantly shone her light on the way forward. She's truly amazing. I also want to thank my beta reader, Staci Motley, for her kind support and her invaluable input. As always, I want to thank my incredibly talented friends Leigh, Tessa, and Lena. You've been with me from the start, and you're always there for me whether I need to cry, celebrate, or fix a plot hole. I don't know what I'd do without you. To my family—Bill, Shannon, Erik, and Sarah. I love you truly, dears.

Printed in Great Britain
by Amazon